Praise for Kate Rhodes and the Alice Quentin series

'Rhodes is a poet whose linguistic precision is very much in evidence throughout the novel and Alice is a vividly realised protagonist whose complex and harrowing history rivals the central crime storyline' Sophie Hannah, *Sunday Express*

'A pacy psychological thriller that makes good use of its London setting' Laura Wilson, *Guardian*

'A terrific new heroine on the block' *Woman & Home*

'Like Nicci French, Kate Rhodes excels at character, pace and sense of place' Erin Kelly

'Quentin is one of a cast of really believable and entertaining characters and both the plot and the writing keep one thoroughly engaged throughout' *Daily Mail*

'Alice Quentin is such a warm character – unique, yet very real. I loved the sense of menace too – perfectly thrilling' Mel Sherratt

'A fast-moving, entertaining mix of sex, suspense and serial killings' *Washington Post*

'First-rate writing' *Publishers Weekly*

'Atmospheric and suspenseful' *The Lady*

The Alice Quentin series

Crossbones Yard
A Killing of Angels
The Winter Foundlings

Kate Rhodes

Kate Rhodes was born in London. She has worked as a teacher and university lecturer, and now writes full-time.

Kate began her writing career as a poet, publishing two prize winning collections. She has held a Hawthornden fellowship and been shortlisted for Forward and Bridport Prizes. She has written five novels in the Alice Quentin series, *Crossbones Yard*, *A Killing Of Angels*, *The Winter Foundling* and *River Of Souls*, the first of which was selected by Val McDermid for the Harrogate Crime festival's New Blood panel championing new crime writers. In 2014 Kate Rhodes won the Ruth Rendell Short Story Award, sponsored by the charity InterAct. Visit her website at katerhodes.org or follow her on Twitter @K_RhodesWriter.

KATE RHODES

River of Souls

MULHOLLAND
BOOKS
HODDER

First published in Great Britain in 2015 by Mulholland Books
An imprint of Hodder & Stoughton
An Hachette UK company

First published in paperback in 2015

1

A CIP catalogue record for this title is available from the British Library

Paperback ISBN 978 1 444 78559 3
eBook ISBN 978 1 444 78558 6

Printed and bound by Clays Ltd, St Ives plc

Hodder & Stoughton policy is to use papers that are natural, renewable
and recyclable products and made from wood grown in sustainable
forests. The logging and manufacturing processes are expected to
conform to the environmental regulations of the country of origin.

Hodder & Stoughton Ltd
Carmelite House
50 Victoria Embankment
London EC4Y 0DZ

www.hodder.co.uk

For my sister Honor Rhodes, OBE, my favourite history expert

'The Thames is in many respects the river of the dead. It has the power to hurt and to kill.'

Peter Ackroyd, *Thames: Sacred River*

'The river had an awful look, the buildings on the banks were muffled in black shrouds, and the reflected lights seemed to originate deep in the water, as if the spectres of suicides were holding them to show where they went down. The wild moon and clouds were as restless as an evil conscience in a tumbled bed, and the very shadow of the immensity of London seemed to lie oppressively upon the water.'

Charles Dickens, *Night Walks*

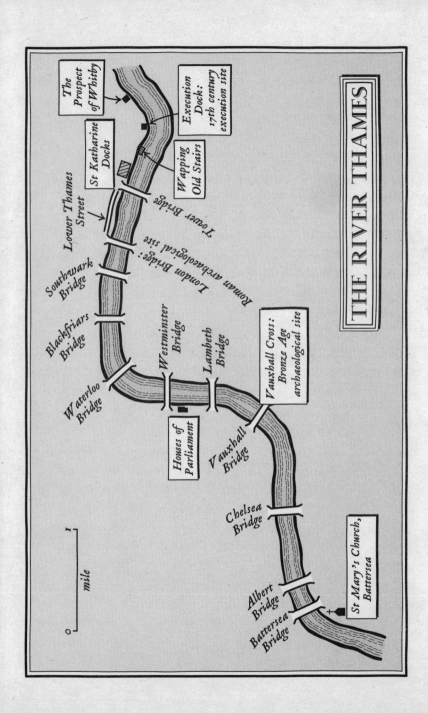

THE RIVER THAMES

The Prospect of Whitby

St Katharine Docks

Execution Dock: 17th century execution site

Wapping Old Stairs

Lower Thames Street

Tower Bridge

Southwark Bridge

London Bridge: Roman archaeological site

Blackfriars Bridge

Westminster Bridge

Lambeth Bridge

Vauxhall Cross: Bronze Age archaeological site

Waterloo Bridge

Houses of Parliament

Vauxhall Bridge

Chelsea Bridge

St Mary's Church, Battersea

Albert Bridge

Battersea Bridge

0 — 1 mile

I

The Thames is preparing to race back to the sea, currents twisting like sinews of muscle. Endless rain has upset its smoothness, reflected lights scattering in a blur of silver. A man stands beside it, gazing across the water's moonlit surface, listening to the voices of the drowned. They whisper to him at night, begging to be remembered. It has taken him hours to walk here, reciting a litany of bridges: Lambeth, Vauxhall, Chelsea, Albert, Battersea. The journey has exhausted him, but the first soul is within reach. He senses it in his quickened breath and the excitement pulsing in his chest.

It's late when he finally enters the churchyard. Traffic hums on Battersea Church Road, and the gravestones jostle him, standing and falling like soldiers in a battle zone. He forces himself to concentrate before stepping over the threshold. There's a stink of incense and stale communion wine, lights bright enough to dazzle. He drops onto a pew at the back of the nave, lets his forehead rest on the balls of his hands until a man's voice addresses him.

'Evensong's over, I'm afraid. I'm just locking up.' An elderly priest, white-haired and pinch-faced, peers down at him. Only his eyes are memorable; cornflower blue, unblinking. 'I've seen you before, haven't I? You're soaked through. Come this way, my friend. There are towels in the vestry.'

Dust motes hang in the air. There's a moment's stillness before the hammer falls. The first blow strikes the priest's temple, his body crumpling. The river's instructions grow louder as the man drags his victim back through the churchyard to the water's edge. He has prepared for this moment, but it still fills him with horror. If he could choose he would walk away and let the priest recover, but the decision isn't his to make. The next stage must be accurate. There's a splintering sound as the chisel enters the old man's skull, followed by a single loud scream. Now he must act fast so everything is complete before his spirit can escape. The priest is unconscious as the Stanley knife swipes along his brow then down his cheek. The blade makes cut after cut, slicing skin from bone. Nausea threatens to overwhelm him, but the man only has moments to complete the river's orders. His fingers tremble as he ties the talisman to his victim's wrist, binding the circle of antique glass tightly in place.

Fast-flowing currents tug at his clothes as he wades into the river. When he's waist deep, the tide seizes his victim from his arms, black robes fanning across the surface. The priest's life-less body drifts east as his soul blends with the river. Tonight the man's duty is done. By morning the Thames will deliver the body to the correct destination, his secret washed clean. The man sinks to his knees, letting the black liquid close over him. Then he wades back to the shore and stands in the graveyard, staring again at the river while its lifeblood drips from his hands.

2

It was still raining when I reached St James's Park on Monday morning. The Thames Barrier had been raised for the third time that week. London's ancient drainage system was failing to cope, murky water bubbling up through the grates. It was tempting to catch the first bus home, but I'd been invited to meet the chief officer at the Forensic Psychology Unit of the Met, and I was intrigued. So I hurried on, with rain cascading from my umbrella.

The headquarters of the FPU was a discreet brown stone building on Dacre Street, four storeys high, a stone's throw from New Scotland Yard. The fact that there was no sign above the door seemed a wise move. Advertising the unit's purpose would make it a target for every psychotic villain the specialists tracked down. The building's interior felt equally anonymous; the foyer more like a dentist's waiting room than the UK's nerve centre for forensic psychology. It had white walls, a small reception desk, and coconut palms gathering dust either side of the door. The receptionist's smile was sympathetic, as though I'd checked in for an extraction.

'Professor Jenkins's office is on the top floor.'

I was looking forward to meeting Christine Jenkins. Her books on personality disorders had been set texts on my degree course, and the urgent tone of her assistant's phone message had sparked my curiosity. Photos of eminent psychologists lined the building's walls. Jean Piaget, Elizabeth

Loftus and Carl Rogers studied me gravely as I climbed the stairs.

The professor's door was open when I arrived. She stood with her back to me by a large window, arms rigid at her sides as if she was marshalling her strength for a fight. She spun round immediately when I knocked: tall and slim, with cropped grey hair, wearing a smart suit. She greeted me with a formal smile.

'Thanks for braving the weather, Dr Quentin.'

'It's no problem. A bit of moisture never hurt anyone.'

'This is the wettest June on record – you must be an optimist.'

I returned her smile. 'Only until circumstances prove me wrong.'

She indicated for me to sit down. 'Do you remember an attack on a young woman called Jude Shelley last year?'

'Of course, the cabinet minister's daughter. The reports said she was in intensive care for weeks.'

Jenkins's smile vanished. 'Someone dragged her into a car after she left a party on Lower Thames Street. He drove a sharp implement into her skull, a screwdriver or a chisel, then slashed her face and threw her into the river. The girl was barely alive when she washed up by Southwark Bridge. She's been in hospital ever since.'

I winced. 'No one was implicated?'

'The MIT closed the case after six months – no credible suspects. Their investigation was flawed.'

'In what way?'

'Let's just say they weren't quite thorough enough.'

'And that's why I'm here?'

'The girl's started remembering details. Her mother's insisting the Met reopens the case.'

I held her gaze. 'Solving it would be a tall order, after letting it go cold for months.'

4

'We can't afford to fall out with Whitehall. The order's come from the commissioner himself.'

'He thinks the Shelleys would go to the press?'

The CO looked uncomfortable. 'This is about limiting damage to the Met's reputation. I'd like you to work on the case for six weeks, starting immediately. Support the family and look for new leads. If nothing comes to light, we'll close it down permanently.'

'That isn't possible, I'm afraid. I return to my hospital consultancy next month.'

'Your boss has given the go-ahead. He's prepared to release you.'

I leaned back in my chair. 'Why me? You've got a whole building full of consultants.'

'The girl's mother's read your book, *Understanding Violence*. She asked for you personally, and I think she's right. You're the best person for the job, Dr Quentin. You've got an excellent reputation.'

Despite her flattery, it irritated me that the decision had been removed from my hands. The CO was fixing me with an intent stare, and my chance of a holiday was slipping away, but I was already hooked. I wanted to know why the Murder Investigation Team had marred their reputation over such an important case.

'When do I start?'

Jenkins looked relieved. 'This afternoon, if possible; the girl's mother wants to meet you. There's a desk for you on the first floor.'

'I'll need the crime file.'

'My assistant will bring it down. I appreciate you stepping in at such short notice; let me know how I can support you.' Her expression grew more serious as I prepared to leave. 'The problem with having a high profile is that people start requesting your help, Dr Quentin. You become a victim of your own success.'

The CO's comment baffled me. It sounded like she was reflecting on her own position, not mine. Her job as the leader of a national organisation placed her head well above the parapet, and the weight of public scrutiny seemed to be telling on her. She started checking her phone before I'd left the room, attention already shifting to her next urgent task.

The desk I'd been allocated was in an open-plan office at the end of a dark corridor. The room contained at least fifteen workstations, but it was almost empty, apart from a few bearded men who appeared completely immersed in their work. I realised that I'd been ambushed. Many psychologists waited their whole lives to be invited to work for the FPU, but this case was daunting. If no new evidence emerged, my next six weeks would be spent consoling a well-known politician and his distressed wife. Despite her promise of support, the CO seemed to expect me to work entirely on my own. There would be no assistant to fall back on as I ploughed through past evidence, and my new colleagues appeared too busy to acknowledge my existence. The elderly man hunched over the desk opposite gave a vacant smile when I introduced myself, then focused again on his computer, as if the prospect of small talk embarrassed him.

The CO's assistant delivered the crime file at half past ten. She looked glad to hand over the thick ream of paper, placing several kilos of confidential facts in my hands. The reports confirmed Christine Jenkins's damning assessment of the investigation. It had stalled soon after it began. Interviews with the Shelley family had been cursory, which convinced me that the senior investigating officer had worn kid gloves because of the minister's position. Under different circumstances, the police would have tested the family's stories to destruction, aware that most violent crimes are carried out by family members, lovers or spouses. I flicked through the file with a growing sense of amazement: the investigators had taken the relatives' alibis almost entirely on trust. Timothy Shelley had claimed that he was with a colleague in Brighton, preparing for a political conference, when his daughter had been attacked. The girl's mother and older brother said they had spent the evening together at the family home. Closer attention had been paid to the victim's boyfriend at the time, Jamal Khan, and to a convicted killer called Shane Weldon, recently released from Brixton Prison for murdering a woman and casting her body into the Thames. The SIO had pursued both men doggedly, but found no forensic evidence linking them to the case. I scribbled their names in my notebook. My first priority would be to interview each family member to build a picture of the victim's social environment, before the profiling process could begin.

I was about to put the reports back when a manila envelope slipped from the folder. It was filled with photos. The first picture showed a tarnished triangle of metal, either copper or bronze, covered in a green patina. There was no information to explain where it had been found. The next photo was a portrait of Jude Shelley at around twenty years old. Her heart-shaped face wore a relaxed smile, light reflecting from her wide brown eyes. She looked pretty and untroubled, as though her life had been full of pleasures. The third image was harder to understand. A raw oval was attached to the same slim neck, but everything else had changed. There was nothing to guide my journey across the blur of exposed veins and bone. Most of the girl's face had been removed. Her lips had gone and so had her nose. One brown, lidless eye stared back at me, unable

7

to close. Even though I'd counselled patients with life-changing disfigurements, I'd never seen such terrible injuries. I pushed the photo back into the envelope, then stared out of the window as the reality of my task hit home.

3

The crime file was locked inside my briefcase as the taxi edged through the Pimlico streets into a roar of traffic. The city seemed to be spinning out of control. I'd spent the last six months working at Northwood Psychiatric Hospital, deep in the Berkshire countryside, and London had shifted into fast-forward during my absence. Pedestrians marched along Grosvenor Row at breakneck speed, as though their existence depended on absolute punctuality. Half-built skyscrapers dominated the view south from the Embankment, the shell of Battersea Power Station still waiting to be transformed into an oasis of deluxe apartments. The riverside to the west was a sheer wall of glass. Factories and warehouses had been replaced by rows of transparent tower blocks. But the Shelleys' house was insulated from modern development, buried deep in the heart of Chelsea, the neighbourhood perfectly preserved for three hundred years. Georgian houses clustered around a garden square filled with rose-beds and cherry trees.

I wondered who owned the neighbouring houses as I sheltered from the rain in Heather Shelley's porch: fading rock stars, probably, and Russian oligarchs. It surprised me that Mrs Shelley opened the door herself rather than sending a housekeeper. She was in her forties, a blonde version of her daughter before the attack, with the same heart-shaped face, but the shadows under her eyes were too dark to conceal. She reached out and grasped my hand.

'Thanks so much for coming.'

There was a warm northern burr to Mrs Shelley's voice and I studied her again as she led me along the hallway. I'd seen her on the news when her husband was re-elected, an archetypal politician's wife, giving the camera a glacial smile. Today she seemed far more human. She wore jeans and a navy blue jumper, a small silver crucifix resting on her collarbone, suede boots even scruffier than mine.

While she made coffee, I glanced around her kitchen. It was large enough to house every state-of-the-art appliance under the sun. A framed photo hanging on the wall showed a family that looked immune to adversity. Heather and her husband sat in a sunlit garden with Jude and a dark-haired young man who I guessed was her brother. He was equally good-looking, but had a heavier build and darker skin tone, his smile more cautious. The Shelleys all looked glossy with health, relaxed in each other's company.

Heather sat opposite me at the table, picking at the skin around her nails. 'Where do you want me to start?'

I gave her a smile of encouragement. 'Wherever you like. I'll need to interview each of you, but perhaps you could begin with some family history. How did you meet your husband, for example?'

'Tim and I met at Oxford.' She swallowed a deep breath. 'I suppose we were chalk and cheese. He'd been to Eton, but my parents ran a greengrocer's in Leeds. I'd won a scholarship to study medicine.'

'Did you ever practise?'

'I never qualified. Tim's career took off, and I wanted to be at home with the kids. It was the logical choice.' Her voice was matter-of-fact, but I wondered whether she'd ever resented sacrificing her career.

'Your daughter studied law, didn't she?'

Her eyes suddenly filled with tears, voice catching as she spoke. 'She did a year of voluntary service in India after leaving school. It made her decide to specialise in human rights. Jude didn't deserve any of this; she wanted to make a difference. She had so many friends.' Her outburst petered into silence, and my sympathy doubled. One more piece of bad news would be enough to shatter her fragile coping mechanisms.

'Can you tell me why you wanted a forensic psychologist to work on your daughter's case?'

'We need someone who understands this kind of violence. The Met were hopeless. My husband insisted on the top people, but they went round in circles. They focused on Jude's boyfriend, but I was never convinced. I only met Jamal twice, but he seemed crazy about her.'

'Did Jude keep in contact with any other ex-boyfriends?'

'I don't think so, but I doubt she'd tell me. My daughter's always been a private person – losing her independence has been terrible for her. She's never been home since it happened.'

'What does your husband think about her case being reopened?'

Heather's expression hardened. 'Ask him yourself, if you can track him down.'

'His job must be very demanding.'

'It's his escape route; he buries his problems under a mound of work.'

Her openness shocked me. Within five minutes she had revealed the strain in her marriage to a total stranger. 'Is your daughter's health improving?'

Heather's gaze locked onto mine. 'Jude was on the waiting list for a face transplant, but she's too weak for such a huge operation now. Last week she spent twenty-four hours in intensive care. The only thing keeping her alive is the dream

that her attacker will be caught. She's terrified he'll hurt someone else.'

'Your whole family must have been affected very deeply.'

'Our son's taken it worst. Guy had a breakdown afterwards.
He only went back to art school at Easter; he's still very
vulnerable.'

I scanned my notes. 'You and Guy were together the night
of the attack, weren't you? Can you tell me what happened
before the police called?'

Her shoulders tensed. 'Nothing unusual. I cooked him a
meal around seven, but I was feeling under the weather. I had
a bath and was in bed by nine. Guy decided to stay rather
than go back to his flat, because Jude was coming over in the
morning. They wanted to catch up.'

'Do you know how your son spent his evening?'

'He was working on an art project.'

'Would it be possible to speak to him?'

'Not today.' Her face clouded. 'Guy won't find this easy, I'll
have to prepare him.'

'I'll keep the interview short, I promise. Was Jude living at
home or in halls of residence when the attack happened?'

'She shared a flat with her friend Natalie, but she always
came home for the holidays.' Her eyes were brimming again.
'We're all so worried. She's got an infection she can't shake off.'

'Maybe the case reopening will give her a boost.'

'That's what I'm praying for,' she agreed quietly.

'Could I see Jude's room while I'm here?'

Heather balked at the idea at first, but after some gentle
persuasion she led me up to the top floor. She stayed outside
on the landing, as though she was reluctant to invade her
daughter's territory. The bedroom walls were a delicate
shade of pink, a pin-board held Polaroid snaps of teenage
faces in various stages of delight, bookshelves loaded with

Stephenie Meyer and J. K. Rowling. I'd been expecting rows of heavyweight law journals, but the space was more suitable for a child than an undergraduate studying human rights. Even though the family must have cleared her apartment, no evidence of Jude's adult life was on display. The room felt like a monument to the pleasures of youth. Her wardrobe held an array of glitzy party dresses, hanging in perfect readiness, as if time might suddenly lurch backwards and render her whole again.

Heather's exhaustion was clear by the end of our meeting. She seemed so focused on her children's welfare that she had forgotten her own. I promised to report back as soon as I'd reviewed the evidence, but the hollows under her eyes looked even more pronounced as I prepared to leave.

'Would it be okay to visit Jude tomorrow morning?' I asked.

'I'd better come too. Meeting new people always upsets her.'

'It's probably best if we meet by ourselves the first time.'

Her smile vanished. 'My daughter's too ill for any kind of stress.'

'I realise that.' I touched her arm lightly. 'She'll have to meet me sooner or later, Heather. I won't stay long.'

Her lips trembled as she said goodbye, then the door gave an abrupt click as it shut behind me.

My head spun as I walked north to a coffee shop on Cromwell Road. It unnerved me that I'd only been working on the Shelley case for a few hours, yet I already felt involved. Heather's suffering was visible to the naked eye, her concentration ruined, all of her answers arriving a beat too late. If she'd arrived for a consultation, I'd have diagnosed situational depression. I could tell she was fighting tooth and nail not to let it erode her strength, but she'd endured every parent's worst nightmare. Dragging herself to the hospital each day to confront her daughter's injuries must have taken its toll.

When I got back to my flat in Providence Square, I made myself some pasta, then peered out of the kitchen window. My plan to go running had been foiled again. Rain was falling in solid sheets, the clouds a relentless grey. A light shower would have been fine, but there are limits even to my masochism, so I opened the crime file and got to work.

The police medic's report on Jude Shelley's injuries described a lacerated throat, which had required a tracheotomy, severe cranial damage, loss of facial skin and tissue, and a broken jaw. On top of that, she had almost drowned. I stared down at the list, trying to imagine emotional triggers for such savagery, but all the evidence would have to be sifted before a psychological motive could emerge.

The graphic details were making me feel queasy, so I switched to the crime scene report instead. Jude had been found on the riverbank below Southwark Bridge at four a.m. on 20 June, almost a year ago to the day. Southwark Police had arrived within five minutes of the emergency call. The next piece of information stopped me in my tracks. DCI Don Burns had been the reporting officer, his outsized signature scrawled across the bottom of the page.

I tried to picture Burns kneeling on the cold mud, keeping the girl in the recovery position until the ambulance arrived. No matter how appalling her injuries were, he would have stayed there, clutching her hand. Thinking about him filled me with discomfort. I'd only seen Burns once since we worked together on the Foundlings case the previous winter. We'd had dinner in a country pub near Charnwood, beside a crackling fire. The signs had been good: he'd kissed me before getting back into his car and promised we'd meet again soon. But since then I'd heard nothing. My phone messages were never returned. When I realised he had no intention of calling, my hurt hardened into anger. The idea of contacting him now made my stomach twist into knots, but there was no alternative. I switched on my computer and hit the Skype key, determined to keep the conversation brief.

Burns answered after three rings. His face refused to come into focus, and his environment looked different. He must have left his flat, because his bookshelves had disappeared and unfamiliar paintings hung on the wall. But when the picture sharpened he was just as I remembered, hulking shoulders almost filling the screen, dark hair in need of a cut, his brown-eyed stare as intense as ever. Only his lopsided smile was missing.

'I've been meaning to call you, Alice.'

Before he could speak again, another face appeared in the corner of the screen. An attractive brunette scowled at me then disappeared from view. It was no consolation that Burns looked as awkward as I felt when I blurted out my request. 'The Jude Shelley case has reopened, Don. I need some information.'

'You want to talk now?'

'If possible.'

'Can we meet tomorrow instead? Eight a.m. at Brown's?'

I nodded then hit the escape button and his face vanished. I had no idea who his new girlfriend was, but the idea of him in bed with someone else started a raw ache at the base of my throat – a classic case of somatising. It had got the better of me dozens of times, emotional pain transforming into physical symptoms. My distress always manifested as headaches or insomnia, but I had no intention of yielding to it again.

I felt calmer after a long bath. I was about to go to bed when a message arrived on my mobile. Lola had texted a picture of herself, marooned on her chaise longue, vastly pregnant. I couldn't help smiling. So what if my day had gone from bad to disastrous? I focused on the prospect of becoming a godmother in a fortnight's time, and wiped everything else from my mind.

4

Burns was waiting for me at Brown's the next morning. He sat by the window in a black raincoat, shoulders hunched as he gazed across the river to Whitechapel, pale skin stretched tight across his high cheekbones. The café had been our regular meeting place in the old days, because it opened early and served good coffee, its dimly lit interior often deserted. I approached his table reluctantly, annoyed that the physical connection was still there. If he'd invited me to check in to a hotel, it would have been impossible to refuse. He looked flustered when he spotted me, half rising to his feet.

'It's good to see you, Alice.'

'Is it?' I observed him steadily as I sat down. 'Look, this won't take long, I just want to ask—'

'Can't I explain why I didn't call you first?'

'There's no need. Let's keep this professional.'

Burns ignored me and carried on. 'The boys weren't coping with me and Julie being apart – Liam wouldn't go to school. Moray kept wetting the bed, crying for hours.'

'You could have told me you'd gone back to your wife. A text would have done it, or an email.'

He studied the surface of the table. 'I didn't know what to say. I felt terrible for messing you around.' His eyes scanned my face as if he was checking for signs of damage.

'That's not why I called. I'm here to talk about Jude Shelley.

The report you filed says you reached the scene before the ambulance.'

At first I thought he wouldn't reply. His attention had shifted to the view, watching a barge dragging itself upstream. 'I had a trainee in tow. It was the poor sod's first call-out; he was off sick for a week afterwards.'

'Was she conscious?'

'That was the worst thing. She kept coming round, even though the pain must have been unbearable.'

'Did you notice anything, apart from her injuries?'

'There was a bit of metal round her neck. Sharp-edged, a couple of inches long, tied to a leather string.'

I remembered the photo from the crime file. 'What do you think it was?'

'The paramedics came before I could get a closer look.'

'Did she say anything about her attacker?'

'Nothing coherent. She kept babbling about souls.'

'Maybe she thought she was dying.'

Burns shook his head. 'It was something about the soul of the river.'

Outside the window, the Thames was blacker than the sky, dense with silt and pollutants. Surely no one could believe that a spirit existed under its dark surface? When I focused again on Burns, he was watching me cautiously. His rugby fullback shoulders were still raised high enough to deflect a rough tackle.

'Have you seen today's papers?' he asked.

When I shook my head, he shunted his copy of the *Independent* across the table. The first headline caught my eye: PRIEST DROWNS IN VIOLENT ATTACK. The story explained that Father Kelvin Owen's body had washed up on the banks of the Thames at Westminster Pier the previous morning with severe facial injuries.

'Just like Jude Shelley,' I said quietly.

'You think it could be happening again?'

'Why would he wait a whole year? The injuries worry me, though. Facial mutilation's so rare, I'd like to know more about what happened to him.' It seemed too coincidental that someone had been attacked in exactly the same way as Jude, on the very day her case reopened. But no one had known about my work apart from the authorities and her family.

'I can get details for you.'

'No need. The FPU gave me a password for the Police National Computer.' I pushed my coffee cup away. 'Did you work on the Jude Shelley case again after you found her?'

He scowled. 'The MIT took over. I met her dad though, the Right Honourable Timothy Shelley. He made a complaint about slow response times. The bloke's everything you'd expect from the English ruling classes: smarmy, vicious and arrogant.' Burns's Scottish accent grew stronger as the chip on his shoulder widened. It irritated me that I could have sat there all day, listening to him rant. I rose to my feet quickly and belted my coat.

'Thanks for your time.'

'Call me again if I can help.' His eyes lingered on my face and it looked like he was planning another apology, so I ducked out of the door before he got the chance.

My throat burned as I walked towards Spice Quay, my heart beating uncomfortably fast. By Tower Bridge I had to stop and counsel myself. I perched on a bench and watched clippers cutting through the drizzle towards Bermondsey. Burns had been at the front of my mind for months, but unrequited love was a slippery slope. It was meant to help twelve year olds test their emotional range, not smart thirty-three-year-old psychologists. My vulnerability made me feel like kicking the nearest lamppost. Maybe I should have yelled at him in the café, but it wouldn't have changed anything. Burns's decision to do the right thing and return to his family only made me like him more. The best option was to wipe him from my mind. I allowed myself one more minute of abject self-pity, then continued my journey along the river path.

Jude Shelley was being treated at the city's most expensive private hospital. The Royal London glittered with luxury. Drinks machines in the echoing foyer dispensed free mineral water and cappuccino, every surface polished to a high shine. The building faced north across the river to the Custom House and Old Billingsgate. It was ironic that the girl's room must have a direct view of Lower Thames Street, where she'd been attacked. In her shoes I'd have begged for an immediate transfer.

A middle-aged nurse led me up to the first floor, examining me from the corner of her eye. 'Have you visited Jude before?'

'This is my first time.'

'Can I give you some advice?'

'Please.'

'Try not to stare. People don't realise they're doing it; under all that damage she's just a normal twenty-three-year-old girl.'

By now we were standing outside room nine, and she gave me an encouraging smile before walking away. I took a moment to compose myself, then knocked on the door. The anteroom smelled of fresh flowers, iodine and stale air, but the thing that hit me hardest was the darkness. The curtains were closed even though it was mid-morning. A girl lay on the bed, wreathed in shadows. She was wearing a hat with the brim pulled down, her face hidden, but her greeting was cheerful as I approached her bed.

'You must be the shrink Mum told me about, Alice Quentin.' Her voice was light and breathless, the words accompanied by air hissing from her respirator.

'Don't worry, I'm not here to psychoanalyse you. Do you mind if I sit down?'

'Feel free. You're saving me from the crap on daytime TV.'

I laughed. 'I know what you mean. Last year I was in hospital for a while – by the end I was almost brain dead.'

'You've experienced the joys of *Flog It* and *Bargain Hunt*?'

'Not to mention *Loose Women* and *Countdown*.' I had no idea if she could see me, but smiled anyway. I got the sense that she was trying to put me at my ease. 'Do you know why I'm here, Jude?'

'My mother's asked you to profile my attacker. She's one hundred per cent certain you'll find him.'

'She's your mum. It's her job to look on the bright side.'

A spluttering sound issued from her oxygen machine. 'The bright side stops working after nine operations in a year.'

'I can imagine.' The nurse's warning echoed as I gazed down at my pad. 'Heather says you're remembering things about the attack. Did the memories come back suddenly?'

'Not really. It's been gradual, over the past few months.'

It didn't surprise me that her recovered memory process had been fragmentary. Victims of violence often kept their experiences buried for decades. 'Do you feel able to talk about it?'

'Of course, but what's the point? The police didn't find him. You won't catch him all by yourself.' Something bitter-edged lurked behind her words. It sounded like she was determined not to raise her hopes.

'I shouldn't brag, but I'm pretty good at my job, and you'll be helping me. Criminals are often brought to justice years after the fact. You remember that from your law studies, don't you?'

'We both know the chances of him being convicted are thousands to one.'

'But that's what you want, isn't it?'

'More than anything.'

'So we're agreed. If you tell me what you remember, we've got nothing to lose.'

She sucked in a long breath before answering. 'It's hazy, but I know he carried me from the car to the river.' She took an aerosol from her bedside cabinet and lifted the brim of her hat by a fraction before spraying something on her face. 'He tied a mask over my eyes until he cut me. I don't remember that part, thank God, but I heard him crying. He said the river was waiting for my soul. Then he threw me in.'

'Do you remember anything else?'

'His voice was muffled, but I think I'd heard it before.'

'It was someone you know?'

'Maybe it was just his accent that was familiar. West London, like mine.'

'Did you see him clearly at any point?'

'Only for a moment. When I try to picture him, there's nothing there.' Her voice faded to a whisper, revealing her exhaustion.

'That's enough for today. I promised your mum not to tire you, but I'd like to talk again. Would that be okay?'

'I'm not sure.' There was a long pause before she spoke again. 'You're afraid to look at me, aren't you?'

'Not at all, but the nurse said it upsets you when people stare.'

'How will you find him, if you can't even face what he did?' The anger in her voice came out of the blue.

'I'd like to see you.' My heart raced as I put down my notebook. 'Working together's going to be easier if we can talk openly.'

In a series of quick movements she flicked on a bedside light then pulled off her hat. I gazed back steadily, trying not to reveal my shock. A waterfall of gorgeous chestnut hair spilled across her shoulders, but everything else was ruined. The photos hadn't prepared me for the extent of her injuries. There was a broad scar across her throat, an oxygen tube feeding into her trachea. Her face was a patchwork of skin grafts, nothing inside her right eye socket except shadows, a livid gash where her lips should have been. But the most disturbing thing was her remaining eye. It explained why she'd used the aerosol. The eyelid had been torn away, leaving her unable to blink, so it would need hydration every few minutes. But it was the one feature she could control. She stared back at me, judging my reactions. I held her gaze for a long breath before speaking again.

'I'll do everything I can to find who hurt you, Jude, but it won't be easy. I'd like to try a technique called memory recovery to help you remember your attacker. It's a type of hypnosis.'

'Ask me any questions you like.' The light flicked off again. 'But I don't believe it'll change anything.'

When I looked up again, her veneer of bravery was cracking apart. Her eye carried on staring at me, unable to close, while air sighed from the ventilator.

5

I stood by the landing window to steady myself. The Custom House dominated the opposite shore, large and prosperous from extorting ships' taxes for eight centuries. Rain spattered the glass, but it no longer mattered that the summer was a washout, or that Burns didn't care about me. Compared to Jude Shelley's suffering, I was the luckiest woman alive.

I was about to leave when a familiar figure marched across the landing carrying a bouquet of yellow roses. Timothy Shelley wore the standard politician's uniform: a dark suit, white shirt and blue silk tie, deliberately inoffensive. He looked younger than his TV persona as Minister of State for Employment, closer to forty than fifty. I'd seen him on the news countless times, justifying why the jobless totals kept on rising. He had the perfect face to break bad news, features bland and permanently fixed in a half-smile, mid-brown hair swept back from his face. He was accompanied by a small entourage. Walking behind him was a taller man, wearing the same type of expensive clothes, about the same age. At a glance he could have been a politician too, but his expression was less certain, as if he was used to taking instructions. Two bodyguards loitered at the top of the stairs, one of them murmuring into his radio. I stepped into the minister's path as he approached his daughter's room.

'Mr Shelley, my name's Alice Quentin. I've just visited Jude. I wonder if we could talk?'

His smile widened by a centimetre. 'My wife said you might be here. Would you mind waiting until I've seen my daughter?'

'Of course not.'

He turned to his companion. 'Giles, could you ask the Home Office to delay my meeting?'

'I'll call them now, Minister.'

The man gave his boss a measured smile before retreating at a brisk pace. He spoke to the bodyguards then babbled softly into his mobile phone.

Shelley seemed to be operating in a slower gear than his assistant, unwilling to be hurried. After twenty minutes he emerged from Jude's room, a little paler than before, which made me wonder if her suffering struck him afresh whenever he visited.

'Why don't we find ourselves some coffee, Dr Quentin?'

He seemed oblivious to the followers trailing behind while we walked downstairs, as though being chaperoned had become second nature. He talked more freely as the machine dispensed cappuccino into white china cups. By the time we found a table, he'd described the excellent care his daughter was receiving, and his sympathy for all families hit by tragedy. Each statement was so perfectly honed, he could have been reciting from an autocue. Maybe I judged him harshly, but I got the sense that he was trying so hard to sound sincere that his words rang hollow. His style was the opposite of his wife's wide-eyed openness.

'Was it your decision to press for the case to be reopened?' I asked.

'Quite the opposite. I was concerned about the impact on Jude. Maybe I'm overprotective, but we've always been very close. I hate the idea of her hopes being dashed, and there's no point in upsetting Guy. Let's be honest, Dr Quentin, we both know that the chances of my daughter's attacker being found are slim. But my wife can be very black and white about things.'

A flicker of genuine emotion showed for the first time, every muscle in his face tensing with displeasure. He and Heather had obviously fought tooth and nail about the family's dirty linen being dragged back into the public eye. He seemed to have no faith whatsoever in my ability to solve the crime, but I didn't doubt the sincerity of his desire to protect his daughter. Maybe the potential impact on his family's privacy concerned him too. If it became common knowledge that the case had been reopened, their ordeal would be replayed in the national media.

'You're in a very visible position, Mr Shelley. Can you think of anyone who might bear a grudge towards you, or your family?'

'Contrary to popular opinion, the Westminster village is a relaxed place to work. I don't have any serious enemies.' His response came a beat too late, but it made me realise how slick he was. Like Blair or Clinton, he could have lied through his teeth in front of a hundred cameras without batting an eye.

'But you must have had suspicions about who attacked Jude?'

'I'm afraid not. I wasn't keen on her boyfriend at the time. He seemed jealous of her other friends, but the police accepted his alibi. The young man in question only visited her here a few times.' His smile dimmed by a few kilowatts. 'Love was obviously skin deep in his case.'

'Can you remember much about the night your daughter got hurt?'

He gave a shallow sigh. 'It's all rather blurred, but I travelled to Brighton with a member of my campaign team. Traffic delayed us, so we stopped for a meal. I don't recall what time we reached the hotel, but I stayed up till after midnight with a colleague planning my speech.'

The minister's aide bore down on us. 'We need to leave soon, sir.'

'Give me one more minute please, Giles.' The man hovered close by, wearing a tense expression, as though his boss's punctuality was a matter of national importance. Shelley rose to his feet slowly, his parting smile a dazzle of bleached white teeth. 'My wife and I appreciate your help, Dr Quentin.'

'One more question, Mr Shelley. Did you hear about the body discovered by Westminster Pier yesterday morning?'

The question made him wince. 'My wife and I were friends of Father Kelvin's. We worship at St Mary's; he christened Jude when she was three months old. The police want to talk to us about it this evening.'

Shelley strode away with his staff in hot pursuit. His well-honed public image was too polished to reveal personal feelings, but the parallels between the attacks must have dawned on him too. His family priest had suffered a vicious assault, carried out in the same style as his daughter's, on the date her case reopened. The only difference was that the attack on Father Owen had proved fatal. I made a mental note to contact the senior investigating officer on the Owen case and set up a meeting as soon as possible.

My head was still buzzing as I hurried along Borough High Street to meet Lola. She was waiting for me at her favourite Turkish café on Park Street. My stress reduced the moment I saw her. She had charmed a waiter into parting with his best table, and she was wearing a mile-wide grin, auburn ringlets cascading across her shoulders. I leant down to give her a hug.

'You look fabulous, Lo.'

'That's a blatant lie. I'm big as a walrus.'

'Believe me, you look perfect.'

Lola's green eyes flickered. 'Are you okay? You seem out of sorts.'

'You're imagining things. What have you been up to?'

'Painting the spare room yellow. I'm hedging my bets.'

Lola had opted for a laid-back approach to pregnancy. She was planning a home birth and had chosen not to know the baby's sex, which was driving her boyfriend crazy. Neal was thirteen years younger, but he liked life to be perfectly controlled. Suddenly she reached across the table and grabbed my wrist.

'You're still going to be my birthing partner, aren't you?'

'Of course. But Neal'll change his mind on the big day.'

'You're joking; one drop of blood and he keels over. Now tell me what's up.'

I considered lying, but Lola's bullshit detector was unbeatable. 'One small thing, one big.'

'Give me the small one first.'

'I've fallen for a married man.'

She rolled her eyes. 'There's a universal cure. Have loads of casual sex until you've shagged him out of your system.' Her lewd expression made me laugh.

'It's that easy?'

'Trust me, it works. What's the other problem?'

'I've been asked to profile an attacker who mutilated someone's face. She's got the worst injuries I've ever seen.'

'Learn to say no occasionally, darling. That might help.'

'Thanks, Lo. You're an endless well of sympathy.'

Lola ploughed her way through a mound of falafel, hummus and pita bread. It was a relief to see her eat a square meal for once. During her years as a dancer, she'd existed on Marlboro Lights, vodka and green salads. It still impressed me hugely that she'd given up booze and fags the instant she became pregnant.

'Have you heard from Will?' I asked.

'Last week. He's moving back to London, isn't he?'

'Your guess is as good as mine.' It still rankled that my brother always phoned Lola instead of me when there was news to report. In the years when he'd lived rough, I'd been dependent on her for information. Even though his bipolar disorder had stabilised, she was still his first port of call.

'Tell me more about the married man,' she said.

'There's nothing to say. His wife kicked him out because he's a workaholic. We had a flirtation, but his sons missed him so much he decided to go back.'

'What are you going to do about it?'

'Nothing, obviously.'

She gave me a sorrowful look then kissed me goodbye. 'Promise not to stay home and mope.'

'Have I ever?'

I kissed her on the cheek and watched her leave. Even in the last month of her pregnancy, Lola could still turn heads. Most of the men in the café gave her admiring looks as she breezed away to her final antenatal appointment.

6

The man shelters between two buildings. He's wearing one of the disguises he keeps in his car, a leather jacket and a short blond wig, grey woollen hat pulled low over his eyes. It's vital that no one can identify him. Taking the priest's life still haunts him, but there's a higher calling now, and he must follow instructions. The river blessed him after it accepted the priest's soul, singing his name for hours.

Pedestrians scurry past on St Pancras Way, hiding under their umbrellas. It would be easy to run at them, knife raised, but the river is more discriminating. It has already chosen its next victim. He searches the faces of the people rushing up the steps to the police station. At last a black woman with a beautiful face emerges and he slips further into the shadows. If she spots him, there's a chance she will see through his disguise. Even from this distance, he can measure how pure her spirit is. He takes time to observe her as she talks to a friend by the station's entrance, her uniform baggy on her slight frame. When she slips through the doorway, he feels bereft. He has memorised her features so accurately, he can see her even with his eyes closed.

It's after two when the man looks at his watch. He must go back before anyone misses him, but seeing the woman's beauty has strengthened him. Even though he's soaked to the skin, he feels elated as he hurries away.

7

My next meeting was at three p.m. that afternoon with Jude's older brother. I'd received a cryptic text from Heather, letting me know that Guy was prepared to see me at his art school on Granary Square. I was curious to know whether he had inherited his father's slick manner and unwillingness to reveal secrets. From the outside, St Martin's Art College was a drab industrial building, but the interior was lined with mirrored walls, glass mezzanine floors, and light flooding across abstract sculptures in the atrium. The students were much more glamorous than the geeks who had populated my psychology course. It looked like they'd spent days foraging in Camden Lock for retro clothes. It made me wish I'd been artistic, but my only talents at school had been a good memory and an obsession with the foibles of the human mind.

I recognised Guy Shelley from the photo in his parents' kitchen. He was in his mid-twenties; tall, with an athletic build and spiky black hair. His skin was so pale it looked like he'd been living underground. He seemed determined to conceal his wealthy background, dressed in scruffy jeans and a black shirt covered in patches of white powder. His handshake felt dusty, as though he'd been sifting flour. He didn't return my smile, which made me wonder if he'd been coerced into seeing me.

'Thanks for making time to meet,' I said.

He gave a rapid nod. 'It's fine. Jude deserves all the time she needs.'

We found a quiet bench away from the main thoroughfare, and I observed his body language. Guy's hands were in perpetual motion, flying up to adjust his hair, or fidgeting in his lap. His mother hadn't described the nature of his breakdown, but it must have been severe to keep him away from college for a whole year.

'I'm trying to build a picture of Jude's life before the attack. Do you remember much about the weeks leading up to it?'

'Not really. I was planning to study sculpture in Rome that summer, but I got ill after she was hurt, so I never went.'

'Did you speak to your sister the day it happened?'

'She called to invite me to a party, but I told her I was too busy. If I'd gone with her, she'd still be safe.' His hands clenched suddenly in his lap.

'That's not how it works,' I said quietly. 'If the attacker was determined to hurt her, he'd have found another way.'

'I suppose so.' His expression was a mixture of sullenness and rage.

'Did you work that evening, at your mum's?'

He gave an awkward nod. 'I had some drawings to finish.'

'But you ate together?'

'Not that night. She had hay fever; after she went to bed I made myself some food.'

His story didn't tally with his mother's description of a cosy shared meal before she went for her bath. Guy's behaviour was twitchy enough to make me concerned, but the shock of his sister's attack might have made him forget the order of events.

'Were you and Jude close as kids?' I asked.

His gaze slipped away. 'I wasn't always the best brother.'

'How do you mean?'

'I was a thorn in her side. Jude's way smarter than me. Most of the time she tried to protect me, even though I'm a year older.'

'Protect you from what?'

'Myself, mainly. I'm my own worst enemy.'

'Why do you say that?'

'I've never had great self-control. Even as a kid it was all or nothing; I'd play computer games all night if I could get away with it. I'd been partying too hard at college last year. My panic attacks started after she got hurt; I'd go and see her then spend days locked in my room. I still struggle with it now.'

'That can't be easy.'

Guy picked at the chalk on his hands. I could understand why he'd been traumatised by his sister's injuries. A single visit had unsettled me, but hours at her bedside watching her suffer could drive a loved one to breaking point.

'Do you talk to your dad about how you feel?'

He let out a sharp laugh. 'You're joking. He thinks emotions are for weaklings, and Jude's the one he's close to, not me.'

'What about Father Owen? Could you talk to him?'

He flinched. 'Not really. I go to church for Mum's sake these days; religion stopped working for me after Jude's attack. But it was awful to hear he'd died.'

'Do you ever go to confession?'

'I haven't for months.'

I studied him again. 'Can you think of anyone who might want to hurt your family?'

He gave me a sharp look. 'Dad's surrounded by weirdoes all day long. These freaks come to his office; I don't know how he stands it. Maybe one of them attacked Jude to get at him.' His skin was growing paler by the minute.

'Do you know if your sister had ever been attacked before?'

His shoulders twitched. 'Why do you ask?'

33

'It's all guesswork at this stage until I fill in the gaps. But this type of attack can be part of a history of violence. Attackers go to these lengths when it's personal, not random. It's often someone with strong feelings for the victim, like a jealous friend or an ex-partner.'

'Jude should talk about her past, not me. She hates people gossiping.'

'Maybe she can't bring herself to look back – any details you remember could help her. Would you mind meeting again over the next few weeks?'

'Of course not.' Guy's face tensed again. 'You know where to find me.'

I watched him walk away, head down, slinking through the crowd. He'd come over as someone whose emotional pain lay very close to the surface, and it interested me that no one greeted him as he passed through the atrium. After a year of absence, his friends would have graduated while he struggled to catch up. Reintegrating must have been hard, on top of dealing with his condition.

I studied the artwork on the walls as I headed back to the exit, wandering through a maze of exhibition rooms. Tables were stacked with sketchbooks, and paintings pinned to the wall. A sign with Guy's name on it brought me to a halt, and I peered into a narrow passageway filled with small white sculptures hanging on transparent twine. A cloud of bridges was suspended above my head, their frets thin as matchsticks, connecting nothing with nothing, each one snapped cleanly in half. The effect was beautiful, but the delicacy of the structures made me even more concerned about his fragile state of mind.

When I got back to the FPU, a copy of the *Guardian* lay on the desk beside mine and I couldn't resist borrowing it. More details had emerged about the priest's death: Father Kelvin

Owen had worked at St Mary's on Battersea Church Road for thirty years, well loved by his community. He had led evensong on Sunday, then returned to lock up at ten o'clock. A parishioner had spotted him entering the church, but when the gardener arrived next morning, the door was open and the chancel lights still burning. The priest's body had been discovered on the riverbank at Westminster at dawn on Monday. The report said he had suffered a savage facial attack. I switched on my computer to hunt for more information.

Christine Jenkins summoned me to her office just as I was trawling the police database. She was perched on her desk, scanning the printed report she clutched in her hand.

'Things are moving fast, Alice. The commissioner wants your work to run in tandem with the Westminster investigation so all bases are covered. Is that viable?'

'Who's the SIO?'

'DCI Don Burns. Do you know him?'

My stomach performed a swift somersault. 'We've solved three major cases together.'

'Good. You already know each other's methods, and I hear he's a safe pair of hands.'

I gave a reluctant nod. 'It makes sense to combine Jude's case with the investigation into Father Owen's murder.'

She gave a crisp smile. 'You can act as Burns's consultant and still report to me. I'll ask his evidence officer to email you now – I appreciate how flexible you're being; let's review progress later this week.'

The loud ring of her phone terminated our conversation and my spirits sank as I closed the door. Burns was the last person in the world I wanted for my new boss, but Christine Jenkins didn't seem the type to discuss personal issues. I sensed that she kept her emotions clear of the workplace and expected the same professionalism from all her employees.

When I returned to my computer, the evidence officer had already sent three emails, including encrypted images from the crime scene. I studied a photo of a white-haired man, dressed in long black robes, limbs splayed across the muddy ground. His face was a blur of colour, all of his features destroyed. There was another connection with Jude Shelley: a large blue bead was bound to his hand. A close-up showed that the glass circle had a bevelled edge, milky and opaque as the bottles that wash up on beaches, weathered by the tide. I stared at it for several minutes but its meaning lay beyond my grasp. I tried to visualise the kind of man who could mutilate a victim's face, then calmly tie a keepsake to his wrist. My one certainty was that the priest and Jude had met the same attacker. Whitehall had prevented the newspapers from printing details about her injuries and the style of the attack, so it couldn't be a copycat. It was becoming urgent to discuss the parallels between the two cases with Burns.

I made my way downstairs, hoping that caffeine would restore my good humour. The café was almost empty. A gaggle of elderly shrinks was holding an intense debate over an article in the *American Journal of Psychology*, which made me wonder if any of them had actually worked with patients before specialising in theories about the criminal mind. The FPU seemed so distanced from reality that most of the consultants had forgotten how to interact.

A stout white-haired man with an unkempt beard appeared as I was struggling with the coffee machine. If he'd been a few stones heavier, he'd have been a dead ringer for Santa Claus. He reached over and jabbed one of the buttons, sending a gush of hot water into my cup.

'You're Alice Quentin, aren't you?' His voice had a broad Belfast accent. 'I'm Mike Donnelly. How long are you with us?'

'Just the next six weeks.'

'Welcome to the madhouse.' He glanced around like he was checking for spies. 'A word to the wise: most of this lot have been incarcerated here for decades. Don't be offended if they take forever to say hello.'

I gave him a grateful smile. 'I'll keep that in mind.'

'We're mostly benign, with a few exceptions,' Donnelly whispered. 'Give me a shout if you need anything.'

He hurried away, as if it was a sin to fraternise with newcomers, but it felt good to have found an ally. When I got back to the office, a middle-aged woman stared at me across a sea of empty desks. I raised my hand in greeting but she only gave a quick nod of acknowledgement before returning to her work. At least the silence allowed me to concentrate on Jude Shelley's file. I ploughed through dozens of witness statements and transcripts of interviews with potential suspects.

The first report concerned Jamal Khan, Jude's boyfriend at the time of her attack. It sounded as if the MIT had been heavy-handed from the start. He was studying at home the night Jude was hurt, his alibi confirmed by his flatmate. Despite having no evidence to implicate him, he was kept in custody for thirty-six hours, and recalled to the station twice for further questioning. The next report gave more background detail. Khan had been completing a Master's degree in social work at the time of the attack, and his relationship with Jude had lasted over a year. When I logged onto the Police National Computer, his name came up immediately. Jamal Khan had been cautioned for an assault in Tottenham five months after Jude was hospitalised, but the victim never pressed charges. I made a note of his current address and phone number and carried on leafing through the reports.

I stayed longer than I'd intended that evening. My last task was to scribble down a list of appointments for the next day.

It was seven thirty before I packed my briefcase. Mike Donnelly was working at his desk, twisting strands of his beard between his fingers, so absorbed in the file he was studying that he didn't register me at first.

'Have a good evening,' I said.

'And yourself, Alice. Take care now.'

He gave me a wide smile, the closest thing to friendship that anyone at the FPU had offered so far. But his reluctance to leave made me wonder if the consultants ever went home at a normal time. The hothouse atmosphere was a reminder that constant exposure to the worst acts of violence could turn even the sanest shrinks into obsessives.

I forgot about my new colleagues when I reached the Tube. The compartment smelled of wet umbrellas, old newspaper and exhaustion. A familiar surge of claustrophobia rose in my chest but I batted it away. My thoughts returned to Jude Shelley. Her assault was different from every other case I'd worked on. The normal motives for vicious attacks on young women were sex or robbery, but Jude hadn't been raped and her purse was still zipped inside her jacket when she was dragged from the river. The fetishistic details of the attack were identical to Father Owen's. The style of the original assault had been replicated with complete accuracy: a mysterious object tied to the priest's wrist, his face ruined, then the baptismal plunge into the river. Judging by his words to Jude, the killer believed in immortal souls, yet he was capable of obscene brutality. But why had the killer waited a whole year before choosing his next victim?

I remembered my mother's hospital appointment as soon as I got indoors. She sounded out of breath when I called, Parkinson's disease making her voice quake, as though she was shivering with cold.

'This is a surprise, darling. It's lovely to hear from you.'

'How did it go at Bart's?'

'It was a routine check-up, nothing more.'

'Did you see the specialist?'

She sighed. 'He's terribly young, still wet behind the ears.'

'Did he say anything helpful?'

'Not really. A lot of medical jargon, then he booked me an appointment with someone else. Passing the buck, I'd say.'

'Can I come with you next time?'

The temperature of her voice plummeted. 'I'm not senile, Alice. I'm perfectly capable of handling this on my own.'

'I know, Mum, but we could have lunch afterwards. We haven't done that for ages.'

My mother's tone only softened when the topic changed. She chatted breezily about a documentary she'd seen on ancient Greece, and how many friends had contacted her since she'd returned from her world cruise. We'd said goodbye before I realised that she still hadn't agreed to let me see her neurologist. Isolation had always been her modus operandi, keeping emotional contact to a minimum to save disappointment. It was a trait I kept trying and failing to remove from my own behaviour.

I took off my coat and listened to a message from my friend Yvette about the walking holiday in Scotland we'd booked for August. Then someone from Stockholm University had left a scratchy, long-distance invitation to speak at their winter conference. My brother's message came last. Will sounded almost as calm as he'd been in the old days, before his drug habit and mental illness took hold.

'I'm in town, Al. Want to meet at the Dickens at nine?'

I swore quietly to myself. I'd have to run to St Katharine Docks to get there on time, but visits from Will were so rare that I didn't want to miss the opportunity. I'd only seen him twice in the last six months, and he rarely answered my calls.

It took me fifteen minutes to jog to the pub. I scanned the crowded bar for a dishevelled figure in worn-out clothes, with a ragged beard and messy dark blond hair. There was no sign of him, so I found myself a table. His low voice reached me before I spotted him. Will was almost unrecognisable – clean-shaven and dressed in brand-new clothes, deep in conversation with a woman I'd never seen before, who was staring at him like she'd forgotten how to blink. A wave of shock crashed over me. My brother hadn't been in a relationship since his illness kicked in ten years ago. It took me several minutes to regain my composure and approach them.

'Hello, stranger.'

Will's face lit up. 'Al, come and sit down. I'll get you a drink.' He gave me a hug then loped off to the bar without introducing me to his girlfriend.

'I'm Nina, it's good to meet you.' Her voice was husky with cigarettes, softened by a rich French accent.

Her expression showed that she was making an effort, but her smile never reached her eyes. It was hard to judge her age. She was a brunette with close-cropped hair, around thirty-five, with the kind of looks the French call ugly-beautiful, her features slightly too large for her delicate bone structure. The blue edge of a tattoo was visible on her collarbone, a sentence in neat italic script, too small to read. We chatted awkwardly until Will returned, and it was clear that she was reserving all her energy for him. He seemed to revel in the attention, like in the old days when girls used to hurl themselves at him. The only difference was the time-lag between his statements, medication forcing him to think more slowly, his sky-blue eyes slightly out of focus.

'How long are you in town?' I asked.

'Three months at least,' Will said, smiling.

'A friend's lent us his houseboat till September,' Nina added. 'Then we'll look for somewhere else.'

'It must be great being on the water. How did you two meet?'

'In Brighton, at Narcotics Anonymous,' she replied steadily.

My mind raced to catch up. She was nothing like the ex-junkies I'd counselled, who emanated vulnerability. Nina was rigidly self-possessed, eye contact so intense she seemed to be daring me to make judgements. It was a relief when she went outside for a cigarette.

'Amazing, isn't she?' Will sighed. 'I knew the right one would come along.'

'It's great you're so happy,' I said, touching his hand.

I reminded myself that forecasting would be pointless. Will was far more stable than he'd been a year ago, and worrying about his fragile equilibrium if the relationship failed couldn't protect him. It crossed my mind to tell him about Mum's illness, but it felt wrong to sour his happiness. He had been out of contact with her all year and I'd have to choose the right moment to explain that she was ill. Nina still seemed tense when she came back. Even though I tried to put her at ease, her smile never revived.

'What are you planning to do while you're here?' I asked.

'Finish my MA dissertation. That should take a few months.'

'What are you researching?'

'Late eighteenth-century Romantic poetry.' She made the statement through gritted teeth, as though the subject was too sensitive to discuss.

My brother spent the next hour chatting about his plans to find work, but Nina stayed quiet. She seemed happiest whenever Will touched her, relaxing visibly when he knotted his fingers through hers.

At eleven o'clock I rose to my feet. 'I'd better get home. I've got an early start.'

'Come and have a meal with us soon on the boat,' Will said, beaming.

From the doorway I saw Nina lean across and kiss him passionately, clearly relieved to have him to herself again.

I still felt shaken when I got outside. It would take some adjustment before the situation made sense. Part of me was thrilled that Will had found someone, but caution told me that partnerships between former addicts rarely worked, and Nina was such a departure from the society girls he'd dated in the old days . . .

I watched the water flowing east, black and viscous as diesel. Small droplets of rain settled on my face as my hands gripped the railing, knuckles calcium-white in the streetlight. I looked at the river again, oozing towards the sea, and realised it was too late to worry. For my sake as well as Will's, it was time to let him go.

8

The next morning was dry for the first time in days, although the weight of the air announced that the next shower could arrive in a heartbeat. Burns had sent an email requesting a meeting the following afternoon, but the prospect of working with him again still worried me. I made myself concentrate on that morning's tasks. My first appointment was with Jude's ex-boyfriend, Jamal Khan. Evidence from the riots four years ago was still visible when I emerged from Tottenham Hale station. Scorched bricks and broken masonry could be seen on the fronts of buildings, but the High Road was teeming with life. Middle Eastern and African shops were selling rugs and hand-printed fabrics; fruit was piled high on stalls with signs promising bargains for a pound. The houses in Bruce Grove were crying out for TLC, rows of Victorian terraces trapped behind broken gates and neglected front gardens.

The Chandos estate was a sea of beige concrete trapped between Lordship Lane and Higham Road. The only greenery in sight came from knee-high weeds thriving on the cracked asphalt. A giant mural by the entrance depicted a waterfall surrounded by lush forests. The town planners must have been hoping to bring some natural beauty into the urban landscape, but the mirage couldn't alter reality. A maze of concrete walkways linked the tower blocks, deserted apart from a few boys slouching against walls, wearing the standard teenage uniform of grey hoodies and outsized jeans.

I realised where the local population were hiding when I reached the main square. The queue outside Chandos Community Support Centre was fifty metres long, a babble of languages spilling from the reception area. I heard French and Portuguese and an elderly man arguing with the receptionist in a rich Jamaican patois. The young woman behind the counter gave me a tired smile.

'Take a seat, if you can find one. I'll tell Jamal you're here.'

Khan appeared just after ten. He was average height and neatly dressed, around twenty-five years old, black-haired with coffee-coloured skin and a serious gaze. 'We'd better get out of here,' he said. 'All the interview rooms are full.'

The café he took me to was on the other side of the square. It looked like a Seventies time capsule, with lino peeling from the floor, plastic chairs and chipped Formica tables. Khan observed me coolly over a mug of tea. I could see why Jude had fallen for him. His features were classically handsome, dark green eyes surrounded by mile-long lashes.

'Can you tell me what this is about?' His expression gave nothing away.

'Jude Shelley's case has been reopened. I'd like to talk about the night she was hurt.'

'I told the police everything back then – not that they believed me.' Khan's tone resonated with controlled anger.

'You're not being singled out, Mr Khan. All of Jude's contacts are being interviewed.'

'I wasn't a contact, I was her boyfriend.' His gaze was as focused as a laser. 'The police treated me like an animal until my lawyer arrived. They kept me away from her for three days. My family made a formal complaint.'

'I'm sorry to hear that. I know this must be hard for you, but you could help Jude by telling me what you remember.'

He stared down at the table's scratched surface. 'It was sunny that afternoon. She met me in Hyde Park; we lay on the grass talking for hours. About seven we went our separate ways. I took a bus to my flat to study, and she went to a party.'

'What mood was she in when you parted?'

He hesitated. 'Not great. We'd just had a row.'

'Didn't you want to go with her?'

'I couldn't. I had to finish my dissertation.'

'Is that why you argued?'

He gave a reluctant nod. 'Jude never had to graft for top grades, she always had time to socialise. It drove me mad sometimes.'

'Were you worried about her going out alone?'

'I wasn't jealous, if that's what you mean.' Khan's eyes blazed. 'We trusted each other. I got angry because she wouldn't confide in me. There was a problem in her family she said she couldn't discuss; something to do with her dad.'

'That's what sparked the row?'

'Partly, but talking about the future made it worse.'

'Forgive me for asking so many questions. I'm just trying to understand your relationship.'

'What's so hard to grasp? A rich Catholic girl falls for a poor boy from a Muslim family. Opposites attract, don't they? But it never works out.' His speech had dulled from rage to exhaustion.

'I'm sorry. I can see this is painful for you.' I let him calm down before continuing. 'Had Jude fallen out with anyone at college?'

'No one.' He shook his head firmly. 'She always kept people on side.'

45

'But she must have attracted attention. Not every student's got a cabinet minister for a dad.'

'Her real friends didn't care about that.' Khan frowned, as if I'd said something crass.

'Did you meet each other's families?'

He gave a grudging nod. 'My parents are practising Muslims but they accept I'm not religious; they let me make my own choices. Her dad was the opposite; he couldn't stand me from the off. It made things impossible.'

'In what way?'

'You want me to be honest?'

'Please.'

'A few days before Jude was attacked, a man came to my flat. I thought it was just some freak who'd picked my door at random; he was dressed in a wig and black sunglasses, so I couldn't see his eyes. Afterwards I wondered if her dad had sent him. He tried to get in, but I shoved him back into the street.'

'What did he say?'

'A load of threats. He said he'd hurt me if I gave away secrets.'

'Can you remember anything else?'

'Something about the river's soul. None of it made sense.'

'And you think Timothy Shelley was behind it?'

Khan stared at me. 'If you were a cabinet minister, would you want your daughter dating a Muslim?'

'Why didn't you tell the police?'

'I didn't want Jude to worry.'

'You never told her you'd been threatened?'

'Things were bad enough already. She'd been tense for weeks about her family, but I never found out why.'

Timothy Shelley's bland face appeared in my mind, his skin shiny with ambition. Why would he risk his position by employing a heavy mob? It seemed more likely that Khan had received a visit from the killer himself. His babble about the river's soul echoing the words Jude had remembered. Burns's team would have to interview Khan in more detail about his threatening visitor, and I needed to question Jude about the family problem she'd refused to share with her boyfriend.

'Your police record says you were involved in a fight last November. Can you tell me why?'

Khan let out a sigh of protest. 'The guy never pressed charges. It shouldn't even be on my record.'

'All police contact stays on your profile for twelve months. You know that, don't you?'

'He tried to mug me. It was self-defence.'

'The report says you threw him against a wall so hard he broke his shoulder.'

'I had no choice.'

When I studied Khan again, his face held despair as well as rage. It was easy to see why the trauma of Jude's attack had left him desperate to punch someone.

'Have you seen Jude since she was hospitalised?'

'The second time she told me never to come back. Her face was covered in bandages, I couldn't even see her eyes. After that the nurses sent me away every time I tried to visit. I don't even know if she got my messages.' He pulled a card from his pocket, his anger finally evaporating. 'Can you do me a favour? Get Jude to call me if she's changed her mind.'

I studied the card then slipped it into my bag. 'Thanks for your time, Jamal.'

He gave a tired smile as he rose to his feet. 'I'd better go. Wednesday's our busiest day of the week; people are collecting vouchers for the food bank.'

I watched him march back to work, arms swinging like a soldier on parade, then began to scribble on a psychological assessment form, recording my impressions before they faded. If Khan had been a patient, I'd have been concerned about the way his manner had vacillated between hostility and despair. The reasons for his hatred of the police were obvious. He had been held in custody despite a complete lack of evidence and kept in their sights long after he stopped being a formal suspect. The pain in his voice was so raw, he still seemed burdened by unresolved feelings for Jude. His claim that she had been troubled by a family issue to do with her father was interesting. Khan's description of the words used by the thug at his door echoed those of her attacker; it sounded like the same man had threatened him because of his relationship with Jude.

I put down my pen and looked back across the square. The queue outside the community centre had grown even longer and I tried to put my impressions in context. Khan seemed like a man with a strong social conscience. His job would require constant patience to deal with the severity of his clients' needs: unemployment, lack of money, and no food on the table. The demands of his work must be keeping his unhappiness at a permanent simmer.

My next meeting was only a twenty-minute Tube ride away, but it felt like entering a different world. Office workers strolled through Holborn, clutching takeaway lunches and giant lattes, the area oozing with prosperity. I inhaled the scent of the world Jude Shelley had once belonged to: Chanel Number Five, cashmere and expensive cigarettes. If she'd finished her degree she would have walked shoulder to shoulder with the sharp-suited young lawyers milling outside Eat and Pret a Manger.

I paused to admire Lincoln's Inn Fields. The wide swath of grass was surrounded by limestone buildings, which housed the city's most expensive legal firms. Jude's closest friend, Natalie Poll, worked for Pembroke's on Newman's Row. She was a pretty, curly-haired blonde with china-blue eyes and a ready smile, her blouse so immaculate it must have been loaded with starch. She shot me an apologetic glance as we entered her office.

'Sorry it's such a squeeze. They keep this room for new recruits to test our grit.' The space barely accommodated a desk and two upright chairs. 'Heather called me last night. I'm so glad you're looking into Jude's case.'

'I'm hoping you can give me some background information. You and Jude shared a flat, didn't you?'

Natalie gave a crisp nod. 'I moved back into halls after she got hurt. The flat had too many echoes. We'd been like twins since our course began – going to the same lectures, sharing meals. She even came on holiday with my family.'

'Were you close to Jamal too?'

Her eyes blinked wide, like a doll being shaken. 'He wasn't my favourite human being.'

'Did he upset you in some way?'

'Their relationship didn't seem worth the anguish.'

'How do you mean?'

'Her family thought he was a bad influence, and I could tell he made Jude feel vulnerable.'

'Was there a specific reason for that?'

'I'd find her crying her heart out some nights. One time her room was trashed after he left, stuff broken on the floor. It looked like he'd been chucking furniture around. I told her to report it, but she didn't of course.'

'Why do you say "of course"? Plenty of women report abusive behaviour, don't they?'

'She'd hate me for talking like this, but I think she had a victim mentality because of her past.'

'You think she'd experienced violence before?'

Natalie pursed her lips, as if she was holding back a torrent of words. 'You should ask Jude about her childhood, and the man she was seeing before Jamal.'

It seemed odd that, despite her friend's injuries, Natalie was still defending her privacy. Jude must have been a strong personality, still commanding loyalty from her friends after so much time had passed. 'Do you know what she and Jamal used to row about?'

'It's obvious, isn't it? Someone like Jude could never marry someone like him, there were too many barriers.' Natalie's cupid-bow lips pressed together in a tight line.

'You still see Jude regularly, don't you?'

'I take her books and magazines. She'd do the same for me.'

We talked for a while longer, but Natalie provided little new information. Her friendship with Jude sounded like it had been intense until Jamal upset the applecart. The two girls had gone to the gym together, partied and shared each other's clothes. Apart from Jamal, she couldn't name a single person who had argued with Jude. When I said goodbye, her handshake was tight enough to burn.

'I hope you catch him, whoever he is,' she whispered. 'Hanging's too good for that bastard.'

It was a relief to escape from the airless room, drizzle blurring the red-brick buildings on the far side of Lincoln's Inn Fields. I thought about the impact Jude had made on the people she knew. Jamal Khan was so haunted that his pain still bubbled close to the surface, but only Jude could explain if their relationship had included violence, or whether someone had hurt her as a child. Natalie Poll seemed to be telling the truth, but she'd kept her distress hidden behind her well-groomed façade right until the end of our meeting. My knuckles ached from the tension in her grip as I walked back to the Tube.

9

There's been no sign of her for hours, but her closeness sings in his veins, louder than the traffic's roar. He takes care to stay in the shadows, sheltered from the rain. His face is hidden under a broad-brimmed hat and dark glasses. He's darkened his skin tone too, with a smear of fake tan. Pedestrians march along St Pancras Way, oblivious to his presence, souls shrouding their faces like mist. None of them interest him. Only the girl will satisfy the river's appetite.

She emerges from the police station at three o'clock, her aura so bright he has to shade his eyes. She trots down the steps, as though she's happy to be chosen. When she stands at a bus stop, he waits by the railing, beyond her line of vision. She's listening to her iPod, locked in her own world, but her closeness is overwhelming. The woman carries on nodding to a rhythm only she can hear. She boards a northbound bus and he finds a seat at the back, his whole body pulsing with her existence. He stares out at the shops on Caledonian Road without noticing a single detail. When he sees her preparing to leave the bus, he stumbles to his feet.

The man glimpses his reflection in a shop window, huddled in a wet raincoat, a bag slung across his shoulder, the brow of his hat concealing his face. He could be one of a million office workers hurrying home from work. The woman takes her time walking through Barnsbury, stopping for a newspaper and a bunch of flowers. Then she walks more purposefully and his breath quickens. He's a few metres behind her when she unlocks her door.

'Can you help me please?' he calls.

The woman is wearing a half-formed smile when he bundles her into the hallway. She has no time to scream, her aura blazing more brightly, blue-white, crackling with electricity.

'Is this some kind of joke?' Her voice quakes with panic.

'There's no point in fighting. I came for this.' He drifts his fingers through the haze of her soul.

'My boyfriend'll be back soon. You should leave.'

'You haven't got a boyfriend.' She reaches for her phone, but he grabs her arm. 'Struggling won't help.'

The woman's teeth sink into his wrist, and he gives a yelp of pain before letting his fist fly. Her body falls unconscious at his feet, red flowers scattering across the carpet, beautiful and scentless. He arranges her limbs neatly, arms straight at her sides. Then he collects the blossoms and arranges them around her face. A flicker of guilt rises in his throat. He doesn't want to hurt her, but she knows too much. If she told her secrets, his world would be broken. The man kneels beside her to enjoy her beauty while it lasts.

10

Jude was awake when I returned to the hospital on Thursday morning. The light filtering through her window was grey as dishwater, and I could tell she was weakening. Last time her hands had gesticulated restlessly, but now she was motionless, only her head slanted in my direction, her eye circled by a network of exposed veins. I noticed again how beautiful her hair was, long strands highlighted with copper, gleaming on her pillow.

'How are you today?' I asked.

'Living the dream. Can't you tell?' A laugh gurgled from the respirator, and I pictured her before the attack, upbeat and full of irony. 'I've been watching Clint Eastwood movies – *Pale Rider*, *Unforgiven*, *Gran Torino*. Films make more sense to me than all this.'

'I bet they do.' Westerns had a clearer moral code, the baddies always caught and punished. 'I've been interviewing some of your friends, Jude.'

'Which ones?'

'Natalie and Jamal.'

She flinched, but her ruined face was impossible to read. 'What did they say?'

'Jamal's quite angry, isn't he? Was he always like that?'

'Not about personal things. Injustice upsets him, that's why he chose social work.'

'Was he ever violent towards you?'

54

Her hands twitched at her sides. 'Of course not. His gentleness was one of the things that attracted me.'

'Natalie thought he'd hit you. She said she came back once and your room was in a mess.'

There was a long pause. 'I can't talk about that.'

'You promised to be open, Jude.'

Her voice was quiet when she finally replied. 'It was me that lost control. He made me so angry I hurled things at him, then felt terrible.'

'What had upset you so much?'

'His defeatism. We never agreed about our future.' Her voice fell to a whisper. 'I wanted to stay with him, but he only saw obstacles.'

'He thought your father hated him.'

'That's Jamal for you – he believes the world's out to get him. Dad's always let me make my own choices.'

'He said that a family problem had upset you, something to do with your dad. Can you tell me about that?'

There was an interval before she replied. 'It was nothing, just the usual chemistry. We're so alike, we wind each other up sometimes.'

'Jamal made it sound much more serious.'

'He misunderstood what was going on.'

'He still wants to visit you. Would you allow that?'

The monitors above her bed bleeped loudly, her heart rate soaring. 'He can't. Tell him to stay away.'

'Are you sure that's what you want?'

'Jamal never saw me like this.' The noise from her machines gradually faded. 'His conscience is too strong. If he'd known how bad it was, he'd have kept coming back, trying to help. I had to let him go.'

'It's your decision, Jude. I won't try and change your mind.' I sat back in my chair. 'Natalie's a loyal friend, isn't she?'

'The best ever.'

Jude talked about her exploits with Natalie in a shaky voice. They had taken a riotous skiing holiday, with so much booze and après-ski that they missed the slopes completely some days. The carefree friend she described didn't match the tense young woman I'd met at Pembroke's. Jude's description of Natalie made me realise that her attack had caused a ripple effect, changing her friends' lives irreversibly. She spoke of a life that had once been full of adventures, which matched the bravery she'd shown in cutting her boyfriend adrift. To have survived so long by herself in a sterile hospital room took more grit than I could even imagine.

'A couple more tough questions. Natalie thought someone might have been violent towards you as a child. Is that true?'

There was no reply. All I could hear was the whisper of people chatting in the corridor, and the breathing apparatus pumping air into her lungs.

'She gets confused sometimes. Take what she says with a pinch of salt.'

'She seemed very clear-headed to me.'

'Why would I lie?'

'Jude, if we're going to find him, you can't hide anything.'

'You're looking in the wrong direction.' Her tone was growing truculent. 'There's nothing more to say.'

I took a deep breath. 'We'll talk about it another time. I need to know everything about your past, including the secrets you'd like to bury.' Her folded arms showed that she had no intention of opening up, so I had to move on. 'I've been through the transcripts of your evidence after the attack. You said Jamal was the only serious boyfriend you'd had, but that's not true, is it?'

Her hands twitched upwards again. 'What makes you so sure?'

'You were a gorgeous twenty-two-year-old girl. I can't believe he was your first.'

'Why? Did you have dozens of lovers at my age?'

'Just three or four. Some lousy choices, actually.'

My candour seemed to unlock her defences. 'There was one serious fling. I was crazy about him but it was a mistake.'

'I need his name, Jude.'

It took ten minutes to wheedle it out of her: Paul Ramirez, one of her university lecturers, a married man. They'd had a six-month affair before she met Jamal, but apart from his name she wouldn't yield a single detail. It seemed incredible that the police investigation hadn't probed deep enough to uncover him. Their incompetence deserved a formal complaint, but I was beginning to suspect that Whitehall had warned them to use a light touch. Jude's body language revealed that she was starting to tire.

'Mum told me Father Owen had died, but she wouldn't say what happened to him.'

'You don't watch the news?'

'It's too bleak most of the time.'

'But you know his body was found by the Thames?'

Her hands froze in her lap. 'You think it's started again?'

'It's not clear yet. The police are looking at the evidence. Were you close to Father Owen?'

Her head shifted by a fraction on her pillow. 'He used to visit me every month. He always said it didn't matter that I'd lost my faith, he had enough to spare.'

Jude's ruined face couldn't reveal her emotions, but I was learning to interpret them from her gestures. The way she'd deflected every question about her childhood made me wonder which members of her family she was protecting. By the time I left, she'd shut down completely. She gave a single nod when I suggested that we try memory recovery techniques next time I visited. The gesture was more a dismissal than an acceptance. Despite her injuries, it was clear that her desire for privacy had survived intact.

I was dreading my next appointment. Now that I was officially included in Burns's investigation of Father Owen's murder, the coroner's office had agreed to let me attend the post-mortem. Despite my squeamishness, the links between Jude's attack and the priest's murder had to be followed up. Burns would be witnessing the procedure too. The building loomed closer as I walked, a huge white edifice that looked brand new, dominating the western stretch of the Euston Road.

The mortuary was so well hidden in the basement that I arrived ten minutes late. A Latin inscription was printed above the door: *Hic locus est ubi mors gaudet succurrere vitae*. There was no time to lament my lack of classical education; the pathologist's assistant rushed out with a worried expression on his face.

'Dr Lindstrop isn't thrilled, she hates delays. DCI Burns is already here.'

The pathologist's expression was thunderous when I entered her theatre. She looked around sixty, grey-haired with a portly figure, anger turning her cheeks scarlet.

'Sorry I'm late. The Tube's at a standstill.'

'And so am I, Dr Quentin, because of your lateness. Do you know how many more autopsies I have booked today?' I shook my head, aware that opening my mouth would increase her rage. 'Three. I won't get home till nine tonight. Stand by the wall, please, and reserve your questions until the end.'

Burns's voice resonated behind me. 'Calm down, Fiona. Remember your blood pressure.'

She dismissed his comment with a swipe of her hand. 'And the same to you, Don. One more noise and you're outside.'

Dr Lindstrop turned to survey the old man's corpse and I nodded at Burns. He looked so ill at ease that I remembered the last post-mortem we'd attended together when he'd passed out cold. I watched Lindstrop circling the marble slab, but avoided focusing on the old man's face, a raw mess of blue and red. His body was pitifully thin, skin sagging across his ribs, naked apart from a white sheet covering his pelvis, as though the pathologist was saving his blushes. I made an effort to steady my breathing and hoped that Burns was doing the same. It was evident that fainting in Dr Lindstrop's theatre would not be tolerated. She was concentrating so hard that she seemed to have forgotten she had an audience.

'You poor old fellow,' she whispered to herself.

The pathologist shone her torch on the priest's damaged face, then stepped back to examine each limb in turn, intoning a list of bruises and contusions into the microphone that hung from the ceiling. It interested me that she handled the man's skin delicately, reserving her tenderness for the dead instead of the living. She examined the glass disc that hung from his left wrist, then cut the leather tie and deposited it on a tray. With an instrument small as a toothpick she scraped under the priest's nails.

'If he fought his attacker, skin or hair cells may still be under here,' she muttered in our direction. 'Even if he was submerged for hours.'

Her assistant labelled the specimen jar and placed it on the tray. Now that she was fully absorbed, Lindstrop seemed to have forgotten her outrage. When she leant down to examine the man's skull more closely, I could no longer avoid looking at his wounds, my empty stomach churning in protest.

'Category A craniofacial injuries,' she told the microphone. 'Total skin excision from mandible to zygomatic, left side. Soft tissue excision from nasal arch to parietal, right side.'

I listened to her reciting surgical terms, but even a layman could see that his entire face had been removed. Only his cloudy blue eyes remained, staring vacantly at the ceiling. Dr Lindstrop peered at the exposed flesh with a magnifying glass, then turned towards us.

'The muscle fibres have been torn vertically, which means that the first cut was made under the chin, then the skin was wrenched upwards.'

'Like removing a balaclava,' I said.

'Quite so.' Lindstrop sounded amused, as though I'd attempted a joke.

Burns gave a muffled groan. He looked even worse than I felt, his face a pallid shade of green. For the next hour Lindstrop was too busy to speak, and my legs were refusing to carry my full weight. I had become intimately familiar with every organ in the priest's body – his heart, lungs, liver and spleen had all been removed and weighed separately. Just as we were about to leave, the pathologist directed her attention to Burns.

'How strong is your stomach today?' The outline of her smile appeared behind her surgical mask.

'I'm still standing, aren't I?' he replied gruffly.

'Come here and I'll show you something interesting.' He didn't move an inch. 'What about you, Dr Quentin?'

A host of smells hit me as I approached the slab: blood, excrement and the dark pungency of tar. Lindstrop raised a measuring jug to the light, half filled with brown liquid.

'This came from his lungs, which shows that he died from drowning. The body fights to breathe, even when semiconscious. The victim ends up inhaling water as a reflex reaction. If he'd died before entering the river, his lungs would have been almost empty.'

'Would the head wound have killed him?'

'That's certain, judging by its depth. The circular bruise on his temple is consistent with a single hammer blow, heavy enough to render him unconscious, then the killer worked on his face and skull. The attack must have been quick for him still to be breathing when he hit the water.' She peered down at the cloudy liquid. 'Finest Thames water, by the looks of it. None too clean.'

'So he was working at speed?'

She nodded vigorously. 'Definitely, or the shock of the attack would have killed such an elderly man before he hit the water. It takes effort and forethought to remove someone's face so neatly.' Her eyes glittered with interest.

Lindstrop showed us the piece of glass she'd removed from the priest's wrist on our way out. It was more beautiful than it had looked in the crime scene photo: a pale blue circle, with embossed markings, its edges delicately curved. It looked ornamental, but I couldn't guess its age or how it had been used.

'What do you think it is?' Burns asked.

'Goodness knows. I'm a pathologist, not a historian. It was attached by a reef knot, double-tied. The victim would have struggled to do that himself.'

She ushered us out, clearly keen to start her next autopsy. I pointed at the inscription above the door before asking what it meant.

'A rough translation is, "This is the place where death rejoices to teach those who are still alive." A fine sentiment, but my schedule allows little time for celebration.' She pointed at Burns. 'You owe me a drink for rushing your victim to the top of my list.'

'Text me, Fiona. I'm at your disposal.'

She hurried away, leaving me convinced that I would make a poor pathologist. Lindstrop's eyes shone with excitement at discovering the reason for a fatality, but death rarely made me feel enthusiastic. In an ideal world, I would never have to attend another autopsy. Burns looked equally fazed, the colour slowly returning to his face. But even now, that unwelcome itch of attraction was still there.

Burns's Audi was parked three blocks away, and I was glad of the exercise, fresh air scouring the taste of formaldehyde from my mouth. Apart from a few grumbled comments about the autopsy, he was monosyllabic on the way to the police station on St Pancras Way. I noticed that the place hadn't changed since my last visit. The walls of the reception area held the same laminated warnings not to smoke, swear or behave abusively towards staff. Burns filled two cups of coffee on our way through the staff room, without bothering to check if I wanted one. He seemed to assume that normal business had resumed. By the time we reached the meeting room, rage was flooding my system, and I was hanging on to my professionalism by the skin of my teeth. The sourness of my expression probably explained why he kept his tone formal.

'I'm glad you're working on this, Alice. I need all the help I can get. I went to see the Right Honourable Timothy Shelley the day after the priest's body was found, but he was just as slippery as I remembered.'

'How do you mean?'

'His answers sounded like he was rehearsing soundbites for the TV. Owen had been his family priest for over twenty years, but there was no sign of real grief.'

'That's how he seemed to me too. His wife and son say he doesn't do feelings; he's about as repressed as they come.'

'Have you found any fresh information on Jude's attack?'

'Not really. So far I've assessed her twice, interviewed relatives and two of her friends.'

'Did they give any new angles?'

'There's a family conflict she won't discuss, to do with her dad, and I think she may have experienced violence before. The first investigation didn't even scratch the surface. The MIT took Jude's family members' word about what they were doing on the night of the attack. They didn't even probe deep enough to find out about her previous boyfriends.'

'I'm going back over the alibis and everything they missed.' Burns shifted forwards in his seat. 'I hope you haven't told the Shelleys you think the police mishandled the investigation.'

'Of course not. But I'm certain it's someone closely connected to the family. Father Owen's death happened the same day Jude's case reopened; only her relatives and the authorities knew about it.'

Burns looked sceptical. 'You think her attacker waited a whole year to kill the man who baptised her?'

'He throws his victims in the river, doesn't he? Maybe he sees it as a kind of baptism.'

'I can't believe a family member attacked Jude. It was them who asked for the case to be reopened.'

I shook my head. 'Only Heather Shelley wanted it. Her husband thinks Jude can't handle the stress.'

'But you don't agree?'

'To survive this long, Jude's tough enough to deal with a few intrusive questions. She's cagey at the moment, it'll take time to win her trust. I think you should run a background check on the man she saw before Jamal Khan; his name's Paul Ramirez. I've arranged to visit him. He's a law lecturer at King's College.'

Burns scribbled the name down, then met my gaze again. 'All we've got so far is that Father Owen visited Jude regularly and he was killed by the same method; Lindstrop confirmed that today. He was alive when he went into the river, just like Jude. I'm not convinced the link to the family's as direct as you say. It could be any freak who's got it in for the cabinet minister, targeting his daughter, then his priest. The date of the second attack could be a coincidence. Security's been stepped up round Shelley and his wife and son, in case they're next on his list.' He rubbed his hand across his jaw. 'You realise we'll face a lot of intervention, don't you? Whitehall don't want the press knowing the two investigations are linked. They're paranoid about a media storm.'

'That could slow things down.'

Burns checked the clock on the wall. 'Do you want to get something to eat and go through the details?'

I took a moment to gather myself. 'Maybe I should explain how I intend to work on the case. I'll attend meetings, answer emails and phone calls, and perform my professional role to the best of my ability. Anything else is off limits.'

For once Burns's cockiness had disappeared. He opened his mouth to speak but swiftly closed it again. His skin was paler than it had been during the autopsy, and his silence continued when I said goodbye.

I I

The man drives back through the darkness to the woman's house. He pulls on sterile gloves then unlocks the door with keys stolen from her bag. She's conscious now, lying exactly where he left her, gagged and bound on the living-room floor, terror visible in her eyes. He loosens her gag to let her breathe more easily.

'Why are you doing this?' she splutters. 'Is it money? Take my bank card. I'll tell you the code.'

'That's not the reason. You know too much, Amala.'

'What do you mean?' She tries to scream, but he wads her mouth more thickly this time, so no words can escape.

'You should have kept yourself clean.'

He takes off his coat, then pulls the knife from his briefcase. For a second the room spins. This is the part he hates most, but the river's voice can't be ignored. He gazes around the room to steady himself. There's a wooden dining table, clothes drying on the radiator, a brass crucifix on the wall. The room smells of washing powder and furniture polish. He raises the knife and steels himself for the first incision. The woman stares back, refusing to pardon him. He's praying it will get easier after he makes the first cut, but his body refuses to comply. Her face is too perfect to destroy. He drops the knife, then staggers to the kitchen and vomits into the sink, tears spilling from his eyes. He shivers as he swabs away the mess with bleach. It shakes him to the core that he can't bring himself to follow the river's instructions.

The man runs upstairs and rummages through the cupboards. When he returns to the living room he forces himself to kick the girl's skull hard, rendering her unconscious again. He lays a suitcase on the floor and lifts her inert body inside. It sheathes her form like a chrysalis, her knees tight against her chest. He waits until the street is silent, lights out in every house, before heaving the case into his arms and carrying it to the boot of his car.

His sense of failure haunts him as he drives south. The river whispers a string of complaints, but he feels stronger by the time he reaches Wapping. He parks his car on the wharf, the suitcase twitching as he cradles it. The Victorian streetlights cast a dull glow, but there's no one around, the pub locked up for the night. He staggers down to the foreshore, wishing he could walk away, but he can't let himself fail again. His heart thunders as he undoes the zip. The rope around the woman's feet has worked loose and she kicks out wildly.

'Stop that,' he snaps. 'The river's waiting for you.'

The man reties the rope, then binds the earthenware bottle tight around her waist with a leather string. He abandons his shoes before wading into the water. The river smells different tonight, metallic as rust, silt oozing under his feet. The woman's limbs are rigid as he drops the noose around her neck, tightens it, then loops it under her arms. It takes seconds to attach the rope to a mooring ring on the wharf, the river's voice rising in ecstasy. She thrashes like a line-caught fish, and suddenly it becomes easier to do his duty. The blade of his knife slices her face again and again. Then he forces her body underwater, her limbs jerking in a frenzy of movement. The river's ecstasy sends a sheen of light flickering across its surface until the last bubbles disappear.

12

I went for a run in Southwark Park early on Friday morning. The buildings around the perimeter looked like they had been soaked in grey emulsion, the boardwalk slick under my feet, but at least my body was glowing when I got home. I was half-way through my bowl of muesli when a text arrived from Will, inviting me to dinner that evening. The prospect of meeting his mysterious new girlfriend again was so intriguing that I accepted immediately.

One of Guy Shelley's statements kept nagging at me. He believed that his father's job exposed him to danger from members of the public. Keen to check whether he was correct, I put through a call to the House of Commons just after nine a.m. Tinny versions of Vivaldi and Mozart squeaked in my ear, then the receptionist announced that she was putting my call through to Giles Moorcroft, the minister's diary secretary. The voice that greeted me was a pleasant Etonian drawl, professionally polite, and I remembered Shelley's sombre dark-haired assistant at the hospital, hovering in the background.

'How may I help?'

'Could I make an appointment with the minister please? My name's Dr Alice Quentin.'

'Can I ask the nature of your enquiry?'

'I work for the Forensic Psychology Unit. I met him this week at the Royal London when he was visiting his daughter.'

There was a long pause, as though he was trying to place me. 'I'll check the minister's schedule and call you back. I'm afraid you may have to wait some time.'

'It needs to be on Monday, please. This is a matter of urgency.'

'I'll see what I can do.'

Maybe I imagined it, but I thought Moorcroft groaned quietly. Perhaps the minister had instructed him to keep me at arm's length, to show his lack of support for the reinvestigation. The thought crossed my mind that he might be avoiding me because he had harmed his daughter, but that seemed too preposterous. Shelley's time must have been in constant demand.

My phone rang as I was about to leave. My heart raced as I answered, on high alert for a call from Lola summoning me to her flat. The woman's raw East End accent was difficult to hear. Background noise was drowning it out – a car engine revving, then a babble of voices. It took me a few seconds to realise that I was talking to DI Tania Goddard, Burns's deputy.

'Can you come to the Prospect of Whitby pub straight away?' Her speech was so terse she seemed to resent wasting a single word.

'What's happened, Tania?'

'One of our officers has been found dead on the riverbank. Burns is asking for you.'

She rang off while I was still processing the idea that the killer might have struck again. I pulled on my waterproof coat and hauled my bike into the lift; there was no point in attempting to drive through the rush-hour traffic. The rapid ten-minute ride to Wapping gave me little time to speculate. The river was at high tide, blacker than ever, vanishing between the ancient buildings on Wapping Wall.

The street outside the Prospect of Whitby was a hive of activity. It had been cordoned off by three police vans and a traffic patrol car. The Met had commandeered the pub, which was heaving with officers. When I headed inside, the dark wooden panelling seemed to absorb every speck of brightness, as though natural light never penetrated the leaded windows. My eyes scanned the interior looking for Burns, but caught instead on a sign over the bar stating that the Prospect was London's oldest riverside pub, open since 1520. The interior had been salvaged from old ships; the bar was made of pewter, walls supported by old barrels and masts. I was still studying the ancient flagstone floor when a young woman appeared. She was almost as small-framed as me, with cropped red hair, her pixie-like face splitting into a smile of greeting. It was Angie Wilcox, one of Burns's detectives from his days at Southwark. The last time I'd worked with her had been on the Crossbones case, but her ability to talk ceaselessly without ever drawing breath was unchanged.

'The boss headhunted me. Last time I saw you I was full steam ahead planning my wedding. It went okay, thank God, apart from one bridesmaid getting rat-arsed at the reception and making a tit of herself. I've had some luck at work too – they're putting me up for my inspector exam next year.'

'Burns must be thrilled to have you.'

'I bloody hope so. It's been full-on since I arrived, and now this happens.'

Angie was as excitable as I'd remembered, but she silenced herself when Burns's deputy arrived. Tania Goddard towered over us, so glossy she looked like she'd been airbrushed; her black fringe bisected her forehead in a geometric line, lips a vivid crimson. Only the bleak look in her eyes revealed her state of mind.

'Are you all right?' I asked.

'I've had better days. The victim's WPC Amala Adebayo, thirty-four years old. She'd only been with us six months. Her body was found tied up twenty metres west along the river-bank. The men who found her brought her up here; they were worried the river might carry her away.' Her voice tailed into silence. 'You'd better go through, Alice. Burns is waiting.'

The wide sweep of the river greeted me when I got outside, acres of charcoal sky with the warehouses of Shad Thames lining the opposite bank. But no one was admiring the view. A white tent had been erected in the patio garden, a police photographer disappearing through the flaps. Burns had his mobile clamped to his ear, his accent growing steadily more Scottish. A business-like young scenes of crime officer scribbled my name on her checklist, then handed me a sterile suit and plastic overshoes. I was about to put them on when a tear dropped from her eye onto the sheet of paper. She wiped it away hurriedly, as though emotions were a weakness best ignored.

'Did you know Amala well?' I asked.

The girl gave a miserable nod. 'We started the same week.'

'I'm so sorry. What was she like?'

'Lovely.' Her eyes were still brimming. 'You could tell her anything. I can't believe anyone would hurt her.'

When I turned round, Burns was facing me. His expression warned me that whatever lay inside the tent wasn't going to be pretty.

'This is worse than Jude Shelley's attack.' He pulled a police ID card from his pocket. 'That's how Amala looked yesterday. I want everyone to remember that.'

'She's stunning.' A young black woman with high cheek-bones and flawless skin gazed back at me.

'Not any more.' His scowl deepened.

Burns pulled back the tent flaps and I stepped inside. The

temperature seemed to fall by several degrees, rain drumming on the plastic roof. Amala Adebayo's corpse was clothed in black shoes and trousers, white T-shirt in tatters. Her hands were bound so tightly that the rope had chafed her wrists. Her legs were constrained too, binds round her knees and ankles. I glanced across at Burns then forced myself to study her face. There was evidence of a frenzied attack. The policewoman's cheeks and forehead had been slashed apart by wounds so deep that white glints of bone were exposed. A single cut had sliced through her eyes, continuing across the bridge of her nose. The river had taken its toll too, her skin grotesquely bloated. A thick rope hung from her neck like a hangman's noose.

My head swam as I stepped back into the open air. For once the rain felt like a blessing, washing away my nausea. 'Did he leave a calling card?'

'It was tied round her waist. Do you want to see it?'

One of the oddest objects I'd ever seen lay on a plastic tray inside a clear evidence bag. It was an earthenware bottle, about three inches long, made of dark brown pottery, with the face of a bearded man embossed on the side. The ceramic features were hard to read, lips almost hidden by his beard, his smile either kindly or malevolent. I leant down to take a photo with my phone.

'What the hell is it?' Burns murmured.

'I need to find out. Tagging the victim's bodies is a big part of his killing ritual. Can I see where she was left on the riverbank?'

He shook his head. 'I'll have to show you from here.'

He led me to the railing and pointed west. The river was moving rapidly, shallow waves scudding along the embankment. A row of buoys marked the spot where the policewoman's body had been found at the foot of a staircase. When I looked

71

back at Burns, his face was tense with frustration. Not only had he lost one of his team, the river had scoured every scrap of evidence from the crime scene.

The rain made me abandon my bike and accept Burns's offer of a lift back to the station, but people kept accosting him with questions. He seemed to be succumbing to shock, his eyes stretched a little too wide. I thought about Whitehall's reaction when they learned that the killer had struck again – their efforts to keep the investigation quiet would be blown sky high. Burns's car smelled as if it had been valeted that morning, the air heavy with polish and lemon detergent. Normally we'd have talked about everything we'd seen, but the atmosphere was still bristling with tension as he explained the arrangements for the case.

'Tania's leading the forensics team and liaising with the media. I'll look after evidence and operations, with help from Angie.' He stared at the road ahead. 'It was like déjà vu when I saw Amala. The style's identical to what happened to Jude.'

'Whoever's doing this seems obsessed by the river. He ran a big risk to carry Amala's body through a built-up area, even in the middle of the night. It would have been a damn sight easier to drive out of town and dump her on waste ground. All the attacks are heavily ritualised.'

Burns didn't reply, and I couldn't help looking across at him. The attraction was difficult to pin down; it might have stemmed from his hulking build, the determined set of his jaw or the fact that he was so focused on doing the right thing. But wherever it came from, I wished I could turn it off at source and concentrate on doing my job.

The atmosphere in the incident room was leaden. Officers from the Met pride themselves on greeting every disaster with gallows humour and a stiff upper lip, but both strategies seemed to be failing. A middle-aged woman was weeping uncontrollably, and I saw Burns crouch down to squeeze her shoulder. Poster-sized photos of Amala had already been posted on the evidence board. I studied one of them closely. She looked much younger than thirty-four, beaming for the camera in a bright green dress, a gold cross dangling from her neck.

Burns waited until the senior investigation team returned from the crime scene to start his briefing. I recognised most of the dozen officers from previous cases, but had never seen them this subdued. Even Pete Hancock looked upset, the station's senior SOCO, who prided himself on being inscrutable. Angie's chatter had lapsed into silence, and Tania stood at the front of the room, gazing straight ahead, arms folded. Burns sounded so outraged when he began to speak that he could have been talking directly to the killer.

'We lost one of our best new recruits last night. Amala Adebayo. She came to the UK from Ghana at eighteen and did nannying jobs until she'd earned enough qualifications to join the Met's training scheme. I know feelings are running high, but you need to keep a lid on them until her killer's put away.' Burns glared at the faces in the front row. 'We know Amala left work yesterday around three p.m. – we have film of her on the front steps. She normally took the bus to her rented house in Barnsbury. I want you to check number-plate recognition and CCTV cameras for the entire journey. Talk to colleagues, friends and family to see if anyone was pestering her. Find out if she visited chat rooms, or did Internet dating. We owe it to Amala to learn all her secrets.' He turned and nodded at Tania to take over.

'This is a manhunt for a serial killer. Father Kelvin Owen was found on the riverbank at Westminster on Monday morning, just three days ago. The hallmarks of that attack are exactly like Amala's. Most of you will remember Jude Shelley being attacked twelve months ago. She survived, but the MO was identical. Her face was destroyed, then she was thrown into the river fully clothed with a piece of metal round her neck.' She glanced down at the papers in her hand. 'One of the investigation team thought the object was an arrowhead. A piece of glass was tied to Father Kelvin's wrist, and a ceramic bottle around Amala's waist, all on thin strips of leather. This guy's so organised, he's even got time to tag his victims.'

My desire to understand the objects' symbolism stepped up a gear. There must be a factor uniting them with the Shelley family, and they had to hold a personal resonance for the killer. Unlocking their meaning would bring me closer to understanding his identity.

There was a ripple of whispers as the team absorbed the information, then Tania and Angie began allocating duties. Search teams were organised to return to the river, another group checking road cameras, the next arranging house to house. The forensic team were conducting a fingertip search of the stairs leading down to the foreshore and part of Wapping High Street, which was still cordoned off. The detectives looked more purposeful as they hurried away, relieved to have something specific to do. Only Pete Hancock looked as concerned as before, black monobrow lowering a centimetre above his eyes, his mouth a thin horizontal line.

I was about to leave when Burns caught up with me. 'Can we have a quick meeting?'

His office had been redecorated. The walls were pristine white, his desk empty, an exercise bike standing in the corner. It made me wonder where the old chaotic Burns was hiding. His hands were buried deep his pockets as he stood by the wall, staring at me.

'Are you with me or against me, Alice?'

'Sorry?'

'I know I'm not your favourite person, but you're the only shrink I trust to work on this.'

'We're after the same perpetrator. That means we're in this together, whether I like it or not.'

Burns looked exasperated. 'Then stop snapping and start communicating. Or are you too angry?'

'Don't patronise me, Don. My role here's professional, not personal.'

'We have to be able to talk openly.'

His tone hovered somewhere between a plea and an order. We stood there for a full minute, like contestants in a staring match. It took considerable effort to swallow my pride.

'I don't appreciate being lectured on how to do my job, but you're right about communication. We need to work together as closely as before.'

Burns gave an emphatic nod, but his expression clouded again as his eyes fell on the stack of papers in the centre of his table. A photo of Amala Adebayo from the crime scene lay on top of the pile, her sightless eyes gazing at the ceiling.

13

Traffic made me late for my 5.30 p.m. meeting with Jude's mysterious ex-boyfriend that afternoon. The taxi dropped me on the Strand and I studied the façade of King's College as I trotted across the road. The colonnaded building was more like a palace than a seat of learning, constructed during the last days of empire, when the economy still held enough cash to support huge architectural projects. I rushed inside, afraid that Paul Ramirez might have left already. Most of the academics I knew were elusive creatures, keen to bury themselves in their books at home.

The law department was on the ground floor, its offices lining a corridor so well used that undergraduates' footsteps had worn a groove in the black and white floor tiles. The building seemed deserted, but Dr Ramirez's door was open by a fraction, and I peered through the gap. The scene inside fascinated me. I'd expected him to be attractive enough to gain a cult following, but he was in his fifties, pepper and salt hair trailing over his collar, dressed in a shapeless linen jacket. A pretty blonde girl sat beside him, staring up at his face, their shoulders almost touching. They were so absorbed by their flirtation that they didn't notice me spying. I wondered whether Ramirez had ensnared Jude in the same way, inviting her to private tutorials after his colleagues had gone home.

I rapped loudly on the door and the girl looked startled, as if her mother had caught her misbehaving.

'Please forgive my lateness, Dr Ramirez,' I said calmly.

He muttered a quiet dismissal and the girl blushed fiercely as she scuttled out. The academic was too cool to reveal his irritation. His bone structure indicated that he must have been handsome once, but now his face was careworn, and there was something unpleasant about his body language. He stood much too close as he offered me a chair. It was only when he spoke that I understood his attraction. His voice was a mellow London drawl, resonating with sex appeal. At least he wasn't pretending to be single: a thick gold wedding band adorned his ring finger.

'Like I said on the phone, Dr Ramirez, I'm reviewing Jude Shelley's case. I'd be grateful for some information.'

'I still don't see how I can help.' His shoulders stiffened. 'What happened is tragic, but she wasn't in my seminar group.'

'I'm interested in her relationships with lecturers and fellow students.'

He appraised me again, his smoke-grey eyes narrowing. 'She's told you about us, hasn't she?'

'Not in detail. I'm hoping you can explain.'

The lecturer allowed a dramatic pause before speaking again. 'Jude wasn't just beautiful, she was the smartest student I've ever taught. I was dazzled by her. She set the pace from day one – it felt like there was no other choice.'

My jaw dropped. 'Of course you had a choice. Students often get crushes on lecturers, don't they?'

'You're quick to judge,' he said irritably. 'But Jude held all the control. When she left me I needed counselling.'

'How did it end?'

'She met a student from the social work department.'

'Jamal Khan?'

His expression soured, as if the name still haunted him. I listened to him talk, surprised by the strength of my animosity. He made it sound like he had fallen prey to a seductress. I'd counselled plenty of sexual opportunists in my time, but Ramirez was deluded enough to be in a league of his own. He seemed to believe that giving his female students a sexual education was a professional duty. He delivered his *coup de grâce* as I was leaving. He stood in the doorway, blocking my exit.

'Surely you realise that women like Jude put themselves in danger.'

'What do you mean?' I stared at him.

'Sexual confidence frightens some men. They find it threatening.'

'You seriously think Jude invited her attack by being assertive?'

The look he sent back was probably meant to be smouldering. 'She approached me, didn't she? Maybe she came on to other men too.'

'I'd like to leave now, Dr Ramirez.' He paused before taking a step back, and I had to suppress my instinct to shove him out of my way.

Adrenalin bubbled through my system as I headed for the exit. My unprofessional reaction annoyed me almost as much as Ramirez's belief that all women were fair game. Normally I could separate emotions from work, but Jude was different. It felt like my duty to protect her interests. The rage on the lecturer's face when he spoke of her desertion made me question whether his wounded pride could have made him attack her. It seemed like a long shot; he had no motive to attack Father Owen or Amala, and I had a growing sense that the attacks were linked to the whole Shelley family. But it would be foolish to overlook Ramirez, like the MIT team had done. I would call Burns in the morning and remind him to investigate his background and alibis.

When I reached the foyer, my gaze landed on a poster for an exhibition organised by the university's history department, called Treasures from the River. Small print explained that the exhibits had all been salvaged from the Thames. I wrote down the exhibition organiser's name and contact details: maybe Dr Hugh Lister could shed light on the strange assortment of objects the killer had used as calling cards.

I made an effort to forget the case that evening, taking my time to get ready. I straightened my hair and put on my favourite jeans, a blue silk top, hoop earrings and thick silver bracelets. But things took a turn for the worse when the taxi delivered me to the Prospect of Whitby. There was a yawning gap where my bike should have been, nothing chained to the railings except thin air. I stood on the pavement, cursing. The bike had cost a cool four hundred pounds and had been my pride and joy. I'd used it far more than my clapped-out car. Bolt-cutters had sheered through the chain, my padlock abandoned on the ground. After a few minutes I forced myself to get a grip: I was lucky to be alive. A stone's throw from where I was standing, Amala Adebayo had experienced the most terrifying death imaginable. I walked back along Wapping Wall, gradually calming down. At the top of Alderman's Stairs I paused to watch a clipper skate across the surface of the river, then hurried on through the rain.

My mood had lifted by the time I reached St Katharine Docks. Will's houseboat was moored to the furthest jetty; a ramshackle Dutch barge called *Bonne Chance*, with rust circling her portholes and rows of plant pots clustered on her roof. A familiar sound echoed from the hold. Lola's laugh hadn't changed since we were at school; it still had an edge of wildness, like she'd been snogging unsuitable men and knocking back tequila all afternoon. She was curled on a window seat, wrapped in an emerald green shawl, full of *joie de vivre* despite being days away from giving birth. The Greek God looked as protective as ever. Neal's nickname suited him: he came from a moneyed background; blue-eyed, athletic and handsome. He'd been Lola's boyfriend for two years but still seemed afraid that someone would abduct her if he blinked. Nina was busy at the far end of the galley kitchen when Will greeted me with a hug.

'What a gorgeous room,' I commented.

The galley was crammed with souvenirs and photos from the owner's travels. Hand-painted mugs and copper pans hung from hooks on the wall, utilising every inch of space. A Lloyd Loom chair stood in one corner, paint blistering from its arms. Interior designers would have described the mismatched crockery and clashing colours as the epitome of bohemian chic. It was nothing like Will's old flat in Pimlico, which had been so minimalist that trinkets never saw the light of day.

Nina gave a tense smile as she passed round a tray of bruschetta, but at least Will seemed relaxed. He sprawled on a bench and told us how he'd spent his day.

'I got a job finally, after a week hoofing the streets.'

'You're too lanky for a hoofer, my friend,' Lola said. 'What's the job?'

'Full-time server in a juice bar in Covent Garden.' He wrinkled his nose.

'Don't knock it,' she said, grinning. 'At least you'll never go short of vitamin C.'

Will swung round to face me. 'What about you, Al?'

'I'm good, except my bike just got nicked.'

'Damn. That thing cost a fortune, didn't it?'

'It's my own fault. I should have used a better padlock.'

'How's work been going?' he asked.

It crossed my mind to admit that I was advising on a particularly grisly case, but it would have soured the atmosphere. 'I'm keeping myself out of mischief.'

'You're not still working for the Met, are you?' His eyes clouded with anxiety.

'Not so much these days.'

'Thank God. You should keep out of all that misery.'

I touched the back of his hand, then changed the subject. Will was convinced that contact with the police was hazardous, and mentioning it only fuelled his anxiety. It was easier to avoid talking about my career.

Will's new girlfriend remained silent as the evening progressed. But Lola and Neal regaled us with a stream of anecdotes about their acting careers. Nina was leaning against the boat's curved wall, her arm threaded through Will's. Their relationship fascinated me. It seemed like my brother had stepped from ten years of loneliness straight into cohabitation without a backwards glance. Nina's quiet presence obviously relaxed him, and they served up a gorgeous meal: aubergine parmigiana, followed by raspberry pavlova oozing with cream. I blinked at him in amazement. A year ago I'd struggled to make him eat a sandwich, but now he could prepare a complicated menu, and appeared to be enjoying every mouthful.

I helped Nina clear the table after we'd finished dessert. She seemed more at ease than the first time we met, no longer struggling to meet my eye.

'What type of psychologist are you?' she asked.

'Clinical, mostly. I do forensic work now and then for the Met.'

'You're not the kind of shrink that locks people away, are you?'

'Hardly ever. Most patients recover better at home.'

'I'm glad to hear that.'

'Why?'

She concentrated on stacking the dishes. 'It's a long story. I'll tell you another time.'

'Sounds intriguing. I'd love to know more about your MA, too.'

'I'm studying the poetry the Romantics wrote here in London. My focus is on Wordsworth and Coleridge.'

'God, that makes me feel like a philistine – I haven't read a book in months.'

'Borrow some of mine.' She gave a tentative smile, then nodded at the stacked bookshelves that lined the galley.

'Thanks, I'll take you up on it.'

I helped her carry the coffee mugs back to the table. The conversation had left me with a set of questions. She'd been more open than before, but seemed to believe that shrinks were inclined to section patients at the drop of a hat.

'We should go,' Lola said at eleven o'clock. 'I'd hate to spoil the evening by giving birth on your kitchen floor.'

Will hugged us all goodbye, but Nina kept her hands safely behind her back, giving a casual nod as we walked away. Lola waited until we reached the dockside before turning to me.

'She's not Will's usual type, is she? A shy one, that's for sure.' Her eyes glinted with concern.

'You think so?'

'Christ, yes,' Neal agreed. 'I wish she'd talk more, that French accent's glorious.'

Lola elbowed him in the ribs. 'You're only noticing other women's sexy voices because I'm a barrage balloon.' Her grin unfurled as he grabbed her for a kiss. 'Do you want to share our taxi, Al?'

'Can you wait a minute? There's something I need to do.'

They sat on a bench while I dug my Dictaphone out of my bag. I walked along the path to record the sounds of the river at night: night buses chugging towards Aldgate, wind hissing through the ornate fretwork of Tower Bridge, and in the distance a couple conducting a blazing row. After ten minutes I switched the recorder off, confident that I'd taped everything the river had to say.

'You're so weird. Why would you need a recording of the Thames at night?' Lola asked.

I grinned at her. 'Trust me, I do.'

Lola kissed me goodbye as the taxi pulled up outside my apartment block. 'How's the unrequited love?'

'Fading nicely, thanks.'

Three glasses of Pinot Grigio had helped to lighten my mood. Will's girlfriend was slowly coming out of her shell, and Lola was impatient for her baby to arrive. At least the people I loved were safe, even though another victim had lost her life. I paused under a streetlamp to check my phone. My heart sank when I saw that Burns had sent two messages: the first was terse and professional, but the second was so rambling and unclear I felt sure he'd been drinking. He was begging me to call him back so we could talk through details of the case. I hit the delete button twice, angry that he'd phoned me out of hours. But by the time I reached my flat, common sense had returned. For Jude's sake I needed to work with Burns to the best of my ability. I sent him a business-like text arranging to meet the next day, determined not to dwell on the past.

14

At night the voices grow louder than ever. The man surveys the river, trying to ignore the calls from unquiet ghosts writhing under the water's surface. He grips the railing and focuses on the view instead. On the opposite bank he sees the outlines of apartment buildings, the spire of a Hawksmoor church, car headlights needling the dark. The skyscrapers of Canary Wharf are half a mile away, their electricity flooding the horizon with artificial brightness.

The man turns his back on the river, but still it calls to him. There's no way to forget what he's done. The brittle sound of metal against bone, the priest's skull shattering. It's the police-woman's face that haunts him most. Her look of terror was unforgettable. Why couldn't she accept that the secrets she knew had to be drowned? He closes his eyes to erase the image of her body thrashing, slick pools of blood collecting on the water's surface.

Two teenage girls sway past in high heels, arm in arm, as he returns to his car. Their spirits glint brightly, tempting him to follow. But he knows there's no point – the river selects its own victims. He slumps in the driving seat, unwilling to go home. The calls grow louder inside his flat and sleep is impos-sible. He rests his forehead on the steering wheel, hands gripping the smooth leather. Already the river is begging for its next soul.

15

I woke on Saturday morning with a hangover and a dull aware-
ness that lying in bed wasn't an option. Burns had cancelled
weekend and holiday leave until the riverside killer was found,
and I agreed with the strategy. For Jude's sake I was prepared
to put rest on hold until her attacker was behind bars. After a
pint of orange juice and two shots of espresso I felt well enough
to call the House of Commons. I half expected to reach a
weekend answer-machine, but a woman's cool voice explained
that Giles Moorcroft had failed to arrange the Monday
appointment I'd requested with Timothy Shelley. I decided to
call Heather later. The minister's reluctance to talk was ringing
my alarm bells; hopefully she would apply pressure until he
agreed. I felt a pang of envy as I left my flat and followed the
river path past Butler's Wharf. Flocks of people were taking
slow weekend strolls, despite the overcast sky. I wished I could
join them, instead of returning to the Royal London.

Jude's room still smelled of sickness and antiseptic. The
pillows on her bed were stacked so high she was raised almost
vertical, as if she was determined to be on an equal footing
when we began our work.

'Are you sure you want to do this, Jude? I could come back
another day.'

'Now's fine, but how do you know it'll work?'

'It normally does.' I smiled at her. 'You don't have to relive
the memory, just take the parts that surface, and let the rest

pass. I'll play you a recording I made by the Thames, about the same time you left the party. It should help you remember that night. You can end the session at any time. Is that all right?'

'I think so.' Her hands were locked together like a mountaineer clutching a guide rope.

'Say the word and we'll stop. Okay?'

Her face was shielded by her veil of chestnut hair, but she gave a light nod. I pressed the play button on my Dictaphone and the room filled with sounds. High heels clacked along the pavement, a plane engine droning, the shrill whine of a motorbike. After a few minutes, Jude's hands fell limp at her sides.

'Can you remember what you wore to the party?' I asked.

Her words hissed out slowly. 'Denim jacket, summer dress, green wedge-heeled sandals.'

'Well remembered, that's brilliant. Did you drink much?'

'Only a few glasses of wine. I chatted for a while, danced with Natalie and some other friends. Then I left about one a.m., by myself.'

'Listen to the sounds and try to remember what happened next. You can surface any time you want.'

Her voice was so calm it sounded like she'd been drugged. 'The street was deserted. There were no taxis, so I decided to catch a night bus to Jamal's, to apologise for yelling at him. It happened fast after that. A man pulled me onto the back seat of a car.'

'Did he get out of the passenger's side?'

'No, he was in the driving seat.'

'You're standing on the pavement now. What do you see?'

'He's taller than me, wearing a hat or a hood. His face is in the shadows.'

'What about his hair colour?'

She hesitated. 'Almost hidden, I think it's whitish blond.'

86

'You're doing really well. Now you're in the car, what can you hear?'

'His breathing. He's on the back seat, whispering something about the river. The blindfold's tight around my eyes. It's all happening so quickly.' She fell silent, as if her energy was draining away.

'What can you smell?'

'Something sickly. Sweetness and chemicals.'

'What does it remind you of?'

'Fake tan or cheap perfume. And his clothes feel coarse when I try and fight him; synthetic, not cotton.'

'Listen to his voice again. What does it sound like?'

'Strained, as if he's trying to disguise it. But the accent's like mine. It's familiar.'

'Can you remember where you heard it?'

'All I can feel is the pain in my head. That's where it ends. There's nothing else.' Her hands were twisting again in her lap, the torn flap of her mouth sealing itself.

'Okay, Jude, I'm switching off the recording. When you hear the click, you'll be back here with me, perfectly safe.'

When I hit the switch, Jude heaved for breath like she was surfacing from a long dive, the respirator wheezing oxygen into her lungs.

I had an hour to kill before meeting Burns. I sat in the library on Euston Road, studying my notes. Jude's reaction to auto-hypnosis had been unusually powerful. She was so eager to remember her attacker's identity that she'd fallen into a state of semi-consciousness as soon as the recording started. But her recall was so patchy there was little hard detail to go on. She'd conjured up a bizarre picture of a man desperate not to be recognised. It sounded like her attacker had disguised every part of his identity – voice, skin tone and clothes. His

87

desire for concealment plus his repeated apologies made me wonder if he was an atypical psychopath, capable of feeling remorse.

I flicked through my notes from previous meetings. Interviewing Jude's close relatives had shown me a family fraying at the seams. Guy's anxiety had disabled him since the attack, and Heather was frantic with worry. Timothy Shelley was so caught up in the pressures of his job that he had little time for anything else. He had probably never noticed the extent of his son's unhappiness and seemed determined to keep out of the reinvestigation. It was taking far too long to visit him at Westminster to discover if Guy was correct about his father's job exposing him to potential threats.

I pushed my notes back into the folder and tried to focus on why Guy's behaviour had concerned me. On a psychological level he seemed even more damaged than Jude, exuding isolation and negativity, locked inside his unsmiling shell. But I was no closer to understanding the killer's choice of victims. Jude and Father Owen had known each other, but no link had been established between them and Amala Adebayo. Killing a newly qualified policewoman seemed to challenge the theory that the Shelley family was the primary target.

Taxis were in short supply on the Euston Road, which was buzzing with weekenders heading for Bloomsbury, but at least the driver who finally collected me seemed happy. Londoners were queuing to use his services rather than face the constant downpours. I arrived at Lambeth Road to find Burns waiting outside a greengrocer's, his collar turned up, wearing a look of abject disgust.

'Dreich,' he muttered.

'You can say that again.'

'Let's get a coffee.' He nodded at a greasy spoon across the road.

Burns sat opposite me in the café. He looked the same as ever, built like a heavyweight boxer, dark eyes giving me a baleful stare. Attraction still nagged at me; but hopefully suppressing it would make it die away.

'Whatever you've got to say, spit it out, so we can clear the air,' I said.

'I still need to apologise.'

'You already did, but I didn't buy it. Men don't go home for the sake of their children. They go because they love their wives.'

His eyes locked onto mine. 'You don't get it, do you? It wasn't easy. You were in my head for years.'

'Rubbish. All you think about is work.'

'That's not true.' His smile creased the corners of his eyes. 'There's always time to fantasise.'

'Don't flirt with me, Don.'

'I wouldn't dare.'

'Good, then we can be friends again.'

Burns looked shocked. 'Have we ever been friends?'

'Not really.'

He gave a slow grin. 'We're back to square one then.'

'Not quite. I've got good reason to hate you now. My bike got nicked from the railings at Wapping.'

He looked mortified. 'Was it insured?'

'Forget it. Let's just get on with the job.'

He nodded. 'I've had some news about Amala. Guess who she worked for when she got her first nannying post?'

'Enlighten me.'

'The Shelleys. She was Guy and Jude's nanny before the MP got his cabinet post, and she stayed close to the family. It was Heather who encouraged her to join the police. Amala visited Jude in hospital every few weeks, regular as clockwork.'

My thoughts raced. Anyone who entered the lives of the Shelleys was in danger: first their priest and now the children's former nanny. Other members of the family could be next on his list.

'What kind of security have the Shelleys got?'

'Category One, Ministry of Defence. They've stepped up travel security round the minister, and the wife and son have been given bodyguards.'

'That's good news. Jude's still sure she knew her attacker's voice, but the memory's buried too deep to access. You need to run a check on everyone who crossed her path: kids from her school, friends, teachers, social groups. It sounds like the guy's heavily disguised when he makes his attacks. He smells of fake tan, wears a hat or a hood, and he may be using some kind of costume. If he's going to that kind of trouble, it's more than concealment. I think he's ashamed, Don. He probably hates himself for what he's doing.'

'The bloke's all heart, isn't he?' Burns's smile twisted. 'Did she mention any names?'

'Not yet. I'll have to keep working with her. Have you got any information on Paul Ramirez yet? I got the sense he's chasing students like it's going out of fashion.'

'Angie's found nothing so far.'

'I wish I knew more about the calling cards.'

'They could just be bits of old rubbish from the riverbank; more proof that the bloke's mad as a hatter.' Burns seemed so focused on the human details of the case he'd forgotten that the objects could be vital clues.

'It's got to be more than that. The arrowhead he tied round Jude's neck might be centuries old, I did a search on the Internet. I'm seeing a historian at King's College tonight to get the pieces identified.'

He looked distracted as he checked his watch. 'Let me know if you want an escort. We should get moving, Shane Weldon's waiting for us.'

'Why are you so keen for me to assess him?'

'The MIT interviewed him three times after Jude's attack, but we know they weren't thorough enough. The bloke killed a woman in Battersea twenty years ago, cut her throat, then dumped her in the river. He's lived at Sinclair House for two years since his release, but something could have sparked his violence again, couldn't it?'

I kept my misgivings to myself as we walked to Sinclair House. The only connection I could see with the current crimes was the riverside location of Weldon's attack. From Burns's description, no other factor linked him to the Shelleys. The hostel turned out to be an austere red-brick building set back from the Lambeth Road, with barred ground-floor windows. It looked like a cross between a prison and a low rent hotel, the carpet in the foyer worn thin as paper. The manager was called Mr Bell, his smile a jumble of grey, mismatched teeth.

'Shane's waiting in the day room. Can you spare me a minute after you've see him?'

'Certainly,' I replied.

He led us down a corridor to the back of the building. Yellowing paint was drifting from the walls, and the air smelled of woodworm, bleach and spoilt milk. Weldon was sitting in the day room, reading the *Sun*. His sandy hair was so badly styled it looked like he'd cut it himself, a ragged fringe undulating across his forehead. Even from a distance there was something disturbing about his face.

'You stayed in specially for this, didn't you, Shane?' Mr Bell addressed his client as if he was twelve years old.

'We need to see Mr Weldon alone, please,' Burns said.

The manager looked affronted as he backed away. When I glanced at Weldon again, I realised why his face had startled me. A deep scar bisected his left cheek. The cut had severed his facial muscles, leaving him with the incomplete smile of a stroke victim. His eyes were tiny and too close together, his gaze flickering from my breasts to my legs, without ever landing on my face.

'What's this about?' His voice had the low rasp of a committed smoker.

'We're looking into the Jude Shelley case and two recent attacks by the river,' I said.

'I don't know anything about that.' His truncated smile vanished.

Burns leant forwards. 'Where were you Sunday and on Wednesday night, Shane?'

Weldon's fingers tugged at his hair, gestures twitchy as a teenager's, even though he must have been in his forties. 'I went to church on Sunday, then for a walk. Wednesday I saw my mum at her flat in Wembley. Last time I checked, all those things were legal.'

'Don't get clever,' Burns snarled. 'It doesn't suit you.'

'Which church do you go to, Shane?' I asked.

He hesitated for a second. 'St Mary's.'

I studied him more closely. 'Did you know that Father Owen was killed a few days ago? His body was found on the riverbank.'

'I just go to the services. It's my nearest Catholic church.' His hands twitched in his lap.

'I'll need to check that,' Burns said, pulling out his notepad. 'What's your mum's phone number?'

'I don't want her upset, she hasn't been well.'

'Write it down for me.'

Weldon clenched the biro tightly between his fingers,

labouring over each digit. I wondered whether the problem stemmed from dyscalculia or a more complex learning difficulty.

'How did you get your scar?' I asked.

'In prison, they did it with a piece of glass.' His expression was unreadable, small eyes refusing to meet mine. 'There are twenty stitches in there.'

'Where did you take your walk on Sunday night?' Burns interrupted.

'Albert Embankment, Nine Elms Road, up to the power station.'

'You came back along the river too?'

He shook his head. 'I did a circle, over Chelsea Bridge.'

'That's where you attacked the girl, isn't it?' Burns said casually. 'Have you been hurting people again like you hurt her?'

Weldon jerked back in his seat. 'I never touched anyone. Ask Mr Bell, I keep myself to myself.'

His gaze settled again on my chest as we said goodbye. I was longing to escape, but the manager was waiting in the foyer, rubbing his hands in anticipation. His office smelled of fresh carpet and brand-new furniture. Clearly he'd blown the charity's meagre budget on improving his own comfort.

'Do you keep a log of your clients' movements, Mr Bell?' Burns asked.

He sucked in his cheeks. 'This isn't a bail hostel, Inspector. Our residents are free agents. We're here to help ex-prisoners reintegrate into society, not to police them.'

'How often do they reoffend?'

'We only had two incidents last year.' The man's grey smile reappeared. 'Shane's one of our success stories. He helps in the kitchen, goes to church, holds down a steady job. We're very proud of him. That's what I wanted to tell you.'

93

Burns's expression remained neutral while the manager extolled his client's virtues, but he voiced his disbelief when we got outside. 'It's too close for comfort, isn't it? I'll call Weldon's mother, and the street cameras will show where he took that stroll. He'll need a surveillance team put on him.'

'He's not a great fit, Don. His attack was spur of the moment: no staging, no signature and no facial mutilation. And why would he admit going to St Mary's Church so easily if he'd just killed the priest?'

Burns returned my stare. 'The bloke would have seen the Shelleys at church, and he knew the priest. Amala's the only victim he doesn't have a link with, but I bet you we'll find one.'

'Killers hardly ever change their MO. He wouldn't just go from hasty opportunism to a planned campaign. I doubt he's got the intellect for something this complex.'

His grumbled reply was too quiet to hear. I was still trying to work out what had struck me as odd about Weldon. His problems with writing made me wonder about his mental capacity. If it was low, he would have fitted in perfectly at Brixton; most of the UK's prison population scored badly in IQ tests. But he was bright enough to drive, which placed him inside the normal range. I felt like reminding Burns that the objects tied to the victims' bodies deserved more attention, but there was no point. The dogged look had returned to his face as he paced across the wet pavement back to his car. He would pursue every lead obsessively until Shane Weldon's life had been turned inside out. Already he was so focused on his task he didn't notice that he was stamping through deep puddles, throwing out enough water to soak passers-by.

16

I'd arranged to meet Dr Hugh Lister in the exhibition hall that evening. The room on the second floor was impressively grand, with pillared walls and a marble floor, but there was no one in sight. Glass display cases lined the walls, and a sign explained that the items had all been salvaged from the banks of the Thames during an archaeological survey. The range of objects was staggering, and some were in mint condition. I stopped to admire a jadeite Roman necklace, stones so glossy it could have been worn yesterday. A thousand-year-old dagger still looked sharp enough to wound. I was admiring an ironwork scabbard when a voice interrupted me.

'You must be Alice Quentin.' A man was gazing down at me with a startled expression in his dark blue eyes. He was medium height, slim and clean-shaven, in his early thirties, with light brown hair cropped close to his skull.

'Thanks for agreeing to help, Dr Lister.'

'I'm afraid Hugh's been called away. My name's Jake Fielding, I run the history department here. How can I help?'

'I've got some objects that need identifying. I'm a psychologist working for the Met, with no historical background, so you'll need to use laymen's terms, please.'

'I'll do my best.' He gave a disarmingly gorgeous smile, still studying my face so intently he seemed to be trying to carbon-date me.

'This is one of the pieces.' I scrolled through the photos on my phone to the ceramic bottle that had been tied to Amala's body.

He stared at the picture. 'It looks like a bellarmine. Where did you find it?'

'That's a long story.'

'Let me show you the ones in our collection.'

Fielding led me across the room, giving me time to observe him. His walk was full of controlled energy, as though he could break into a run at any minute. He didn't fit my stereotypes about historians. I'd been expecting grey-faced professors in tweed jackets and corduroys, but he wore faded jeans and a grey shirt that clung to his muscular arms. By now we'd reached a small display case, which held a row of clay bottles just like the one in my photo. Fielding's hand brushed my shoulder as he pointed them out.

'They're three centuries old,' he said.

'What were they used for?'

'Witchcraft rituals. The name bellarmine comes from a cardinal who was unpopular in the seventeenth century. His face was always embossed on the side. The witches called them spirit jars. They believed that human souls existed separately from the body and could be coaxed into the jars, then cast into the river, imprisoned forever. A neat trick, don't you think?'

'Was the Thames used for sacrifices?'

He nodded vigorously. 'Since prehistory. People living by the estuary have always feared its power. We've found hundreds of valuable items like jewellery, daggers and swords. They must have believed that rituals could keep it in check.'

'What about human sacrifice?'

'That's likely too. Hundreds of decapitated skulls were found a few years ago; the victims were probably executed after losing a battle.' He gazed at the bellarmines again. 'Some of these are still sealed. The witches did a good job of trapping their victims' spirits.'

There was something unsettling about the intensity of his gaze, so I returned my attention to the row of clay flasks and tried to imagine the kind of man who thought that human souls could be imprisoned for all eternity. Over Fielding's shoulder, I saw a caretaker rattling his keys with an irate expression on his face.

'I've outstayed my welcome, haven't I?'

'Come back another day. Hugh's our Thames expert, he can tell you everything you need to know.'

'Thanks, I'll call him on Monday.'

'Let me walk you to the exit.'

'There's no need.' I glanced at his clean-cut profile as we fell into step.

He gave another attractive smile. 'I could use the exercise. I've been trapped inside all day.' When he paused by the doors, I assumed he was about to share one last piece of historical information. 'Listen, my team's working by the river tomorrow afternoon. If you meet me on London Bridge at five, you can meet Hugh then.'

My answer blurted out before I could edit it. 'That would be great, thanks.'

He tapped my number into his phone, then walked back into the building at a rapid pace, as though nothing could break his stride. We'd spent the past twenty minutes chatting, yet I'd formed no clear impression. He was well spoken, with a crisp west London accent, and he'd been unselfconscious about studying me during our conversation, but that was the extent of it. For all I knew, his clean-cut exterior disguised a multitude of sins. He might be even more predatory than Paul Ramirez, his bedpost covered in notches.

My brain fizzed with ideas on the bus ride home. Maybe the killer had found the bellarmine beside the river. When I closed my eyes I could almost see him, stooped on the muddy ground, as the high tide raced past. I still felt sure Jude could identify him if she could summon the courage to access her memory.

On Sunday morning I woke up dry-mouthed, from a nightmare that refused to clear. I'd dreamed myself back at the Prospect of Whitby, the pub empty apart from Jude behind the bar. She seemed unaware of her injuries, turning her ruined face towards me as she poured my drink.

I stayed under the shower a long time, rinsing the images away, then took longer than normal to get ready. My mother was bound to criticise every flaw, so I clipped my hair into a French pleat, selected a knee-length dark red dress, black low-heeled boots and my Whistles raincoat.

I only had to wait five minutes for a boat from Tower Pier. Clippers are one of my favourite ways to get around the city, cutting back and forth along the Thames between Putney and the Thames Barrier, with no traffic to slow them down except cargo ships heading for Tilbury. I stood by the railing, watching the Tower of London shrink into the distance, wash streaming from the propellers. The sky was gunmetal grey, the water two shades darker. It smelled of brine and decay, three millennia of human waste trapped in its depths.

It took half an hour to reach Greenwich, and I hurried to the covered market, hoping to arrive first, but my mother had beaten me to the coffee shop. Even from a distance I could tell something was wrong. She had always prided herself on choosing expensive clothes and styling her hair perfectly, but today she looked dishevelled. Her stiff deportment was letting her down. She was slumped awkwardly in her chair, as though she lacked the strength to sit upright. I steadied myself before marching through the shoppers who were queuing to buy flowers and bric-a-brac from the busy stalls.

'There you are, darling.' Her tremor passed through my hand as I touched her shoulder.

'What can I get you, Mum?'

'Something milky, please. Not too strong.'

It was the first time in years that I'd seen her without makeup, her hair uncombed. I remembered watching her dab powder onto her cheekbones as a child, painting on lipstick with a brush, gradually turning herself into an artwork. I rushed inside to place our order. When I joined her again, it was obvious she was in no mood for questions.

'Don't fuss, Alice. Mornings are shaky, but by lunchtime I'm myself again.'

'Why not let me see the specialist?'

'Let's not waste time arguing. Are you on holiday at the moment?'

'I'm working for the Forensic Psychology Unit. They tell me it's meant to be an honour.'

Her pale eyes studied me. 'More murders and misdemeanours; I don't know how you stand it.'

'Neither do I sometimes. This latest case is fascinating, but it's the worst yet.'

'What about boyfriends?'

'Nothing serious, but I'm seeing a historian this afternoon.' My meeting with Jake Fielding couldn't be called a date, but at least the white lie brought a smile to her face.

'And what about Will?'

'He seems well. He's living on a houseboat at the moment.'

My mother's defences faltered. 'He never answers my calls.'

'You know how forgetful he can be. I'll remind him.'

Coffee slopped from her cup when she tried to drink, hands performing a Saint Vitus's dance across the table. The quake in her voice sounded like Katherine Hepburn's, with an odd rattle behind her words. I racked my brains for facts about Parkinson's, remembering that symptoms could accelerate suddenly, without warning. My mother's condition had worsened visibly since the last time we met.

Normally she would have said goodbye promptly, then marched home through Greenwich Park to her flat in Blackheath, but today she was lingering.

'Let's get a taxi, Mum. I can catch the train home.'

She protested, but I could tell she was relieved. The short walk across the market square seemed to tire her, and when we reached Wemyss Road she took forever to climb the stairs to her maisonette in the small Victorian building. It looked shabbier than when she'd first bought it. She'd been overjoyed to find a self-contained apartment with its own entrance and stairway, but her front door was crying out for a fresh coat of paint. Her shaking was even more pronounced when we reached the landing.

'No need to come in, darling. Go and get ready for your date.'

'Don't worry, there's plenty of time.'

When she finally opened the front door, I took a sharp intake of breath. Her apartment had always been immaculate, the kitchen sterile as an operating theatre, but today it looked like a bombsite. Dirty dishes and takeaway cartons were piled in the sink, a stack of ironing sat on the kitchen table, bags of rubbish waiting to be taken down to the bins.

I put a mug of tea beside her armchair. 'We should find you a home help, Mum.'

'Don't be ridiculous. I'm just a little slower than before.'

'A few hours a week would make all the difference.'

'You can't bully me. I'm not one of your patients, Alice.' Her grey eyes had turned glacial.

I retreated to the kitchen and spent the next hour cleaning and carting rubbish bags outside. When the time came to leave, my mother stood by the window, doing a good impersonation of herself before her illness arrived. She was so thin as I embraced her that she felt insubstantial in my arms.

My thoughts refused to stay still on the train back to London Bridge. Mum had always been invincible; even my father's violence had failed to slow her down. It seemed unfair that poor health had ambushed her at the age of sixty-three, after living so cautiously. I'd never seen her smoke a cigarette or take one drink too many.

The housing estates of Lewisham and Catford streamed past the train's window, a hinterland of grey concrete, stretching to infinity.

17

Nerves got the better of me as I walked along the river path. Dates had been so thin on the ground that even a casual meeting felt like a major event. I ignored the knot tightening inside my ribcage and reminded myself that Burns deserved no loyalty whatsoever. I could flirt with anyone who crossed my path. When I passed the Royal London, I remembered Jude Shelley, struggling to breathe, her unblinking eye gazing down from her window. The main reason for today's meeting was to discover the origins of her attacker's calling cards so I could understand his motives.

Jake Fielding was standing in the middle of London Bridge when I arrived at five o'clock, sheltering under a large umbrella, too busy studying the river's surface to notice me. He was so distracted that he looked startled when I tapped his shoulder.

'There you are.' His gaze drifted across my face.

'You're in a dream world, aren't you, Dr Fielding?'

'Jake, please.' His face relaxed slightly. 'It's work, I'm afraid. The Archaeology Trust has promised us funds to excavate here if we can find more evidence of a Roman sacrificial site. Three archaeologists will be out of work if we don't raise the cash.'

'And that's why you're working weekends?'

'Hugh's running the project, but I've spent every spare minute here for months. Come on, I'll introduce you.'

As we walked along Lower Thames Street, it struck me that only a year ago Jude had been abducted from the same stretch of pavement, while the river churned at low tide. Even at half strength the currents had been strong enough to haul her body to the opposite bank in moments.

'I hope you can handle wading through a sea of mud,' Jake said.

'It can't be worse than Glastonbury.'

'Believe me, it is.'

I followed him down the wooden steps at Grant's Key Wharf, each tread slick with dark green algae, the river's stench rising to greet me. It smelled of decay and port wine, mixed with an undertone of cinnamon; a reminder that the city had once been the spice trading capital of the world. A dozen people clad in waterproofs were gazing earnestly at the ground. Some of them were attacking the mud with trowels and small shovels.

'We've been here since low tide,' Jake commented.

'It looks like they're beachcombing.'

'That's pretty much correct. The tides carry objects down from Lambeth and Battersea, but we're planning an under-water excavation by the bridge's foundations.'

'What do you expect to find?'

'This stretch of the river was sacred for centuries. The Romans made offerings to the river gods. There are all sorts of relics buried in the silt: glass, silver, gold. We've only discovered a fraction.'

A thickset man of around fifty with a short grey crew cut made his way over; his face was so angular it looked like it had been chipped from a block of granite. He glowered down at me. 'Found a new volunteer, Jake?'

'This is Alice Quentin, she wanted to speak to you,' Jake said, turning to me. 'Meet Hugh Lister, the man in charge.'

There was something intimidating about Lister's body language, and his handshake nearly wrenched my arm from its socket. His skin was carved with such deep lines it looked as if he'd spent years in the tropics.

'It's good to meet you, Dr Lister. I understand you know all there is to know about the Thames.'

'Hardly, it's still full of secrets.' His voice was a refined growl, which sounded vaguely familiar, although I couldn't place it. 'I hope you'll stay a while and help us search.'

'I've got some pieces I'm hoping you can identify. Would you mind looking at some photos?'

He frowned at me. 'Pictures are no use. Bring them to the department and I'll do my best.' It was obvious he had no time to waste on chatting to strangers, striding back to the point where he'd been foraging. Lister struck me as a typical historian, short on social skills and unperturbed about his scruffy image, dressed in an outsized cagoule and mud-spattered jeans.

When I turned round Jake was yards away, leaning down to inspect something he'd unearthed. All I could see was the city's profligacy: torn carrier bags, beer cans, punctured bicycle tyres. Gradually details started to emerge. I picked up a coin and studied its tarnished surface carefully. When I straightened up a man in his early twenties was giving me a polite smile, dark brown eyes fixed on my face. He was a head taller than me, his cheeks pock-marked by acne scars, skull haloed by short blond curls.

'You're new, aren't you? I'm Mark Edmunds, one of Hugh's PhD students.' His voice was at odds with his appearance, a mellow baritone that seemed to belong to an older man.

'I'm just visiting, but I envy you. This feels like a glorified treasure hunt.'

'There hasn't been much glory today, but you're spot on. We're just overgrown kids mucking about on the riverbank.

Most archaeologists would go mad if you stuck them behind a desk.' His gentle smile reappeared. 'Have you found anything yet?'

'Just this.' I held out the coin in the flat of my hand.

He gave a soft laugh. 'No need to alert the British Museum. That's a shilling, less than fifty years old.'

'Now I'm disappointed.'

'Don't be, it takes time to find buried treasure. Give me a shout if I can help.' He raised a hand in farewell, then returned to the tideline.

I thought about the exchange as I carried on studying the ground. Something about Mark Edmunds's diffidence made him seem vulnerable. Maybe all history departments were populated with benign oddballs, escaping the rigors of the modern world. A few minutes later I spotted something else, bone white, protruding from the silt. As I rubbed the mud away a clay pipe revealed itself. When I straightened up Jake was watching me, blank-faced, as though he'd seen a ghost. He seemed to recover himself in the time it took to stride across the mud and take the object from my hand.

'Nice find; it's eighteenth century. We don't often see them in mint condition.'

'Beginner's luck,' I replied.

I watched him wrap the pipe in foam, trying to forget his intense stare. The historians were stretched out across the riverbank, most of them working in pairs or small groups, but Hugh Lister seemed determined on solitude. He bristled when I asked him what he'd found, yet he'd collected far more than anyone else – buckles, pipes, and a smoky piece of glass which he assured me was sixth century. The rain was worsening. Even with my hood up, moisture trickled down my backbone. I was about to make my excuses when I heard Jake exclaiming under his breath as he rinsed dirt from a piece of clay.

'As if by magic. Look at this, Alice.' He held out a shard of earthenware, embossed with a sprite-like face.

'That's part of a bellarmine, isn't it?'

'The tide probably carried it upstream from Execution Dock.'

I looked at the face's malevolent grin and shivered. Jake was studying it in fascination and I got the sense that he could have carried on scouring the riverbank until dawn.

'You look cold. Why don't we go for a drink?' His hand glanced across mine as he turned away.

Hugh Lister and the rest of the group carried on with their search, but we ended up in a crowded pub on Tooley Street. The barmaid bustled over to serve Jake, wearing a flirtatious smile. I observed him while she poured brandy into shot glasses. His fine bones and deep set blue eyes were compelling; the kind of classic good looks that photograph well from any angle. A jolt of panic passed through my chest as I searched for a table. The best course of action would be to ask my questions then run before life got complicated. The drinks Jake placed on our table were full to the brim.

'You got doubles?'

'A single hardly wets the glass.'

'Then I should eat something before I fall over.'

He was watching me again. 'I can't imagine you drunk. You're too composed.'

'Not true. I can dance on the tables with the best of them.'

His eyebrows shot up. 'You like to dance?'

'Six years of ballet as a kid, but I wasn't much good. Anyway, there are some things I need to ask.'

'Not now. Sunday's meant to be a day of rest.' His fingers skimmed across my wrist, the sudden physical contact unsettling me. 'It's too late for professional questions.'

Normally I avoid personal details, but Jake seemed comfortable talking about himself. His passion for archaeology had taken him around the world; he'd worked on excavations in Brazil, Peru and Egypt before becoming an academic.

'Lucky you. All I've done is backpack across Europe, and a few trips to the US.'

He smiled. 'They work us pretty hard out there. I was researching with Hugh last year, diving in the Mexican Gulf. His specialism's marine archaeology, but he knows a hell of a lot about rivers. His latest book's about the Thames estuary.'

'He seemed in his element today.'

'That's the trouble. The guy's a bona-fide obsessive; he never switches off. His PhD student's nearly as bad.'

'Mark Edmunds?'

He nodded. 'Most nights we have to eject him from the library.'

'I liked him, he was very welcoming.' I checked my watch. 'It's time I went home.'

'Not yet. You haven't told me about your job.'

'What do you want to know? I combine hospital work with forensic psychology. Right now I'm helping the Met on two murder cases, the ones where the bodies ended up in the Thames.'

He did a double take. 'The priest and the policewoman. I saw it on the news.'

'That's why I asked for help. The bellarmine I showed you was found at one of the crime scenes. Judging by what I saw today, I'm guessing that all the objects came from the river.'

'You think a serial killer's been hunting by the Thames?' His eyes widened. 'You should read Hugh's book. I've got a copy at my flat, why don't you collect it?'

'I really ought to go.'

He gave me a quizzical look. 'Because you're seeing someone else?'

I hesitated. 'Not any more.'

'But you've still got feelings for him.'

'What are you, a mind reader?'

He laughed. 'It's just a book, Alice. No strings attached.'

The booze must have affected me, his insistence making my head swim. Burns's face appeared briefly, then vanished as I fastened my coat.

Jake's apartment was less than half a mile from mine. We strolled back along the river, my head muzzy with brandy. The boardwalk was so slick that I almost fell, but he steadied me, and his arm circled my waist as we walked in silence. It had been a long time since I'd strolled arm in arm with a man, and it felt intoxicating. Part of me longed for the simplicity of waking up with the same boyfriend every day, even though the intimacy would smother me within weeks.

By Butler's Wharf the drizzle had become a deluge. We sheltered in a doorway, the river's surface pitted by droplets large as pebbles.

'Damn, I left my umbrella in the pub,' Jake muttered.

'Let's wait here till it passes.'

When he leant down to kiss me it was intense enough to wipe away Burns's image, and neutralise my anxiety about the case. Rain carried on ricocheting from the wall above our heads.

'Come on. Let's make a dash for it,' he said.

He set off at a sprint, but by New Concordia Wharf his pace was slowing. Water poured from the hem of my coat as I trailed him up to the fourth floor. I stood in his living room while he went to the kitchen to make coffee; the river shore was visible from his window even in darkness, Whitechapel's lights pulsing in the distance.

When he returned I was curled up on his sofa, admiring the view. He gave me a towel to dry my hair, but it made little difference – my clothes were saturated. With the light switched on I saw that his living room was packed with objects from his travels: small North African figurines, a hand-woven kilim on the floor, rows of brightly coloured bowls. Even the air smelled exotic, patchouli and the desert odour of baked clay. I felt sure he must have bartered for every item, or dug them from the ground. He handed me a glossy hardback with an aerial view of the Thames on the cover.

'Handle with care. Hugh ploughed three years of obsessive research into this.'

'I will, thanks.' I started leafing through the pages.

'Don't read it now – peruse it at your leisure.' He sat beside me, his hand closing around mine. 'It's still chucking down out there. I don't think you should leave.'

'What's the alternative?'

'Stay with me, obviously.'

'There's just one snag. I'm in love with someone else.'

'But it's over, isn't it? You said so already.'

It was easier to kiss him than explain. Odd thoughts pulsed through my mind as the kiss deepened and his hand stole inside my blouse. I'd slept with two men in the last three years, and the number of times I'd had sex could be counted on the fingers of one hand. My skin was crying out for attention, even though relationships never worked for me. Jake kissed me again until I could hardly catch my breath, then he dragged me to my feet.

His bedroom was different from the lounge. It looked temporary, with little furniture except his outsized bed. A light bulb hung from a wire in the centre of the room, casting a fierce yellow glare.

'That's too bright,' I said.

'It's perfect.' He lounged on the bed, observing me. 'I want to see every detail.'

Undressing for a man has always unnerved me, because I'm out of proportion. Skinny and five foot nothing, breasts a size too large for my frame. But a combination of booze and desire had made me brazen. I took my time unbuttoning my blouse, watching his eyes chase across my body, his gaze growing cloudy. When he pulled me onto his lap, the sex was quick and uncomplicated, and he was in too much of a rush to undress. The zip of his jeans chafed my hip as he entered me, my thighs tight around his waist. We came at exactly the same time, his head thrown back, muscles taut across his chest. It showed me the value of keeping the lights up high – I'd seen desire ebb and flow across his face, the way his skin flushed when he came. Afterwards he lay on his side, his arm heavy across my waist.

'Where do these come from?' I touched his thickened biceps.

'Digging mainly, swimming now and then. I can't stand gyms.'

'Me neither.'

'Something else we've got in common. Where did you get these?' He skimmed his hand up my thigh, making me shiver again.

'Running. I did a marathon last year.'

'Next time I'll come and watch.' His hand closed around my jaw, thumb brushing my lower lip. 'I missed a few things just now. Can we try that again? I promise not to sprint this time.'

The second time was more relaxed, me on top of him, hips rocking fast then slow, refusing to let him climax. Afterwards he carried on watching me with his unfocused gaze, as though he'd lost something.

'It's unnerving, the way you stare.'

'A man can look, can't he?'

'If you must.'

'Take it as a compliment, Alice.'

The bright light didn't prevent Jake from falling asleep soon after. I got up to use his bathroom and couldn't resist nosing around his flat. It was smaller than mine, with just one bedroom but a perfect riverside view. A smear of blood was oozing from the graze where his zip had caught me so I hunted for cotton wool in his bathroom. The contents of his cabinet made me do a double take. It was crammed with every beauty product a girl could desire: mascara, Clinique eye shadow, Liz Earle foundation. Unless he regularly transformed himself into a woman, it was proof positive that he didn't live alone.

I sat on the toilet seat to take stock. It had never occurred to me to ask whether Jake was single. For all I knew he was happily married, his wife away on a business trip. The brandy I'd drunk was starting to sour, my mouth filling with bitterness. The place was too small to share with anyone other than a partner. Sex with him had been exhilarating, but after my experience with Burns, I was in no mood for complications. I rushed back to the bedroom and retrieved my clothes before taking a last look at his perfect body sprawled across the bed. I considered turning out the light but the sudden change might have woken him. Instead I grabbed Hugh Lister's book from his living-room table and escaped into the dark.

18

The man's bed is empty when he wakes at dawn, his eyes bleary with sleep. For once the river is quiet. The silence frightens him; his life would be meaningless if the voices stopped. He dresses quickly and peers out of the window. The water looks the same as ever, stretching for miles, the city's diluted history stored in its memory. He listens intently until he hears it at last: a faint whisper, calling his name like a lover, soft but insistent. He finds his coat and rushes down the steps, scarcely noticing the rain. Soon he's at the water's edge, no one in sight. The sky to the east is already turning pink, leaving little time to complete his task. The river's calls coax him as he unlocks his car, odours of brine and tar enveloping him, like an exhaled breath.

It takes quarter of an hour to drive to the abandoned wharf. Builders planned to develop it and erase another stretch of the river's memory, but luckily the foundations were too weak. There's nothing here except condemned warehouses, holes gnawing through their roofs. The dock is home only to ducks and pigeons, but it contains everything he needs. The man picks his way between fallen tiles and abandoned scaffolding, then pulls open a metal trap door and descends the rusty steps. Even at low tide the cellar floor is drowned by water, a few rats swimming across its surface. When the warehouses were built, the basement would have been dry enough to store grain, but three centuries have seen water levels rise. The incoming tide laps the ceiling of the vast room every day, tons of water gushing through the broken windows, forcing the rats from their riverside home on a daily basis.

The man squats on the stairs to inspect the space. The river led him here days ago, and it's the perfect hiding place. The voices are louder now, suddenly jubilant as he splashes across the uneven floor, jeans drenched to the knee. When he reaches the opposite wall he leans down to inspect his handiwork. Two metal brackets are embedded in the bricks. The man pulls hard to test them, relieved that they still hold his weight. The tides have left them intact. It's impossible to yank them from the wall. He pictures himself following the river's instructions. Its voice is growing impatient, demands harder to ignore.

A new sound spills through the window, a church bell pealing six a.m., chimes resonating from the opposite bank. The man's sense of guilt quickly fades. Religion helped him once, but it's a long time since he lost his faith. The river's instructions are all he can rely on now. Everything else has abandoned him.

19

Lola looked tired when she opened her door at eight on Monday morning. Since the start of her pregnancy she'd been waking early, inviting me to breakfast several times a week. Her cat-like eyes observed me closely as she kissed my cheek.

'Been partying, Al?'

'A touch of insomnia, that's all.'

'Liar.' She smirked at me. 'You've been shagging that policeman out of your system, haven't you?'

There was no point denying it, so I kept my mouth shut. Lola's uncanny ability to read my mind had irked me ever since secondary school. I watched her rubbing her back while the kettle boiled.

'How are you feeling?'

'Hormonal. I've cried enough salt water to raise the sea level.' She rested her head on my shoulder. 'Don't say anything kind, it'll only set me off again.'

I carried the tray into the living room and she wolfed down a croissant without bothering to chew.

'I'm huge, but I can't stop stuffing myself.' She curled up on her chaise longue, her green dress stretched tight across her bump, a torrent of wild red curls cascading across her shoulders.

'You still look glorious, for what it's worth.'

The compliment seemed to be the final straw, because she burst into tears, cheeks flushed with exertion. All I could do was sit there clutching her hand.

'What's wrong, sweetheart?'

She blotted her eyes with a tissue. 'Neal's gone to an audition. We had a huge row before he left; he's still refusing to be at the birth. He says he's scared of flaking out. You won't let me down, will you?'

'Of course not, I made you a promise.'

She was soon back to normal. Her outbursts were like tempests, powerful but quickly blown over. 'Tell me about your love life, Al. I need distraction.'

I helped myself to more coffee. 'There's not much to report. I've been seeing a history lecturer, but it's a non-starter.'

'How come?'

'His bathroom's got more beauty products than Boots.'

'Maybe he's into personal grooming.'

'Eye shadow and blusher? And sometimes he looks at me like I don't exist.'

'But he's good in bed?'

'Hell, yes.'

Lola gave a dramatic shrug. 'So ask about the crap in his cabinet and find out one way or another.'

She was right, of course. But I couldn't see myself rushing to Jake Fielding's flat to confront him about his absent lover. I changed the subject quickly, and spent the next hour listening to Lola's birth plan. It included soft music and lavender oil instead of anaesthetic. I didn't have the heart to tell her about my month on a maternity ward during med school: in all likelihood she'd end up yelling for an epidural after three hours, like everyone else. By the time I got up to leave, her mood had brightened.

'Thanks for listening, Al. Sorry I'm such a misery guts.'

'At least I got a sumptuous breakfast.' I gave her a tight hug then set off down the stairs.

★   ★   ★

I still felt calm when I reached the FPU. My ability to separate personal from professional issues had revived. All that
mattered was finding Jude Shelley's attacker: so long as I
could deliver my work commitments, my private life was
unimportant. Even the solemnity of the office felt less unnerving. A row of grey faces glanced up at me, then swiftly
returned to their computer terminals. Apart from Mike
Donnelly, no one had responded to my overtures with more
than a few monosyllables. I was longing to learn more about
their work because some of the senior consultants were working on famous cold cases, but everyone seemed too busy for
idle conversation.

I flicked on my computer and concentrated on my profile
report. It was less than four pages long, even though I'd
included every fact at my disposal. All three attacks carried
the same idiosyncrasies, and the only clear link between the
victims was the Shelley family. Father Owen had known Jude
since he baptised her twenty-three years ago, and Amala
Adebayo had worked as the children's nanny. The attacks
appeared to have nothing to do with criminality as none of the
victims had been robbed. There was no overtly sexual dimen-
sion and the time lapses between the bouts of violence were
unusual. The killer had waited almost twelve months before
striking a second time. It still struck me as odd that his violence
had resumed on the same day the original case reopened, as if
he had received a warning. But Burns's team had checked that
the only people who had known were his family and the
authorities.

I still couldn't rule out the possibility that one of Jude's
close relatives had attacked her. I scanned the computer
screen, flicking back through the evidence. The police had
spoken again to Timothy Shelley's colleagues, who had
confirmed his presence in Brighton on the night Jude was

attacked. Heather and Guy's alibis were more questionable. Their recollections of how they had spent the evening differed, and they relied on each other to corroborate their stories. But Heather's involvement seemed unlikely. She had insisted on having the case reopened and had no motive to attack her own daughter. I could imagine Guy's emotional volatility turning into violence. And it still seemed possible that an unknown killer had developed an unhealthy fixation with Jude, extending his obsession to people she cared for. Or maybe his obsession was with the minister, and anyone in his orbit was vulnerable. Now that his appetite had revived, he was working at speed, striking twice in less than a week. He might have killed more victims in the interval since Jude was mutilated. If his MO was consistent, he could have cast them into the river, their undiscovered bodies washed out to sea.

The killer's modus operandi revealed some key facts: attacking at night suggested that he was risk averse and organised enough to lead a double life. He might even be bucking the trend for most convicted serial killers and holding down a day job. Each of the attacks would have required considerable planning, but there seemed to be an element of calmness in his temperament. He had attacked Jude on the back seat of a car, dropped her body into the river, then driven into thin air without leaving a trace. Conjuring tricks that effective required a high degree of forethought. Despite his capacity for violence, he was composed enough to plan each attack rigorously before killing again.

The other clear link between the crimes was the Thames itself. I felt certain that the objects he attached to the victims' bodies had a symbolic value, as well as a historic one. They wouldn't have looked out of place in Jake Fielding's exhibition of artefacts. Although the fetishistic element of the killing ritual remained unclear, the attacker's confidence seemed to be growing. Amala's death had shown an escalation in violence; her ordeal had lasted longer, and binding her feet and hands before tethering her to the riverbank had been the worst cruelty yet. Even if she had survived her injuries, she could never have swum away. I closed my eyes and tried to picture the kind of man who could calmly destroy someone's face, then stand back and watch them drown.

I flicked open Hugh Lister's book on the history of the Thames. It explained that the river had been sacred since prehistory. Bronze Age settlers had made human sacrifices and cast jewellery, swords and arrows into the water to appease their gods. They had lived in fear of immense floods that ravaged their settlements. The Romans had made offerings too, sacrificing bronze, gold and glass to the tides. But the chapter on the seventeenth century interested me most. It showed pictures of bellarmines just like the one tied to Amala's body, the ceramic bottles small as the palm of my hand. Like Jake had said, the spirit jars had been used in witchcraft rituals to cast spells and capture spirits.

I scanned the pages until I spotted a fact that startled me. During the seventeenth-century witch trials, hundreds of women had been put to death at Execution Dock. They were tied to ducking stools or bound to the riverbank. Three tides had to wash over their corpses, to rinse away their wickedness, before their bodies could be buried. Maybe the killer had been sending a message by executing Amala using the same method. The end of the book revealed another surprise: bellarmines had a high monetary value. A German museum had paid thousands of euros recently to acquire an intact one. I closed the book and gazed out of the window at the pedestrians sidestepping puddles on Victoria Street. The killer must either be combing the Thames foreshore regularly, or have access to large sums of money.

I spent the rest of the morning checking assessment forms from my interviews, then studied my printout of the evidence gathered so far. HOLMES 2 – the Home Office Large Major Enquiry System – was a blunt instrument at the best of times, taking similar fact evidence and crunching it into a crude formula. Shane Weldon's name was first on the suspect list it threw out, but I remained unconvinced. Despite the fact that he'd known Father Owen and killed a woman in the same vicinity, there had been no planning or ritualised violence in his first attack. None of the suspects identified by the profiling software struck me as a good psychological fit.

I studied my own list and thought again about Guy Shelley. His edgy manner, instability and isolation were all signs of a violent personality. Paul Ramirez had seemed incensed by Jude's desertion, but Burns's team had discovered nothing suspicious in his past, and his wife claimed that he'd been at home on the nights of each attack. Even if his rage towards Jude had made Ramirez violent, why would he kill her priest and her former nanny? My report felt thin and unsatisfactory as I folded it into an envelope.

Heather Shelley looked tense when I arrived at midday. Burns had been keen to interview her about Amala's death, but I'd managed to keep him away, convinced that she'd be more open if I met her alone. It had been a week since our first meeting, but she seemed to be regretting her request for frequent progress reports. She sat at her kitchen table, raking her fingers through her hair, barely able to keep still.

'First Father Owen and now Amala. I can't believe it's happening again,' she whispered.

'Can you tell me about your relationship with Amala?'

Her eyes were glassy with shock. 'She was eighteen when she came to us. We employed her as our au pair through an agency, but the kids adored her, so I helped her apply for a permanent visa. She stayed on for three years as our housekeeper after they went to secondary school, then I encouraged her to get some qualifications.'

'When was the last time you met?'

'Two weeks ago. We visited Jude together, then had coffee.' She shook her head in disbelief. 'Someone must know who's doing this. His wife, or a relative.'

'Killers can be incredibly devious, unfortunately. Concealment's part of the thrill. They love to feel they're controlling the rules of the game.'

She glared at me. 'How can you call it a game? My daughter's fighting for her life and two of our friends have been murdered.'

'I wasn't describing my point of view. I have to enter the offender's mind-set; a lot of convicted killers are competitive. They see successful attacks as victories.'

Misery was clear in her face. 'I shouldn't have snapped. I'm sorry, yesterday was a tough day.'

'Something else upset you?'

'Guy's in a terrible state. He drove over from his flat on Bankside yesterday and he hasn't left his room. The news about Amala hit him hard. He only stays here when he's ill.' She stared down at her clasped hands. 'The GP's upped his anti-depressants, but they don't seem to be working.'

Heather's distraught expression made me feel guilty for keeping her son's name on my suspect list. It seemed ironic that Guy Shelley's flat was on the riverside, a stone's throw from the Tate Modern. He was surrounded by enough cultural stimulation to fuel his creativity for years, yet he was too frail to enjoy it.

'Would you like me to speak to him?'

She looked optimistic for the first time since I arrived. Maybe she thought that a psychologist could wave a magic wand and restore her son's mental health. But I felt sure he would need dozens of therapy sessions to address his problems. I'd made the offer more for Heather's benefit than his. Despite her husband's glamorous job, I didn't envy the strain she was under. Seeing Guy would also let me assess his psychological state and help remove his name from my list.

I paused on the landing when Heather led me to the top floor. She managed to persuade Guy to let me in, but it was clear he was in no state for conversation. His room was modest compared to the rest of the house, grey light filtering through the window. A few sketchbooks were stacked on a table littered with screwed-up paper. He was hunched on the edge of his bed, forehead balanced on the heels of his hands. I sat on an armchair a few metres away.

'No need to speak unless you want to,' I said. 'I'll stay for ten minutes. If you feel like talking, I'm happy to listen.'

Silence is the first rule of psychology. Over the years I'd drawn hundreds of confessions from patients and prisoners, simply because I'd kept my counsel. At first I thought Guy would say nothing; he didn't move a muscle, his chest curled tightly over his knees as though the outside world had ceased to exist. There was a row of charcoal drawings on the wall. One showed a demolished house, with bricks and girders spilling from its structure. Beside it was an aerial view of the Thames, frayed as a torn strip of silk. It seemed odd that all his sketches focused on dissolution.

Guy's voice was almost too quiet to hear. 'It's happening again. I can't stand it any more and she's making it worse.'

'Your mum?'

'Not her.' He shook his head vehemently, still unable to meet my eye.

'Try to explain why you're upset, Guy.'

The silence thickened until it felt like a layer of foam insulating the room. I was about to leave when Guy finally looked up, his skin chalky, eyes reddened. 'You can't see it, can you? Lies are the only thing holding my family together.'

'What do you mean?'

'There are secrets everywhere you look.'

I asked him to explain, but he closed his eyes, his head lolling forwards over his knees.

Heather Shelley looked shocked by her son's claim when I got back downstairs. 'He's upset. Guy often talks nonsense when he's stressed.'

'If there's a family secret, it would help me to know.'

'I'm not hiding anything.'

I smiled at her. 'Most parents tell the odd white lie to protect their kids.'

'Guy could be talking about his adoption. We mishandled how we told him about it. He'd always been so fragile, we waited until he was twelve. When he finally heard he went off the rails. He was furious everyone had known except him.'

It took me a moment to absorb the information. The photos in the kitchen made the family look like the perfect unit, but Guy's build and colouring set him apart. 'Has Guy seen a therapist since Jude was attacked?'

'It didn't help. I keep asking him to go back, but he refuses. The pattern's always the same; he comes here in a dreadful state, stays a day or two, then leaves without saying what's wrong.'

'That sounds painful.'

She rubbed her hand across her cheek. 'Tim doesn't notice half the time. By the way, his office has arranged your meeting for tomorrow morning.'

'Thanks. I want to find out whether the attacks could be linked to his job.' I made the statement to reassure her. It seemed unlikely that anyone from the minister's political sphere would choose to attack Amala, but I wanted to reduce her worry about the family connection.

'You'll have a hard time getting anything out of him. Tim's got an amazing knack for detaching himself from anything personal.'

'Try not to worry too much.' I reached out and touched her hand. 'Your son might find cognitive behavioural therapy useful. It won't fix deep-seated emotional issues, but it can relieve anxiety.'

She gave a grateful smile then checked her watch. 'Jude's expecting me, but you'll come back soon, won't you?'

Heather's stance seemed contradictory. Her body language was hurrying me out of the door, but her words were begging me to return.

20

I puzzled over the meeting with Heather and Guy during my taxi ride to St Pancras Way. A family therapist could have written a book about the Shelleys. Only the minister seemed immune to suffering, his stellar career distracting him from family concerns. I still had the sense that the killer must be so closely linked that any of the Shelleys could have identified him. When I looked out of the window, rows of police officers were marching along the riverbank by Blackfriars Bridge. Despite the inclement weather, search parties were scouring the foreshore at low tide. Rain was still coursing along the gutter as the cab pulled up outside the police station. A huddle of journalists was waiting outside under giant umbrellas, but I managed to bypass them without being accosted.

The incident room was busy as I headed for Burns's office. Angie was babbling into her phone nineteen to the dozen, and Tania was giving one of her male underlings a dressing-down. She had a six-inch height advantage, and was applying the full force of her frown, glossy black hair tucked behind her ears. Detectives were racing from desk to desk. I'd never seen an investigation team working so purposefully, their urge to find Amala Adebayo's killer going into overdrive.

Burns looked disgruntled when I reached his office, tie loose around his neck, as though he feared strangulation. His expression was a mixture of anxiety and poorly controlled rage. He nodded a formal greeting but gave no sign of a smile.

'I've brought my profile report,' I said. 'Do you want me to talk you through it?'

'I can guess what it says. Jude's the trigger, isn't she? He's attacking anyone close to her. But what's the cause? Someone's picking off people she cares about.'

I shook my head. 'You're ignoring his obsession with the river and the fact that each attack hurts all of the Shelleys. I've included details of people I've interviewed and a couple of names to investigate more closely, but I need to push Jude harder for information tomorrow. Her whole family seems weighed down by secrets, especially Guy. The pressure's brought him close to cracking point.'

'Heather's his alibi for the night of the attack, isn't she?'

I nodded. 'They've got different stories about how they spent the evening.'

'Do you want Tania to interview them again?'

I shook my head. 'Leave it with me. The situation's too volatile for more intervention.'

'Can I come with you to see Jude tomorrow? There are some things I want to ask.'

It crossed my mind to refuse, but I nodded my agreement. On a selfish level it would be easier than visiting on my own. Confronting that ruined face without revealing my pity was one of the toughest things I'd done. 'Is there any other news?'

He glanced down at a printout. 'Now they know the attacks are linked, the higher-ups are pushing me to chase suspects from Jude's investigation. Shane Weldon's still in my sights. A street camera picked him up the night Father Owen died, heading for Battersea. He was in the right place at the right time so we're watching him round the clock. If it's him, I need to know why he'd target the Shelleys.'

'I'm not convinced. Like I said, it's rare for a killer's MO to change so radically.'

He dumped my report back on his desk. 'I brought Jamal Khan in yesterday, but he didn't remember much about the bloke who threatened him before Jude was attacked. He kicked up a big fuss about being questioned again.'

'Are you surprised? The MIT stopped him seeing his girl-friend while she was in hospital fighting for her life; he's got reason to be angry.'

Burns frowned. 'Taking sides, Alice? That's not like you. I thought you prided yourself on being level-headed.'

I bit my lip to stop myself retaliating. People had been call-ing me guarded and emotionless ever since I was a child. 'Injustice makes people angry. I'd say that was a fact, not a feeling. Have you found anything else on Paul Ramirez?'

'A student accused him of sexual harassment ten years ago when he taught in Manchester, but she dropped the charge. It looks like he transferred to London with his tail between his legs.'

'But his behaviour stayed the same.'

'He may be a creep but his alibi's rock solid. We still can't find any reason why Amala was targeted, apart from her link to the Shelleys – her computer's clean, and there were no ex-boyfriends hanging around.'

'She was single?'

'Her last relationship ended a year ago – some guy from her church. He was in France when she died. There's no evidence anyone followed her the day she was attacked. Nine people got off at her bus stop. Five have been identified, but the picture's too blurred for facial recognition of the rest. The photo boys are working on it now. She passed a street camera on her way home, but if anyone was following, he kept to the other side of the road. We've drawn a blank with house to house too. A neighbour saw a dark saloon car parked on her drive that night, but that's all we've got.'

I changed the subject to lighten his gloom. 'I found some information about the calling cards. It's likely they all washed up on the banks of the Thames, and they're centuries old. Our man could be a history buff.'

Burns gave a shallow groan. 'That narrows it down to half the population. Have you seen all the telly programmes about past civilizations?'

'I still think the objects could unlock the case. One of the lecturers at King's College has agreed to identify them.'

Angie appeared in the doorway before he could reply; her irrepressible cheeriness had dimmed by a few degrees. 'Can I have a word, boss?'

'Come on in.' He cleared space at the table.

'It's a logistical nightmare. Marylebone have lent us forty uniforms, but we need more. Most of them are doing house to house in Barnsbury, speaking to people at Amala's gym, her church and all her regular haunts. I need at least thirty extras to finish searches at Wapping and input reports. No one's giving. I've tried the DCIs at Holborn, Marylebone and Aldgate.'

Burns nodded. 'I'll call in favours. They'll be here by the end of today.'

'You're a lifesaver.'

Angie's smile revived before she scurried away, but it was clear that stress levels were building.

'A hundred and twenty uniforms chasing our orders, and she's taking the lead, poor kid,' Burns commented.

'How's she doing?'

'Good, but it's a baptism of fire.' He looked at me again. 'How are you getting on with the Shelleys?'

'It's a complex picture. The mother's falling apart, and Guy's got mental health issues. Out of them all, Jude seems strongest, psychologically. I think she's determined to stay alive until we catch him. The Minister for Employment's been elusive, but he's agreed to meet tomorrow.'

'Tell him my lot need a pay rise.' I was halfway to the door before he spoke again. 'Can you come back tonight to go through your report?'

When I turned round Burns looked more dishevelled than ever, dark hair in need of a cut, shirtsleeves rolled to the elbow, revealing muscular forearms. He'd have been more at home on a building site than shuffling papers across his desk. It took considerable willpower to refuse.

'Ask me tomorrow during working hours.'

I felt a minor sense of victory as I escaped into the corridor.

21

The man is sheltering under his umbrella on Westminster Bridge. It's six thirty and people are flooding from the City, their auras glittering too brightly, like candle flames before they expire. The man is tense with anticipation. His next target is familiar, and he's been watching him for months. Today he must track him all the way home without being seen. He keeps his head bowed, even though his disguise is convincing: pale blue contact lenses, skin darkened to a healthy tan, a short black wig. When he stood in front of the mirror in a public toilet, he hardly recognised himself.

He finds it hard to concentrate as the crowd barges past. A young couple block his line of vision; the girl kisses her boyfriend right in front of him, her tongue slipping inside his mouth. The boy's soul is filthy as cigar smoke, smothering his face.

'Disgusting,' the man hisses.

'Shut up, you freak.' The boy reddens with anger, but his girlfriend tugs his sleeve.

'Don't, Steve. Can't you see he's off his head?'

She drags her boyfriend back into the crowd and the man focuses again on his task. Big Ben's face is already illuminated, tourists braving the weather for one last photograph, but there's no sign of his target. The man looks over the railing at the water. Ghosts appear under the surface, chalk white, then dissolve again. They are so beautiful. He wishes he could capture one in a spirit jar to keep in his pocket.

The next victim appears at seven fifteen. He's in his twenties, handsome and dark-haired. A friend is with him, dressed in the same expensive clothes, as if they had shopped together for matching items. The companions walk side by side, enjoying each other's jokes.

Once they have crossed Westminster Bridge, they disappear into a pub on Addington Street. The man is angered by the delay, catching glimpses of them through the window, deep in conversation. But the river's voice reminds him that the prize is worth waiting for. It's growing dark when his victim finally emerges. He squeezes his friend's shoulder before turning away. The man's heart rate increases as he pursues him into the Tube station. His soul is easy to spot, a haze of sulphurous yellow rising above the crowd.

The man stands at the end of the compartment. He hates the press of flesh, the tainted air. It's a relief to leave the train at the Oval and breathe more easily. He follows the young man past the entrance to the cricket ground, maintaining a fifty-metre distance. The man dips his umbrella carefully as he reaches Clayton Street, concealing his face as he passes a CCTV camera, then watches his target enter an apartment block. He waits until a window lights up on the first floor. After fifteen minutes he stands by the security door, and smiles politely at a young woman as she emerges. She's in such a rush that she doesn't register him as he slips inside the building.

The young man is still dressed in his suit when he answers the door.

'Sorry to disturb you. I'm here about the noise downstairs,' the man says calmly.

'What noise?'

The first punch sends the young man reeling as the door slams shut. The next blow knocks him out cold, the river's voice flooding the room. The attack has already ruined his looks, his dislocated jaw stretched in an exaggerated yawn. The man steadies himself before opening his satchel and sealing the victim's mouth with gaffer tape. He lays him on his side, fastening his wrists behind his back with a length of rope, then tying his ankles. Once he's finished, he speaks directly to the man's spirit.

'I'll come back for you, I promise.'

The soul flares upwards, longing to be released.

22

A text arrived from Jake Fielding on Tuesday morning, inviting me to dinner. Despite his mysterious bathroom cabinet, it was tempting to accept. I hedged my bets by sending back a message to remind him that Hugh Lister was identifying the crime-scene objects that evening, and suggesting a drink afterwards. Hearing from him raised my spirits as my bus trundled through the early morning traffic towards Westminster. I stared out of the window across the river to the South Bank. Even on an overcast day, it was a Mecca for tourists. My eyes panned past the Royal Festival Hall, and the London Eye, glittering like a charm bracelet, to the sculptures in Jubilee Gardens. Guy Shelley's flat must be hidden somewhere between public monuments.

I got out at Westminster Bridge at nine a.m. and hurried to the House of Commons. All I remembered from my obligatory school trip was being led through endless dark chambers, which echoed with silence. Security levels had risen considerably since then. Two armed officers were stationed in the lobby, automatic machine guns strapped to their chests, checking the crowd for potential assassins. The hall was grand enough to take my breath away, its vaulted wooden ceiling carved with heraldic symbols. A throng of lobbyists was braying at top volume, company logos dangling from their necks. After five minutes Giles Moorcroft arrived to collect me. He was wearing another expensive suit, cufflinks with a club insignia and highly polished Oxford brogues. A cloud of discreet aftershave wafted in my direction as he extended his hand. He looked older than I remembered from seeing him at the hospital, dark brown hair greying at the temples. His face bore a solemn expression, but no distinguishing features whatsoever, not a single blemish or scar. Even his voice was anonymous, the clipped authoritative tone affected by most politicians and bureaucrats.

'Sorry it took so long to find a meeting slot, Dr Quentin. I'm afraid the minister's been called to the House; you're welcome to wait in my office.'

He ushered me down a poorly lit corridor. The building smelled of beeswax and dust, with an undertone of alcohol, as though MPs were already drowning their sorrows in sherry behind closed doors. Mr Moorcroft's desk was in a small anteroom, below a gloomy portrait of Disraeli, volumes of Hansard lining the walls. But at least he had a direct river view: the grand outline of Lambeth Palace rose from the opposite bank as clippers shuttled between the piers.

'Can I offer you some coffee?' he asked.

The black liquid in his percolator smelled like it had been brewing for days. 'I'd better not, thanks. I'll exceed my caffeine limit.'

'So will I.' He gave a dry smile. 'It's my biggest vice.'

Moorcroft sifted through a stack of papers, signing and organising them into piles. His job obviously involved far more than filling Timothy Shelley's diary, and I wondered if it gave him professional satisfaction. He looked like a throwback from the days when civil servants made a virtue of discretion, his dark blue tie clipped neatly to his shirt. I peered around the room for a sign of his real personality, but found little, apart from a black raincoat hanging behind the door and an old-fashioned umbrella with a wooden handle.

When the phone rang, Moorcroft picked it up without saying a word, then replaced the receiver. 'I'm afraid the bill's delayed. Could you come back another day?'

'I'd rather wait, if possible. I've got some urgent questions.'

He took off his reading glasses to study me. 'Mr Shelley told me about your efforts to help Jude. I saw a lot of her as a child. She was always a chatty little thing when she came to the constituency office. It's hard to believe the suffering that girl's gone through. Is she beginning to recover?' His mouth snapped shut when his statement ended, as though he regretted his candour.

'I'm afraid she's very weak. She's got pneumonia.'

His grey eyes clouded with pity. 'That's a terrible shame.'

'Could I ask a question, Mr Moorcroft? Do you know if anyone has ever threatened Mr Shelley during his time in office?'

His guard rose in an instant. 'I don't see your meaning.'

'A letter from a member of the public perhaps, or an unpleasant email?'

'That's not unusual; constituents often criticise their MPs.'

'Including Mr Shelley?'

He replaced his glasses. 'I'm not at liberty to share private information.'

'Don't worry, I'll ask him myself. I'm just trying to find out if anyone might be targeting his family.'

'The minister works under considerable pressure. Sometimes that makes people a little thoughtless towards those closest to them.' Moorcroft delivered his cryptic speech slowly and with full eye contact, as though he was transmitting a coded message. Then he returned to his work, remaining silent until Timothy Shelley blustered into the room at ten o'clock, exuding bonhomie.

'Forgive the delay, I'm afraid they're a fact of life here. Come on in.'

His office was considerably plusher than his underling's. It contained a huge mahogany desk, and a suite of sofas for ministerial powwows. The walls displayed beautiful artworks, including a Hockney landscape vibrating with sunlight, which must have been worth a fortune. Shelley looked exactly as I remembered, pink-faced and blessed with an aura of absolute entitlement, wearing a placatory smile.

'How can I help, Dr Quentin?'

'I'm still gathering information. I wondered if anyone has ever threatened you while you've been in post.'

His eyes narrowed. 'Did Giles tell you about the incident at my constituency office?'

'He's too discreet. I couldn't get a word out of him.'

He gave a satisfied nod, as if his assistant's loyalty was a matter of pride. 'A man threatened me the April before Jude got hurt. When the police investigated, he'd given a false name and address and they couldn't track him down. But it didn't strike me as particularly serious.'

'Do you remember what he said?'

Shelley's gaze evaded mine. 'I'm afraid not. He seemed rather unhinged.'

'And that's the only incident?'

'One or two unpleasant phone calls, but nothing personal.'

Shelley went on a charm offensive after that. He regaled me with anecdotes about threats his colleagues had received, including a junior minister who had almost had his house burned down. It seemed odd that even though his daughter was gravely ill and two people in his immediate circle had been killed, he seemed emotionally removed, just as his wife had predicted. I was about to thank him and leave when I remembered Guy's comment the previous day.

'I don't mean to pry, but your son mentioned something about family secrets. Can you think what he might have meant?'

Shelley's smile faltered. 'Guy's always believed in conspiracies. It's part of his creativity, I suppose. The only secrets in my family are open ones, like the fact that he's adopted.'

'Can you think of any other secrets that might affect your family?'

Anger flared in his eyes. 'Shouldn't you be finding out who attacked Jude, not putting me through the third degree? Inspector Burns questioned my family at length the evening after Father Owen died. He seems to think we're existing under some kind of curse.'

Shelley's character revealed itself in the depth of his frown. Under his smarmy exterior, he resented criticism, and his aggression helped me understand his assistant's statement. If anyone crossed him, I felt sure he would treat them abominably. The door swung open before I could reply and Moorcroft entered the room, head bowed.

'Time for your next appointment, Minister.'

Shelley gave a crisp nod. 'I'd appreciate it if you spoke to my wife about these matters from now on, Dr Quentin.'

Moorcroft escorted me back to the lobby in silence, but I handed him my card as I said goodbye. 'Please contact me if you remember anything unusual about the months before Jude's attack.'

I felt sure he was longing to say something, but loyalty held him back. He gave a tense smile before slipping the card into his pocket furtively, as if that gesture alone could get him fired.

23

I thought about Timothy Shelley's ability to bury his feelings as I arrived at the Royal London. Jamal Khan's claim that Jude and her father had been locked in a secret feud had stayed with me. I was still wondering what Shelley had done to upset his daughter when I saw Burns, standing by the hospital's reception desk, glowering. His expression only softened by a fraction when he spotted me.

'You're late, Alice.'

'By approximately three minutes. Sincere apologies.' I rolled my eyes. 'Did your team check Timothy Shelley's alibi for the night Jude was attacked?'

He nodded. 'One of his assistants shared a car with him down to Brighton. Shelley went to his room alone around nine p.m., to rehearse his speech. The call came through to the hotel about three a.m., but he wasn't in his room. He said he'd left his mobile there and gone for a walk in the hotel grounds. Apparently he was sleepless, thinking about the conference the next day.'

'If you wanted to put him in the frame he could have driven to London at nine p.m., attacked his daughter and been back in Brighton two hours later.'

'You've got a vivid imagination.'

'The whole family's lying. Shelley told me he worked with an assistant until midnight before going to bed. Guy and Heather have different versions of how they spent their evening too. She told me she cooked him a meal, but he says she went to bed early with hay fever.'

'What are you saying?'

'We need to know why none of them are telling the truth.'

Burns gave a curt nod. 'I'll talk to Shelley again, and see what I can get out of him.'

'I'll speak to Heather and Guy. Shock could have confused them all, but I'd like a clearer picture.'

We signed in at the reception desk and headed for the first floor. Burns's lumbering stride was slower than normal, as though he was reluctant to reach the destination.

'Does Jude know I'll be with you?' he asked.

'I phoned her doctor yesterday.'

The set of Burns's jaw revealed that he was nervous, not that he'd have admitted it. He always retreated behind a wall of Scottish machismo when his emotions were exposed. We waited at the nursing station by Jude's room, and the sister crossed our names from her list. She was a pretty Indian woman with a sympathetic smile, as if she believed that visitors deserved as much tenderness as patients.

'She's very weak today. I'm afraid she may not be able to see you; I'll have to check.'

'Is her chest infection improving?' I asked.

'Not yet.' Her smile faltered. 'But she's a fighter. If anyone can beat it, she will.'

The sister's words hit home. Jude's life hung in the balance; she was weakening every day, but we were no nearer finding her attacker. Burns refused to meet my eye as we stood on the landing, still as a method actor preparing to go on stage. After a few minutes the sister returned, her expression concerned.

'The consultant says you can have ten minutes, maximum.'

The room felt different this time. Jude normally kept the light dim, but now it flooded the room, the ventilator beside her bed hissing quietly. The air smelled of medicine and the bitter tang of aloe. She lay motionless against a mound of pillows, and I could tell she was past caring who saw her injuries. All her strength seemed to have vanished. Behind me I heard Burns take a sharp intake of breath.

'Who's my new visitor?' Jude's voice was a raw whisper, followed by a gush of oxygen.

'DCI Burns from the Met,' I said. 'Do you remember him?'

'I don't think so. Do we know each other?'

'It doesn't matter. Are you well enough to talk?'

'That's all I'm good for these days.' The next sound was a cross between a sob and a laugh. 'Guy told me about Amala. That's why you're here, isn't it? It's the same man.'

'I'm afraid that's possible.' I sat beside her bed. At this distance there was no avoiding the extent of her wounds, thick sutures holding her skin grafts in place. Each one must have been harvested from a different part of her body, a patchwork of skin types and textures. Her words emerged from the raw slit where her lips should have been.

'Did he cut her face too?'

Burns stepped forwards. 'It was a different kind of attack.'

'Oh, God,' she whispered. 'He did, didn't he? He hurt her just as badly.'

'She died of drowning, but her facial injuries were severe.'

'I knew it.' Her voice was shrill with distress, a monitor bleeping above her bed, her pulse hitting a hundred and twenty. 'Why the hell haven't you caught him? Can't any of you do your jobs?'

'We will, I promise you.' Burns's reply was calm. 'It's just a matter of time.'

'You can help us, Jude,' I said, 'by talking openly about the past. Before the attack you'd had a row with your dad. Can you tell us what that was about?'

'Just the usual father–daughter stuff.'

'Like what?'

'We disagreed about the internships I'd applied for. Nothing serious.' Her words came out in a breathless gush and I could tell she was hedging.

'Jamal said you were really upset.'

Her shoulders twitched. 'He misread the situation.'

'What about your relationship with Amala? Were you close?'

'Very.' There was a pause while she steadied herself. 'I confided in her. She was amazing to me and Guy when we were kids.'

'Did she mention anyone threatening her?' Burns asked.

'Never. Last time she talked about how she loved working for the police.'

Her blood-oxygen monitor had fallen so low that the sister was bound to throw us out at any minute. 'Look, Jude, we'll have to let you rest soon. Have you remembered anything else about your attack?'

'It was weird, after you left. All I could smell was cheap fake tan, and I kept hearing the strain in his voice. I thought about it for hours.'

'What about facial details? Can you remember any of his features?'

Her voice weakened. 'I keep trying, but I can't see him.'

'Maybe you're trying too hard. Let the memory float back, in its own time. There's something else I wanted to ask. Can you think of anyone you ever fought with? Even someone you knew as a child.'

She sighed. 'I thought I was surrounded by friends, but someone hates my guts.'

'Why do you say that?'

'He's attacking people I love, isn't he? This is my fault.'

'You shouldn't think like that,' Burns said quietly. 'There's no clear picture yet. It could be nothing to do with you.'

Jude's eye roamed in his direction. 'I know your voice, don't I? Come nearer so I can see you.' When Burns walked forwards her hands fluttered at her sides. 'You're the one who stayed with me in the ambulance.' Her voice was quieter now, her bloodshot eye focused on him. 'If you'd let me die, Father Kelvin and Amala would still be alive.'

The sister whisked in and politely shooed us outside, giving Burns no time to reply. By the ground floor he was still white-faced and silent, so I fetched him some water from a dispenser.

'I made a mistake,' he muttered. 'With injuries like that, maybe I should have let her go.'

'What choice did you have? You had to call the ambulance.'

'I could have taken my time. If I'd left it five minutes she'd have slipped away. Her quality of life doesn't bear thinking about.'

'Don't punish yourself, Don.'

'She must hate my guts. I would in her shoes.'

He sat there in mute discomfort and I reached out to touch his hand. He looked shocked for a moment, then his fingers closed around mine. Anyone passing through the foyer would have assumed we were a pair of grieving relatives. The gesture probably helped me more than him, because it neutralised my anger. Giving Burns comfort put me back in control. I reminded myself that he was the type of man who would fight tooth and nail to protect his kids, which was his strongest draw. The best thing I could do was let him get on with it and hide my feelings from plain view.

It was a relief to spend the rest of the day in silence, while my colleagues at the FPU slaved over their desks. When I bumped into Mike Donnelly in the café that afternoon he produced his usual encouraging smile.

'How's it going?' he asked.

'I've seen more relaxed environments. Why's everyone working so hard?'

'The Met keeps threatening to cut our funding, so people are worried about their jobs. The boss likes results in double-quick time.' He slipped into a stage whisper. 'And there are plenty of weirdoes here. Most of us make Freud look normal.'

'You think so?'

'Christ, yeah.' He nodded vehemently. 'There's a woman on the second floor who's been looking for the Sutton strangler for four years; dealing with the worst murders ever committed. She wanders about chatting to herself. Spend too long here and you go crazy or start wearing sandals all year round.'

I scanned the glum-faced individuals in the café, noticing their dubious footwear, and couldn't help giggling. But that was all the levity the afternoon provided. When the CO called me to her office at three o'clock, an overweight man of around sixty was standing by her desk, sparse grey hair combed flat across his scalp, his skin reddened by anger or high blood pressure.

'Alice, this is Mr Leigh, the director of Whitehall's press office,' Christine said. 'He wanted to meet you.'

The man's handshake was so cold it felt like he'd rinsed his hands in ice water, his eyes glittering like chips of jet. 'I've heard a lot about you, Dr Quentin, most of it positive. But questions have been raised about your approach. In future, please don't contact the minister directly. Submit questions to my office and we will obtain answers for you.'

'I'm afraid I don't understand.'

'The tone of your inquiry has been judged inappropriate. If you approach Mr Shelley again, Whitehall will press for your removal.'

I gazed at him, too flabbergasted to reply. Mr Leigh's collar was at least one size too tight, double chin trapped behind the starched material. Our meeting seemed to be increasing his tension, his overstretched skin turning puce. Eventually I found enough calm to speak.

'My work doesn't just concern the minister's daughter. Two other victims have been killed. My colleagues from the Met will interview Mr Shelley again, and I may need to speak to him too. This is a murder investigation; nothing can obstruct it until the killer's found.'

Mr Leigh's small eyes bored into my face. 'It would be unwise to ignore my advice. If you trouble Mr Shelley with any more intrusive questions, I'll complain to the commissioner myself.' He swept out of the room, leaving an odour of outrage and wet gabardine.

'Admirable self-control.' The CO gave a wry smile. Maybe she hadn't realised that I was capable of standing my ground, but it took several minutes for my anger to neutralise. It was clear that Whitehall and Scotland Yard were united in their desire to protect the Shelleys from scrutiny. Christine's body language was jittery as we reviewed my work, her heel tapping a staccato rhythm on the lino. It made me certain that the top brass were passing pressure down from above.

At five o'clock I caught the Tube to Euston to collect the crime-scene objects from the Met's Forensic Services Lab. It was hidden behind Euston Square, a Seventies concrete box that was yielding to decay, metal window frames patchy with rust. The basement smelled of rat droppings and damp, as the forensics officer wrapped each item in foam, then placed them inside a polystyrene box, like family heirlooms. The woman wore her white hair in an austere bun, and looked alarmed by my request to take the items away.

'These are classified objects. I'll come with you, then they'll be brought straight back here after your meeting.'

She insisted on carrying the box herself while I hailed a taxi. Our only moment of small talk came during the journey, after I mentioned that the history lecturers at King's were a bunch of well-meaning oddballs.

'I can imagine,' she replied. 'My brother's an academic and he struggles to do up his shoelaces.'

When we arrived at King's she was still cradling the box protectively against her chest. Jake's office was filled with faces I recognised from our expedition along the riverbank. There was a hubbub of chatter, Mark Edmunds's soft baritone throbbing in the background. Only hatchet-faced Hugh Lister seemed immune to the excitement. It still looked like he'd been spat out of bed on the wrong side.

'Is it okay if this lot see your finds, Alice?' Jake asked.

'The more the merrier,' I replied.

Lister led the way to a classroom packed with benches and scuffed wooden tables. His face was grave as he removed the objects wearing sterile gloves. It reminded me of Fiona Lindstrop conducting an autopsy, focused and methodical, leaving nothing to chance. He laid the sharp piece of metal that had been tied to Jude's neck on a foam-lined tray and leant down to examine it. The lines on his face were more deeply carved than I remembered as he frowned in concentration.

'A Bronze Age arrowhead, from around 1000 BC, in poor condition. The patina's oxidised, it's been in the water so long. It needs careful cleaning.' Lister cast me a scathing look, as if I'd brought him substandard goods. But his expression brightened when he picked up the opaque glass circle that had been tied to Father Owen's wrist. 'Flux glass, made from sand and lime. It's Roman, probably early sixth century. This would have been the centrepiece of a necklace. It's like one we found at London Bridge; unbelievable it's still in one piece.'

The rest of the team took turns peering down the microscope, while Lister waited, arms crossed. His engrained frown suggested that it had been years since he cracked a smile, irritability pouring from him in waves. Only Jake seemed unperturbed by his bad mood.

'Come and look, Alice,' he said. 'The scratches are typical of ancient glass from a river sacrifice. It's been damaged by rubbish the tide's dragged over it for centuries.'

Under the microscope, the glass was covered in minute cracks and whorls, and the same pattern covered the earthenware glaze of the bellarmine. Lister confirmed that all the objects had come from the Thames, which made me see the killer differently. He possessed enough patience to wander the muddy shore, collecting the treasure yielded by each high tide. But why did he feel compelled to return it with the corpses of his victims?

When I looked up again, the room was emptying. Now that the identifications were finished, the historians were retreating to their dusty world of books and artefacts. Lister turned his harsh gaze in my direction.

'Can we keep these pieces for our archive?' he asked.

The forensics officer looked horrified. 'Not while they're police property.'

Lister scowled deeply but didn't reply, his worn-out jacket flapping behind him as he left.

'Hugh's not great on social skills, I'm afraid.' Jake gave her an apologetic look. After she'd gone, he turned his attention to me. 'Let's get out of here and find somewhere to eat.'

I waited in the corridor while he collected his things. The office next door belonged to Hugh Lister and I couldn't resist peering inside. There was no sign of him, but the room was packed to the ceiling with belongings. Towers of books were stacked against the wall, papers spewing from a filing cabinet's open drawers. A pillow and a rolled-up sleeping bag sat on his desk, and lying in one corner there was an aqualung with a wet suit thrown across it. Lister seemed to have forced all his worldly goods into a room less than four metres square.

'It's quite something, isn't it?' Mark Edmunds appeared beside me. 'Management keep asking him to clean up, but it never happens.'

'How does he get to his desk?' I asked.

'With difficulty, I imagine.'

'Why does he keep an aqualung in there?'

'Hugh's been diving shipwrecks and reefs for years. He made a TV series about it in the Nineties.'

I finally realised why Lister's face was familiar. I'd watched his programmes as a child, featuring marine excavations in exotic seas, hunting for buried treasure. Back then he'd been a typical enthusiast, explaining each find in excitable tones. Either he'd produced a different persona for the camera, or some tragedy had killed his optimism. Edmunds was still standing attentively at my side, short blond curls swept back from his face.

'Would you like to come to the pub? A few of us are having a drink, you'd be welcome to join us.'

'That's kind of you, but I'm waiting for Dr Fielding.'

'In that case, enjoy your evening.'

His face flushed with embarrassment before he marched away. I was still wishing I'd handled the encounter better when Jake reappeared.

'Are you okay?' he asked.

'I think one of your PhD students just invited me on a date.'

'Which one? I'll give him a written warning.'

'Mark Edmunds.'

Jake gave a slow nod. 'That doesn't surprise me.'

The Strand was full of escapees from shops and offices as we headed for Charing Cross. The air was dense with drizzle, but it wasn't heavy enough to bother with an umbrella.

'I wish this would stop. I hate being permanently drenched.'

'I don't,' Jake said, grinning. 'You look great soaked to the skin.'

Salvador and Amanda's was packed with couples poring over trays of tapas, so I left him searching for a table and queued at the bar. He raised his eyebrows when I delivered our drinks.

'What's this?' he asked.

'Tequila with a shot of lime.'

'Good choice. I haven't drunk that since I left Cancún.'

'Tell me about Mark Edmunds.'

His eyebrows rose. 'He's got mental health issues; apparently the guy suffers from paranoia. It was a gamble, pairing him with Hugh, but they connect pretty well and studying has a calming effect on Mark. To be honest, I couldn't refuse his PhD application.'

'Why?'

'His family gave the department a big donation last year.'

'But he struggles with social situations?'

'We've only had one major incident – last term he threw a punch at another student. Mark thought the bloke was mocking him. Afterwards he apologised profusely and there's been nothing since. He's a workaholic, though, which explains why he gets on with Hugh.'

The information confirmed my suspicion that the history

147

department was even more dysfunctional than the FPU; students and staff using it to shield themselves from the outside world. I took a slug of tequila and decided on direct communication. Now that I was clear of Burns, honesty seemed like the best policy, wherever my relationship with Jake was heading. Secrecy had only led to confusion in the past.

'Who lives with you? Your bathroom's full of cosmetics.'

An emotion crossed his face too fast to identify: guilt perhaps, or panic. 'I live alone. That stuff belongs to my sister Annie. She stays over when she's in town. Did you think I had a secret romance?' His erratic eye contact proved that he was lying.

'Just curious, that's all.'

'I'd like to know more about you too. You're not exactly open.'

'What do you want to hear?'

'The usual stuff: family, relationships, the past.' For once his dark blue eyes focused on my face rather than the middle distance.

'I grew up in Blackheath. My mother worked in a library, Dad at the tax office. He had a drink problem that we all paid for. I've got one brother, Will, who's bipolar. The illness kicked in ten years ago. He's had a bumpy ride since then, but right now he's madly in love.'

Jake looked stunned. 'That's quite a life story.'

'You can have the full psychological case study, but I'd hate to bore you.'

We picked through olives and white anchovies while we exchanged details about our relatives. It sounded like his family was on the opposite side of the spectrum from mine.

'They're solid law-abiding citizens. One older brother and a younger sister, both much more savvy than me. I grew up in Weybridge, beside the river. Dad's a retired surveyor, Mum's

148

a lawyer. All very suburban.'

'Sounds idyllic to me.'

'Most of the time it was tedious as hell.' He reached out and touched my hand. 'Why don't you come back for coffee? We've talked enough for one day.'

24

Apart from one shot of tequila, I was stone-cold sober, which helped me make judgements instead of acting on impulse. I watched Jake brewing coffee in his kitchenette, humming quietly to himself. His physique certainly gave no cause for complaint. He had the lean build of a dancer or a gymnast, and his deep-set blue eyes had appealed to me from the start. He was the opposite of Burns, whose giant scale suggested he could easily knock down walls. Jake was ideal boyfriend material: interesting, good company, great in bed. But one vital ingredient was missing. His body language told me he'd lied about living alone, and I was intrigued enough to find out why.

'Tell me how the police work's going,' he said.

'Slowly. The Shelley family wanted a forensic psychologist to re-examine their daughter's case, that's why the Met recruited me.'

'So you're a one-woman hit squad.' He sounded amused. 'Have you found anything new?'

'Only that more attacks are being carried out. Someone's tying objects from the river to the victim's bodies; it's got to be the same man.'

'Is it definitely a male killer?'

'Probably. Ninety per cent of violent attacks are carried out by men.'

His gaze flickered with curiosity. 'What was the MP's daughter studying?'

'Human rights law.'

'Sounds like your culprit's not keen on morality.'

'How do you mean?'

'A human rights lawyer, a priest and a policewoman. He's gunning for do-gooders, isn't he?'

It was an interesting point. All three victims had been defenders of strict moral codes. Maybe the killer harboured a dislike for all legalities, seeing himself as a maverick, following his own belief system. I made a mental note to consider the idea later.

'Jude was studying at King's, two floors below you. Her tutor was Paul Ramirez. Do you know him?'

His smile vanished. 'Not personally.'

'But you've heard his name.'

'There was an investigation last year. A couple of students made a complaint.'

'Sexual harassment?'

'There was a lot of hearsay, but it can't have been serious. He didn't lose his job.'

I studied his face. 'I'd still like to know how the killer's finding his treasure trove.'

'From the riverbank, probably. Amateurs sometimes forage down there, but he'd need to spend days searching. It took me months to find an intact bellarmine. Or he could be buying the pieces through auction houses that sell to museums.'

'Can you tell me their names?'

'I'll write them down for you.' He trailed his index finger slowly across my collarbone. 'Don't you ever switch off?'

When I looked at him again, his eyes had slipped out of focus. It was a trait I often saw in patients with conditions like attention deficit disorder; there was something disturbing about the emptiness of his stare.

'You're drifting, Jake.'

'Sorry.' He rubbed his temple. 'That keeps happening. I'm fine one minute, then I'm in another time zone. Tiredness, probably.'

'It might help to sleep in the dark. You'd get more rest.'

His smile broadened. 'That way I'd miss things.'

'I'd better go home. Big day tomorrow.'

'I'd rather you stayed.'

'I can't tonight.'

A flash of anger crossed his face, but he quickly hid it. 'Then I'll walk you home.'

'There's no need. I'll get a taxi.'

I kissed him lightly on the cheek then rose to my feet. I couldn't understand why my thoughts were racing. Plenty of things about him appealed to me, but those odd moments when his attention lapsed were off-putting. After my experience with Burns, I needed someone whose focus was on me alone.

My phone had been on silent all evening and three messages had arrived when I got home. My instinct was to ignore them, but duty overrode tiredness. If it was Lola telling me her waters had broken, I'd never forgive myself. There was a rambling diatribe from Burns, then a greeting from Will, followed by something that terrified me. When I listened again, my mother said my name twice in a breathless whimper, before the line cut out. I closed my eyes and tried to keep calm. Her flat was an hour away – far too long, if her illness had taken a sudden turn for the worse. My hands shook as I rang her neighbour, Mary. The elderly woman sounded shocked, but agreed to ring Mum's doorbell and use her spare key if she failed to answer.

'Call an ambulance if she needs one,' I said. 'Don't wait for me.'

The drive to Blackheath was a test of nerve. I wanted to speed through Elephant and Castle, but the roads were clogged with taxis and night buses. By Lewisham my patience had evaporated. One thought kept repeating itself: I should have visited her more, instead of running from the past. It was too late for childhood anger, and it was shameful that I'd left her alone. Speed cameras flashed as I raced through Blackheath Village, but I'd stopped caring how many points I racked up.

My mother's neighbour met me by the entrance. Mary was older than Mum, but pink-cheeked and robust by comparison, dressed in no-nonsense slacks and a crisp cotton blouse.

'She wouldn't let me call 999. I haven't moved her in case something's broken.' Mary looked embarrassed, as though she'd failed in her duty, so I thanked her profusely.

Mum was lying at the foot of the stairs, curled on her side, covered by a blanket. I clicked into safety mode as I crouched beside her, remembering the basics from medical school.

'Try and move your hands. That's it, now wiggle your feet. Where does it hurt?'

'Nowhere. I shouldn't have called you, I only fell a couple of steps.'

'Don't be daft, Mum. We're going to A&E to get you checked over.'

She explained that she'd been coming down to put the rubbish out. Her speech was clear at first, but I could see she was fading. It was a struggle to help her into the car. She was limping heavily, so weakened by shock that I almost had to carry her. It concerned me that she said nothing during the ten-minute drive to Greenwich District Hospital, keeping her eyes closed. If she'd had even an atom of any strength, she would have protested bitterly. When I checked the mirror she was huddled under her blanket, face pale as alabaster.

A junior doctor examined her in the corridor because the triage bays were busy. It sounded like the building was full of drunks, howling for pain relief. Maybe it was a blessing that Mum was too dazed to notice.

'No broken bones, thankfully, but I don't like the look of that bump on your head,' the doctor told her. 'We'll take an X-ray, then keep you overnight.'

'There's no need.' The quake in my mother's voice had grown even stronger.

'People always say that.' The doctor gave a gentle smile. 'But concussion can be nasty. If you're well tomorrow, you can go straight home.'

By now her strength was returning and my mother spent the next hour complaining bitterly about being detained against her will. It was after midnight when I helped her into a bed on a general ward, the bruise on her forehead darkening from pink to crimson.

'Call me tomorrow, Mum. I'll come and collect you.'

'No, darling. You'll be at work.'

'It doesn't matter. Give me a ring as soon as you get the X-ray result.'

When I kissed her cheek she accepted the embrace for once, rather than flinching, and I had to blink back a tear. She seemed to be shrinking right in front of my eyes.

25

The flat is exactly as the man left it when he returns in the middle of the night. The front door is still latched open and the victim lies motionless, weakened by a long and pointless struggle. The man pulls a torch from his pocket rather than turning on the lights. The scene fills him with disgust. Blood has spilled across the floor because the victim has tried to work his hands free, showing a pathetic cowardice. The man releases a savage kick, silencing his whimpers. Now his task is easy. The victim is a dead weight as he drags him downstairs and piles his body into the boot of the car, his spirit glimmering in the dark.

It doesn't take long to reach the abandoned warehouse, the river crooning his name. Its music caresses him in the darkness, as though he's standing in a concert hall with an orchestra playing for him alone. But he can't let himself be distracted. He drags his half-conscious victim down to the basement and there's a muffled protest as the man ties him to the metal brackets. He considers listing the terrible deeds that will cost him his life, but no courtesy is required. His only duty is to sacrifice him to the river.

The man runs his torch across the ground, rats fleeing from the light, through a welter of deep puddles. The room smells of tar and saturated brick, the metallic odour of the river's sediment. Soon water will trickle through the glassless window, then the flow will become a torrent, and the victim will understand his fate.

For safety's sake the man drags a concrete block back over the hatch, so the victim couldn't escape even if he broke free. In twelve hours' time the river will receive its next sacrifice.

26

Seeing my mother so frail had left my head reeling: she'd been indomitable during my childhood, always smiling and presentable, no matter how bad things got. The thing that shook me most was how little I knew about her needs. Our relationship had been too fragile to ask about the care she wanted when she grew old. She'd reached that stage in a few short months, instead of decades. My worries simmered quietly while I ate breakfast the next day. Normally I shielded Will from family crises, but this one was too big to handle alone. At eight thirty I set off across Tower Bridge, the river brown as shoe leather, a flood of commuters gushing towards the City.

Will looked shocked to see me tapping on the window of the *Bonne Chance*, his smile slow to appear. I felt like hurling myself into his arms, but displays of emotion always made him panic so I kept my arms stiffly at my sides.

'Come on in, I'm just making coffee. Nina's still in bed.'

'Sorry to drop by so early. Aren't you at the juice bar today?'

'I'm on late shifts, two till ten.'

'How's it going?'

'Good,' he said, nodding vigorously. 'The people are from all over: Estonia, Brazil, Poland. Soon I'll be fluent in five languages.' My brother threw himself down on the bench opposite. 'Is something wrong?'

'It's Mum. She's been ill for a while with Parkinson's and

last night she had a fall. It's probably nothing serious but the hospital kept her in overnight.'

'Parkinson's? Why didn't you tell me?' My brother gazed at me in stunned silence. The last time he'd seen Mum had been a year before, when they'd had a huge row. I'd never understood how their relationship functioned; he seemed to blame her for our road-crash childhood, even though Dad was the violent one. Maybe he resented her remoteness. She had stayed away when his life fell apart, as if bipolar disorder was a malady you should be able to snap out of overnight.

'I didn't know how to handle it,' I admitted. 'To be honest, I still don't.'

'That's not like you. You're always in control.'

'This time I haven't got a clue.'

His expression calmed suddenly. 'Tell me where she is, I'll go and see her.'

'Are you sure?' The prospect of visiting Mum normally sent him running for the hills.

'Positive. Leave it with me.'

He seemed like a different man when he fetched the coffee. Normally he moved slowly, like he was wading through water, but now his gestures were swifter and more decisive. It made me wonder how long he'd been waiting to become my big brother again. He wrote down the hospital's address and the name of the ward, then shooed me off the boat so he could take charge. I had no time to worry about the fireworks that would explode when the pair of them clapped eyes on each other. There was a briefing at the police station that I had to attend.

Media interest had risen dramatically since last time. Press vans were double-parked across the yellow lines on St Pancras Way, oblivious to the threat of parking fines, several dozen journalists clustered on the steps. The story's appeal was obvious: a cabinet minister's daughter, a priest and a copper all thrown faceless into the river by a savage killer. But experience had made me wary of press involvement. It always slowed investigations down and raised levels of panic. The hacks' morose expressions revealed that there had been no new information, so I put my head down and raced for the entrance.

The incident room was rammed by the time I arrived. Burns gave a quick nod of greeting and I noticed that he looked calmer, as though Amala's death had finally sunk in, or maybe he was just relieved that no more attacks had been reported. His grave expression made the room fall silent when he rose to his feet.

'This is turning into the biggest manhunt London's seen for years. The killer's MO seems simple. He damages people's faces then drops their bodies into the Thames. Except it's not that easy. The uniting factor between all the victims seems to be the Shelley family. First Jude was attacked, then their priest, then the children's former nanny. But we still don't know why they're being targeted. The other thing we need to keep in mind is how dangerous the killer is. This guy gets a kick out of mutilating his victim's faces then letting them drown.' Burns swung round to face me. 'Alice, can you tell us any more about his profile?'

The tension in the room hit me with full force when I rose to my feet. 'Something's sparked this man's violence again, a year after he attacked Jude Shelley. It could be a personal tragedy, or a recurrence of mental illness, or it could have been triggered by the reopening of the Jude Shelley case. He's selecting victims from her family or closely connected to them. It's almost certain to be someone they all know. Jude recognised his voice, but can't name him, which confirms that he's from inside their world. The fact that the last two attacks happened so close together makes it likely to happen again soon, and his violence is escalating. In some ways he's a typical serial killer, hungry for bigger thrills. People who kill in this way tend to be males between the ages of eighteen and forty who gain pleasure from this level of ultra-violence. The calling cards he's choosing are pieces of history gathered from the riverside. Hundreds of years ago they would have been sacrificial objects, but we need to know why he's binding them to the bodies of his victims. It's too soon to tell what they symbolise, but I think we're looking for someone with two obsessions: the Shelley family and the river Thames.'

Most of their faces were blank with disbelief. Coppers operate in the world of facts and evidence; for most of them the mention of history and symbolism was a step too far. A few old-timers were struggling to disguise their scorn as Burns rose to his feet again.

'We have to take the psychological angle seriously. The killer told Jude Shelley that the river was waiting for her soul, and Amala was killed at Execution Dock. Take a look on Wikipedia; thousands of people died there over the centuries. Maybe our man's trawling the Internet, looking for kill sites where lives were sacrificed. Or he could believe that Amala did something to deserve punishment.'

The disgust on Burns's face showed his contempt for the killer's methods. I watched him issuing a raft of instructions. His build as well as his voice made him ideal to lead a large team, shoulders wide enough to deflect any criticism. The Scottish burr helped too: it gave a hard edge to his orders, every member of the team quick to acquiesce. It took less than fifteen minutes to send everyone on their way. Their work focused on deeper investigation into Jude's social contacts, Amala's private life, and the victims' links to the Shelley family. I wondered how Mr Leigh, director of the Whitehall press office, would feel about the family being subjected to yet more questions. Even though Heather had pressed for her daughter's case to be reopened, she could never have imagined the level of renewed scrutiny.

I was about to return to the FPU when Burns caught up with me.

'Have you got time for a catch-up?'

'Of course.' I followed him through to his office. 'I got a verbal warning from Whitehall yesterday to leave the Shelleys alone. It made me realise what the MIT were up against on Jude's investigation. Apparently my conduct has been inappropriate.'

'What did you say?'

'That I'll do whatever the case requires, with or without their permission.'

Burns looked amused. 'Scotland Yard are twitchy too. The seniors want me to focus on suspects from Jude's case as well as chasing new leads. I'm keeping Shane Weldon in my sights. They need to report progress to Whitehall, and he's our closest fit.'

'How can chasing the wrong man be seen as progress?'

His eyes narrowed. 'Did you know that Timothy Shelley's tipped for deputy prime minister in the next reshuffle?'

'So they'd do anything to bury this.' It didn't surprise me that the minister's bland affability had won him friends in high places, but I was stunned that Downing Street was prepared to accept any arrest to shift media attention from their blue-eyed boy. 'That doesn't make the links between Weldon and the new attacks any stronger. He went to Father Owen's church, but that's all you've got.'

'Shane would have seen the Shelleys every Sunday. Maybe it's a case of jealousy; they've got everything and he's got nothing.'

'He killed a woman on impulse, two decades ago. The man we're looking for researches, plans and covers his tracks. I've checked Weldon's prison records. He had a whole year of counselling to address his violence, and there's every chance that it worked. I think we should focus our attention on people with a specific interest in the Thames: students, history specialists, museum curators. Have you run a check on the academics at King's yet? It's where Jude studied, and their exhibition hall's crammed with exactly the type of objects the killer uses for calling cards. That's the line we should be pursuing.'

Burns looked sceptical. 'We did that already. None of the staff has a record. How are we meant to find a lone history fanatic in a city this size?'

'I'm just asking you to go deeper into the backgrounds of students and staff at King's.'

I listened in silence as he explained why he intended to carry on doggedly pursuing Shane Weldon. After a few minutes he fell silent.

'What's wrong, Alice? You're never this quiet.'

'I think you're taking the wrong approach, and I'm a bit distracted. My mother had a fall last night; I had to take her to Casualty.'

He shot me a sympathetic glance. 'Getting old's not an easy ride, is it?'

'You can say that again. Are your parents alive?'

'Dad's hanging on, still smoking like a trooper. I don't get much time to visit.' He gave a grunt of disapproval, but I couldn't tell whether his father's cigarette habit concerned him or his own lack of care.

I rubbed my hand across my forehead. 'Tell me what Weldon's been up to recently.'

'The blokes at Sinclair House say he doesn't come back some nights, but if he's got a girlfriend he's keeping her quiet.

His release contract says he's got to declare any relationships or he's in breach.'

'I can see why he's on your radar. The killer knows the river intimately; there are dozens of stairways and dockyards that are invisible from the road, and Weldon's walked that route hundreds of times. But has he got the mental capacity to pull off a complex series of attacks? The perpetrator's taking an intellectual approach, and he's targeting the Shelley family's circle for a reason. That's a poor psychological fit with Weldon.'

Burns's face set in a scowl. 'Maybe he went to St Mary's last Sunday night to confess, and Father Owen wouldn't absolve him. I'm getting a warrant to search the hostel. I want him in for a full assessment.'

'There are no grounds for that, but I'm prepared to compromise. If he breaches his licence, I'll interview him again.'

'That's your idea of a compromise?' he growled.

My refusal to comply seemed to destroy Burns's peace of mind. His jaw clenched so tightly I decided to stay silent; if he ground his teeth any harder, the bones might crumble.

27

It's early evening by the time the man sets out for the warehouse, in full disguise, resentful about being delayed. He takes the back streets, hoping that no one is following. The river is calling incessantly, begging him to act.

When he reaches the dock he looks around cautiously, then drags the concrete block from the hatch. The first sound he hears is a raw scream. The river's work is almost done, water lapping at the victim's throat, his eyes round with terror, broken jaw gagging. The tape across his mouth has soaked away and his shrill cries echo from the walls of the chamber.

'Let me go! Please. Why are you doing this?'

He crouches on the wet stair, the young man's pleas silenced by the river's victory cry. The tide is the predator; he only has to position the souls correctly so it can claim them. A dozen rats swim across the surface, preparing to escape through the open window. Water laps tenderly at the victim's face and his spirit flares in a burst of yellow light, sending out sparks like a Roman candle as he begins to drown. Then the water closes over his head. He fights to the surface one last time, bubbles spewing from his mouth.

The event is more beautiful than anything the man has witnessed. Heat rises to greet him as the river claims its new victim, the water shimmering gold, lights arcing across the walls. Then all that's left is a hymn of gratitude, and his panic dropping away. Now he has time to relax. Two more tides must cleanse the young man's body before he can work on his face.

28

It was early evening by the time I caught the bus boat to Greenwich. I'd heard nothing from my mother, but Will had texted to let me know that she was being kept under observation for another day. I bought a coffee and made my way to the front of the boat. The river journey was preferable to the endless drive through the suburbs. I stared at the northern bank as the clipper passed Wapping Pier. The Prospect of Whitby was doing a roaring trade, a crowd visible through the large windows, even though the terrace where Amala Adebayo's body had been laid was still cordoned off. The letter E was stencilled high on a brick wall, marking the site of Execution Dock, the old gallows still in place. If buildings had memories, the bricks and mortar of Wapping Wall must be replete with them. The death penalty had once been applied so regularly that the condemned waited in line for hours, listening to the screams of the dying before being marched to the hangman's noose.

The clipper passed a procession of old wharfs. Some had been converted into expensive housing developments, while others remained derelict. It was the abandoned ones that interested me, their architecture almost untouched. Rusting hooks and rope-pulleys were a reminder that cargo would have been lowered to the ships anchored below. The reason why the developers had neglected the warehouses was obvious: they must be riddled with damp, water gushing into their basements. My gaze traced the outlines of disused piers, trying to guess which stairway the killer had dragged Amala down. At Canary Wharf, dozens of city workers piled onto the boat, grey-faced from hours of calculations. The majority wore sharp suits; they were younger than my brother was when the finance world's expectations burnt him out. Anxiety welled in my stomach. It took a stretch of the imagination to picture Will and my mother spending time together without the usual fireworks.

The nurse at the hospital informed me that Mum had been moved to a separate room. When I peered through the observation window, she was relaxing on a cloud of pillows. The wide bruise on her forehead had darkened, and Will was sitting beside her. As far as I could tell, no missiles had been thrown.

'Hello, darling,' she greeted me calmly. 'I didn't know you were coming.'

'How are you feeling?'

'Much better. Will's been marvellous, he made them give me this room.'

'He's a miracle worker.' I wondered how he'd achieved the impossible. From experience I knew that single rooms in NHS hospitals were reserved for the mad or the dying.

Nina was lurking in the corner wearing black trousers and a dark red blouse, which made her slim figure look chic instead of boyish. I nodded a smile of greeting in her direction.

'Nina's been telling me about her thesis,' my mother enthused. 'It sounds fascinating.'

The whole thing felt like a dream. Not only was she communicating peacefully with Will, but she had accepted his new girlfriend too, even though her tattoos were on full display. Lines of ornate script scrolled down the side of Nina's neck, statements half hidden by her clothes. It fascinated me that she seemed to be turning her skin into an essay.

'You've made some decisions, haven't you, Mum?' Will said quietly.

She gave an obedient nod. 'I'm going to find a home help. And Will's getting a stair-lift fitted for me.'

The information rendered me speechless. In just one day my brother had achieved more than I had in months. Mum's relief at being reunited with him after such a long absence had probably given him an advantage, but the method was unimportant. All that mattered was the outcome. She was accepting help, for the first time since her diagnosis.

The visit to the hospital gave me another chance to observe Will and Nina's relationship first hand. She was a million miles from the chatty, ambitious career girls he'd chosen in the past, so self-contained that she could become invisible without vacating the room. But her presence calmed Will instantly. If a look of irritation crossed his face, she could remove it with a single touch.

At eight o'clock a nurse advised us that visiting hours were over, and I watched in amazement as Will bent down to kiss Mum's forehead, her smile broadening. For a few seconds it hurt that she never showed me that much affection, but I quelled the thought immediately. The last time she'd seen him, his bipolar disorder had been at its worst. She must be overjoyed that he was more in control. I squeezed her hand as I said goodbye but she barely responded, her eyes already closing.

Will and Nina travelled back with me on the clipper. There was a stunned look on my brother's face, as though he couldn't believe his luck.

'Did you cast a spell? I've been telling her she needs a home help for months.'

'I'll manage things from now on, Al. It's my turn to deal with her.' He made negotiating with my mother sound like the emotional equivalent of lion taming.

'She seems okay to me,' Nina said quietly. 'A bit cantankerous, but her illness can't be easy.'

I stared down at the water as the wash unfurled like a bride's train. When we reached Cherry Garden Pier, I gave them both a hug, then stood on the dock as the boat headed for Tower Bridge. Will's expression was still blank with disbelief, and I crossed my fingers. Not long ago, seeing Mum would have signalled a downturn in his mental health – hopefully Nina's support could prevent that from happening.

I checked my phone for messages when I got home. One had arrived from Jake, inviting me out the next evening. The decision was so tricky that I considered phoning Lola for advice, but it was too late to disturb her, so I accepted on impulse. Seeing him again might help me understand why he was permanently distracted. An evening with Burns would have been far more interesting, even though it was out of the question.

My brain was fizzing with the day's events, so I checked my email instead of going to bed. Christine Jenkins had sent a cryptic request to meet me and Burns the following day at her office. I noted the appointment in my diary then leafed through my papers, studying the map I'd printed from the Internet. It showed the Thames snaking through London, bisecting south from north. The killer's territory stretched between Battersea Bridge and Wapping. I'd marked the site of each crime scene in red ink, beginning with Jude Shelley's abduction from Lower Thames Street in the affluent north, her body washing up by Southwark Bridge. Then Father Owen had been taken from his church in Battersea, his mutilated body discovered at Westminster Pier. And the final attack had shifted to the East End. He had left Amala's corpse hanging from a rope at the city's infamous execution site in Wapping. It was the escalation that alarmed me, the killer growing more assured with each new challenge. I gazed at the map again and considered Burns's favourite suspect, Shane Weldon. He could have passed between the ten bridges hundreds of times, memorising hiding places. But Jude was certain that she knew her attacker's voice, and she had never encountered Weldon. His south London drawl was nothing like the refined accent Jude had described. The history connection made me doubt his involvement even more. I couldn't imagine him possessing enough patience to search for relics on the riverbank, then developing a complex and symbolic killing ritual.

When I checked my watch it was quarter to eleven, but I took a gamble on my hunch that Burns would still be working and picked up my phone.

'Any news?' I asked.

'Yes, indeed.' His voice was low with tiredness, but I detected an edge of triumph. 'Our Mr Weldon's breached his licence. He couldn't resist bragging at the hostel about having a girlfriend. I'm interviewing the lady in question tomorrow, and I'd like you to be there.'

I gritted my teeth. 'What's the address?'

The street was in Vauxhall, not far from the Tube station. I put down the phone in a state of amazement. Why would anyone date a man who had served a life sentence for killing a woman then chucking her body into the river like a piece of litter? The question repeated itself as I climbed into bed and switched out the light.

29

The morning's visit intrigued me, even though Burns was bound to crow. I'd always been fascinated by the psychology of relationships between women and violent male offenders. A behaviourist would probably say that it stemmed from watching my father beat my mother during my childhood, powerless to help. It amazed me that many of the UK's most notorious prisoners had dozens of female pen pals. It seemed like a problem of misinterpretation: they saw violence as a form of potency. But hundreds of prison visits had given me a different view. The most violent offenders were often profoundly damaged, lashing out at their victims through a combination of hatred and fear.

Burns was waiting outside a council block on Black Prince Road when the taxi arrived in Vauxhall. It was a ten-minute stroll along the river from Sinclair House, which probably explained Shane Weldon's passion for night-time walking. The building sat right by the road, the daily grind of traffic darkening its windows with exhaust fumes.

'Not the classiest postcode,' Burns commented.

We peered into the lift but decided against it; the metal chamber stank of urine, vinegar and cheap booze. Rain dripped from the atrium as we climbed the stairs, and I tried to ignore the dark brown stains smeared across the concrete.

Sue Rochford must have been waiting for us, the door of her fifth-floor flat hanging open. It was a chilly day but she was dressed for summer in cropped black trousers and a turquoise vest top. The woman was so thin that I glanced at her arms, but the skin was unblemished. If she was a user, she was canny enough to shoot straight into her thigh.

'Thanks for giving your time, Mrs Rochford,' Burns said.

'It's Ms, actually. My husband fucked off years ago, thank God.'

Her lounge was full of mismatched furniture, armchairs upholstered in emerald green fabric, which clashed with her orange settee. The air had a synthetic smell, as though she'd emptied an entire can of air freshener in preparation for our arrival. She studied us nervously, grey roots visible in her dry blonde hair. Her age could have been anywhere between thirty-five and fifty, deep grooves bracketing her mouth, eyes spiralled by a network of lines.

'We'd like to hear about your relationship with Shane Weldon,' Burns said.

She rolled her eyes. 'The bloke made one stupid mistake. You lot need to get over it.'

He returned her gaze steadily. 'Do you mind me asking your age, Ms Rochford?'

'Thirty-eight. Why?'

'Shane killed a woman of thirty-six. He slit her throat, then dropped her body in the Thames. He didn't know her from Adam.'

Her expression didn't flicker. 'I thought about topping my ex plenty of times. I had it all planned.'

'But you didn't, did you? Shane told his trial judge he wanted to know how it felt to kill a woman. No other reason.'

She frowned at him, then examined her nails. 'I still don't get why you're here.'

'Your boyfriend's serving a lifetime sentence. He'll be on probation till he shuffles off this mortal coil. His bail conditions mean that he's got to report whenever he starts a relationship so his lady friends know about his murder conviction.'

'Now you've told me, you can fuck off.'

'Charming,' Burns muttered.

'How did you meet Shane?' I asked.

Rochford's blurred gaze shifted in my direction. 'He walked me home from the Lord Nelson one night. I thought he was a real gent, he didn't lay a finger on me.' She still seemed blithely unconcerned by her boyfriend's violent past.

'Have you got a job at the moment?' I asked.

'I was a care assistant, but these Filipinos agreed to take less money.' She gave me a poisonous look. 'There should be a law against them flooding the country.'

'Cash must be tight,' Burns said. 'Your benefits can't leave much for clothes or trips out.'

'I get by.' Rochford scowled at him.

'How much does Shane give you? Forty quid a week? Fifty?'

'You filthy bastard,' she snapped. 'I'd never sell myself to anyone. I could report you for saying that.'

Burns gave a relaxed shrug. 'Shane told a mate at Sinclair House that he pays you a few quid to keep your door open. But I'm not here to arrest you for soliciting, I just need some facts. Have you got a car, for example?'

The anger in her voice gave way to exhaustion. 'A blue Ford Escort, ten years old.'

'How often does Shane borrow it?'

She blinked rapidly. 'Just to visit his mum now and then, over in Wembley.'

'I'll need the keys, and the dates when Shane's used it.'

Rochford protested but finally offered the information. Afterwards she jumped to her feet to show us out, as though we were polluting her environment.

'One more thing, Sue,' Burns said. 'Has Shane ever been violent?'

'Do I look stupid? I've had enough of that to last me a sodding lifetime.'

She slammed the door so hard the casement rattled, but Burns said nothing. When we reached ground level he tipped his head back, staring up at her window.

'Why in God's name is she seeing him?'

'We don't know her history,' I replied. 'And we haven't proved anything. Maybe Shane killed a woman on impulse, served his time, and now he's reformed.'

Burns gave me a pitying look. 'Even if I'm wrong, he's not exactly love's young dream, is he?'

We took shelter from the rain in a café before the meeting with Christine Jenkins. I felt a pang of regret for the days when our conversations were full of flirtation and banter, but Burns was sticking to the letter of my warning. Oddly enough his remoteness made me want to touch him more, although he didn't seem to notice. He used the time to update me on his team's hard work.

'Hancock found something weird in Amala's house at the spot where she was tied up. There are strands of synthetic blond hair on the carpet.'

'That fits Jude's description. It sounds like he wears a wig and disguises himself in other ways too. Maybe the victims know him, and he's afraid he'll be recognised.'

He gave a distracted nod. 'I've got a warrant for a finger-tip search of Shane's room and I'll get one for his lady friend's flat.'

'The killing ritual matters as much as the attack. If it's Weldon, you're going to find objects he's salvaged from the river. Those pieces are costing the killer a lot of energy or money.'

'I don't think he bought them. We've checked all the main auction sites.'

'I'm still more interested in the students and staff at King's. I'd like to know about a history PhD student called Mark Edmunds. If we're looking for someone with an obsessive interest in the Thames, he fits the bill.'

Burns looked unimpressed. 'Do you want me to widen the search to every history teacher and GCSE student in London?'

'Intellectuals sometimes kill, you know that. Some of the researchers at King's are so passionate about history it's bordering on madness.'

'Angie's organising more detailed checks. What's the head of department's name?'

'Jake Fielding.' It crossed my mind to mention that I'd been seeing him, but it would have broken our rule about keeping our personal lives separate, so I kept my mouth shut.

Christine Jenkins looked solemn when we reached Dacre Street. It was so cloudy outside that her office was full of shadows. She perched on the edge of her desk when we sat down.

'Whitehall's getting concerned. The longer this drags on, the worse the impact on public confidence. I've had Mr Leigh on the phone twice already today.'

'With respect, ma'am, my team's working to capacity,' Burns said calmly. 'I should be in the incident room now, supervising them.'

She gave an apologetic nod. 'The commissioner wants me to give an overview to the exec at Scotland Yard when I report on Alice's work, otherwise I wouldn't have brought you here.'

'We're pursuing a key suspect from Jude Shelley's attack. And we've got strong lines of enquiry for the recent murders,' said Burns.

'You're aware that the commissioner wants loose ends from the first investigation tied off. They need assurances that no stone's been left unturned.' She gazed down at a stack of reports on her desk. 'So many things got missed last time, we can't make the same mistake twice.' She turned to face me. 'And what about you, Alice?'

'I think it's a mistake to get distracted by the original suspects. None of them are a good fit for this killing series. It still seems odd that these attacks started just as Jude's case reopened, as if the killer was forewarned. I'm almost certain Jude Shelley knew her attacker, even though she's buried the memory. He's in disguise when he attacks, so it's possible that he's known to all the victims, but I'm not getting much help from the Shelleys. The minister's keeping us at arm's length. His adopted son has an anxiety disorder, and his wife's at breaking point.'

She shot me a look of sympathy. 'Far from ideal working conditions. What's your take on the psychology of the offender?'

'He's highly ritualised and likely to be a functional psychotic. Our man's shown strong self-control so far, only allowing himself to attack at night, planning meticulously. He's obsessed by the Shelley family and clearly a risk taker, gambling with exposure by abandoning the bodies in public places. I think he may have a delusional interest in the Thames. His rituals use ancient sacrificial objects at historic killing sites. The objects he's tying to the bodies seem almost as important to him as the violence.'

The CO gave a grave nod. 'He's having a ball, in other words.'

She peered out of the window at the heavy sky, as though we'd ceased to exist.

30

The man wishes he could return to the warehouse to finish his task. But one more tide must rinse the victim's soul before the river claims it. He's sitting in a busy café, sifting through newspapers borrowed from a rack by the counter. Most of the headlines are lurid enough to make him wince. The tabloids are calling him the Riverside Killer, pedalling theories about his ruined childhood and the nature of his sadism. All nonsense, of course. It makes him wish he could phone the news desks and explain the simple truth. He has no choice in the matter. He has to kill the ones who know the secret, and the river instructs him, its clear voice forcing him to act against his will. There's no pride or glory, just the elation of the moment, quickly followed by remorse. Yet he can't ignore the thrill of reading about himself. Even if their speculations are wrong, the world is taking notice and the attention is dazzling. He reminds himself to stay focused on the river's mission. Everything else is flattery and glitter.

The papers will carry on fabricating their lies, it won't change his duty. He can't afford to let anything slow him down. The secrets have to be erased, and without a steady supply of victims, the river's currents would grow sluggish, water pooling in the shallows, refusing to flow. He gazes down at the *Telegraph* until a young girl approaches his table, her skin pale and translucent. She points at one of the newspapers in the pile beside him.

'Could I borrow this, please?' Her voice is almost as pure as the river's.

'With pleasure.'

The man hands her the newspaper with a flourish and she offers a gentle smile in return. He watches her avidly as she turns away, wishing again that he could select his own victims.

31

'Sorry I moaned so much last time,' Lola apologised when she picked up the phone.

'I wasn't expecting a comedy show.'

'Come round and help me finish this huge chocolate cake. I promise not to cry.'

'I can't. I'm going out for dinner. But call if anything happens, won't you?'

'Thanks for being on standby. Who's the hot date?'

'The historian. It's his last chance to prove he's keen.'

'Of course he's bloody keen.'

'Maybe he's just lonely and sex-starved.'

'Jesus, Al,' she groaned. 'You'll die alone, surrounded by cats.'

'No I won't. I'll wait till your kids grow up and leave home, then move in with you.'

It took me ages to choose an outfit. Hunting through my wardrobe was a welcome distraction, but it proved that I needed to go shopping. There were a few lacklustre suits, and a floaty skirt from Ghost that would disintegrate with the first drop of rain. I chose a Liberty's black cashmere dress, which had cost a small fortune, but had been a good investment, because the fabric still felt gorgeous. I made an effort with my hair too, fiddling with my straightening tongs until it hung to my shoulder without a single kink. Then all that was required was a pair of boots and a dash of red lipstick. The hall mirror showed a gaunt-faced blonde, bright lips making me paler than ever, but the taxi had already arrived and it was too late for adjustments. If Jake was genuinely interested, it would take more than garish war paint to scare him away.

We'd agreed to meet at the Prospect of Whitby. I'd considered suggesting a different venue, but didn't want to stop visiting just because it featured in my nightmares. The bar staff were busy serving a throng of punters. There was no sign of Jake amongst the crowd, so I made my way to the beer garden. Lanterns glowed on the newly reopened terrace, a few couples watching the lights pulse on Butler's Wharf. I peered down at the expanse of silt glistening on the riverbank, and caught a whiff of brine mixed with the pungency of ripe fruit. Hundreds of years ago crowds would have gathered here to watch condemned men being pushed from the jetty. Their necks would have broken instantly, bodies twitching as the Thames lapped at their feet. But why had the killer ended Amala's life here? She was a confirmed Christian and an upholder of the law. Maybe he believed she was guilty by association. Years ago she had worked for the Shelleys, and I felt certain that both the minister and Jude were still hiding information, despite the danger they faced. My determination to peel back their layers of secrecy grew stronger every day.

When Jake tapped me on the shoulder I almost jumped out of my skin. He was out of breath, hair glistening with rain. 'Sorry, Alice, my meeting overran.' He took a step backwards and scanned me from head to toe. 'God, you look glamorous.'

'You mean I normally look a total mess?'

He laughed. 'You're impossible to compliment. Come on, let's go somewhere else, this place is heaving.'

We ended up in a curry house on Wapping High Street, which suited me perfectly. Candles glowed on each table, and the waiters performed their duties in dignified silence. They provided us with bottles of Tiger beer, dishes of sag aloo and lamb madras. Jake watched me heaping pilau rice onto my plate. The seriousness of his expression was still there, but his air of distraction had vanished, and he was even more handsome than I remembered. His cropped hair revealed his strong bone structure and soulful eyes. For the time being his looks were enough to wipe Burns from my mind.

'What made you become a historian?' I asked.

'I wanted to be the next Indiana Jones.' He gave a wry smile. 'I was an evangelist for archaeology. I thought all human secrets lay underground.'

'Does the present day bore you?'

'Not at all. But there's something incredible about finding pieces of Aztec treasure in the middle of a desert. The past can be addictive.'

'You still feel that way, don't you?'

'Sometimes, but I'm not as bad as Hugh. He's abandoned modernity completely.' He tried to look grave. 'What's your opinion of my condition, Dr Quentin?'

'Incurable, I'm afraid.'

'Diagnose me anyway.' His eyes lingered on my mouth. 'I'm prepared for the worst.'

'You're a perfectionist, so highly driven that your passion for your subject borders on obsession.'

'Wrong on all counts, Doctor. That's not the root of my insomnia.'

He refused to explain, but the teasing went on all evening, his upbeat mood putting me at ease. I was determined to stay sober, so I drew the limit at two beers. I was still curious to know why he seemed so relaxed.

'You've had good news, haven't you?'

He grinned. 'The Archaeology Trust is funding our excavation; all those muddy weekends finally paid off.'

'Congratulations! You must be thrilled.'

'Relieved, more than anything. Now no one gets fired.' I felt his hand touch mine under the table, then his fingers skimming the bare skin of my thigh. 'Come home with me, Alice. And this time promise not to run away.'

I studied him again. 'I could. But promises often get broken, don't they?'

Going back to Jake's flat was an easy decision. He was good company, and I had professional questions to ask, but the main reason was pure self-interest. The only thought in my mind as we climbed the steps was the pleasure of watching him undress.

'Another beer?' he asked when we got inside.

'Just water, please.'

I stood in his lounge surveying the walls, while he dug around in his fridge. There was a pin-board I hadn't noticed before. It held a tide table, a calendar with several dates crossed out, and a large-scale map of the Thames, with sections of the river marked in different-coloured inks. I shivered as Jake dropped a kiss on the back of my neck.

'Why do I get the feeling you're investigating me, Alice?'

'Don't flatter yourself, it's the river I'm interested in. What are these marks for?'

His finger trailed across the map. 'Sacred sites. The Romans built a bridge where London Bridge stands now, for sacrifices. And Vauxhall was important in the Bronze Age. The place was more significant than Stonehenge.'

'How come?'

'It's where the Thames is most powerful. Two underground rivers, the Tyburn and the Effra, merge with it at Vauxhall Cross. Hundreds of objects have been dredged up there

– gold jewellery, silver talismans and coins. There's a display in the Museum of London.'

'So Vauxhall's the most historically important location on the river?'

'Definitely.'

I stared at the map again, trying to make sense of the fact that human lives had been sacrificed at all three of the recent murder sites. Jake's arms were closing round my waist.

'Tell me about the amateurs you see on the foreshore. What kind of people are they?' I asked.

'Dog walkers, history buffs with guidebooks, the odd loon waving a metal detector. Why?'

'The killer knows his history, that's all.'

'Come on, it's midnight. It's time to switch off.'

He pulled me down beside him on the settee and my mind emptied when he kissed me. I liked the fact that he was greedy about taking what he wanted, because it allowed me to make demands too. At some point we travelled from the sofa to his bed. I woke at three a.m., face down on the divan, the light bulb burning overhead, its fierce brightness piercing the surface of my dreams. When I stumbled along his hall to the bathroom the cabinet door hung ajar and I couldn't resist peeking inside. This time it was empty, apart from toothpaste and shaving foam. The transformation was intriguing – either Jake's female visitor had reclaimed her beauty kit or he'd wiped out all trace of her existence.

The mystery had banished sleep completely, so I went back to the living room and gazed at the objects on his shelves. There was a row of half-burned candles, a bottle of tequila with a bright red skull grinning from the label, and some post-cards of Cancún Bay. I studied them closely. I'd always wanted to dive there, in the world's bluest ocean, but Jake's phone distracted me. Its buzz was shrill and insistent. I reached out to turn it off in case it woke him, but a woman's image appeared when I hit the button, and my heart lurched inside my chest. It was a photograph of me, taken a year before when my hair was shorter. I stared down at myself then closed my eyes. After the shock cleared I looked again. The girl wasn't me after all, but she looked so similar that an identity parade would have been pointless. Her light green eyes matched mine, and her mid-blonde hair held the same wave that refused to straighten.

Panic cancelled out my intention to stay the night. I was in such a hurry to escape that the phone clattered to the floor as I stumbled into my clothes. Jake was moving around in his room, his voice calling as I rushed outside. The sky was a light-polluted brown, no stars in sight. The river's odour held the memory of every substance it had been forced to swallow: wine, spices, rotting meat. I'd always loved its earthiness, but now it was making my stomach churn. I was sick of complications, and too shocked to care where Jake Fielding had found a picture of a woman who looked like my identical twin.

32

It's almost six a.m. when the man forces himself out of bed. Standing in front of the bathroom mirror, he begins to shave. His appearance is the same as ever, only the river's voice marking him out from the crowd. He thinks of the methods he used in the early days to try and silence it. Turning up the radio, or watching TV, but the water's instructions always filled the room. Today it's little more than a whisper, words slipping through his mind like a brook's babble. The thought of what lies ahead fills him with disgust. He's close to tears as he stands under the shower. Sometimes he wonders how long he can continue doing as he's told.

He studies his tide table carefully, then selects the items he needs from the kitchen: a butcher's knife and a smaller one with a sharp blade. He drops them into his satchel beside a towel to wipe his hands. He's about to leave when the phone rings in his bedroom, but he knows he mustn't answer. Nothing must distract him until his task is done.

He feels less afraid when he gets outside, the water glistening under the fading streetlamps. The river is slipping west, surface blank with innocence, as if it wants nothing more than to return to its source. A woman from his apartment block walks by with her dog, and he raises his hand in greeting as he unlocks the car; he must act normally, so no one will suspect that anything is wrong. She grins back then sets off along the road, her pale blue soul hovering innocently around her shoulders.

He reaches the old warehouse by seven a.m. This time no sound emerges as he descends the steps, but there's a skitter of activity. Rats are crawling over the victim's body; in forty-eight hours they have almost completed his work. The victim's face is already ruined, purple bruises covering his forehead, skin bloated by the tides that cleansed his sins. Even his friend from the wine bar would fail to identify him. The man opens his bag and reaches for his knives. Rooted to the spot, he listens to the water's instructions then forces himself to begin. The task is worse by daylight because he can see every incision, flesh slicing from each bone. He works fast, determined to suppress his nausea.

Once the victim's skin is loosened, he makes one final cut then throws it into the corner; another meal for the rats to enjoy. It takes moments to tie the piece of flint tightly around the victim's neck, then haul him to the open window. The river laps at the wall below, and the man peers out cautiously. No boats are passing and there's no one visible on the opposite shore, so he heaves the body over the lintel and listens to the splash as it hits the water. The river claims it immediately, currents dragging it into the deepest channel.

The man watches the river play with its latest toy, pulling it deep then letting it bob to the surface. Rats cluster in the corner, enjoying their feast, and a fresh wave of sickness rises in his throat. He tests the wall brackets, checking they are still secure. Then he escapes from the dark space with the river's praise echoing in his ears.

33

Jude was propped up in bed when I arrived on Friday morning. I had spent most of the night puzzling over the photo on Jake's phone, but seeing her put my worries into perspective.

'I'm surprised they let you in. It's good to see another human being.' Her voice had reduced to a breathless whisper, and she looked weaker than before, patchwork skin grey with exhaustion.

'Did you have a bad night?'

'This thing doesn't let me sleep much.' She tapped the oxygen machine rasping loudly at her side.

'I wanted you to know they're making progress finding Amala's killer. It sounds like she didn't have an enemy in the world.'

'I still can't believe she's gone.'

'Did she ever mention any relationships?'

'Not since last year. She was waiting for someone with the same beliefs.' There was a long pause while Jude's exposed eye roamed across my face. 'Why did you come, Alice? I can tell you're not here to talk about Amala.'

'I wondered if you knew anyone from the history department when you were at King's.'

'A few, it was a relaxed place. Everyone chatted in the coffee bar.'

'Did any of the men flirt with you?'

'There was one guy who used to chat in the lunch queue. He asked me out once. Mark somebody, I can't remember his surname.'

I looked up abruptly. 'Mark Edmunds?'

'That's him. Blond guy – sweet but a bit odd. He backed off after I said I had a boyfriend.'

'Did he seem angry about that?'

'More disappointed. He was nice about it; he said Jamal was a lucky man.'

'Was there anyone else?'

'I don't think so; most of the historians kept themselves to themselves.'

'That's helpful, but I still need to know about your childhood. You always steer away from it. Are you ready to say who hurt you back then?'

She flinched. 'I told you, my past has nothing to do with this.'

'Was it your dad?'

The nurse burst into the room before she could reply. 'Jude's consultant needs to see her now.' She held the door open but I stood my ground.

'I hate to push you, but next time I really need to know.'

Jude didn't reply, lying passively while the nurse tidied her bedding. As soon as I reached the landing I put a call through to Burns but got no reply. I left a message on his voicemail, asking him to find out about Mark Edmunds as a matter of urgency. Afterwards I sat in the foyer, gathering my thoughts. It seemed wrong to pry when Jude's condition was so serious, but I felt sure her friend Natalie had been correct. She was shielding someone who had hurt her in the past. Even in her weakened state, Jude made a practice of concealment; she had recognised her killer's voice and seen his face, but hidden both facts under layers of memory.

I pulled my folder from my briefcase and sifted through my reports, hoping that a pattern might emerge. The first thing I found was the lab analysis of the contents of Father Owen's lungs. The water he'd inhaled had returned the expected result: he'd drowned in Battersea. Grains of chalk dust from a concrete factory that flushed its waste into the river confirmed that he'd died in the borough he'd served. I stuffed the papers back into the folder with a sense of frustration. If Mark Edmunds had carried out the attacks, what had driven him? Jealousy could have made him target Jude. But Father Owen seemed as blameless as Amala. According to Burns, the priest had encouraged homeless people to sleep in the community centre beside his church, and he'd run a soup kitchen there for twenty years. His only known vice had been an occasional glass of whisky. Everything I learned about the victims made me believe that the killer saw them as guilty by association. Being close to the Shelleys had made them targets. But if he hated the family so much, why hadn't he attacked Guy or Heather, or even the minister himself? His motivations refused to make sense.

I was about to leave the hospital when my phone buzzed loudly in my pocket. Angie's voice was babbling nineteen to the dozen.

'It's happened again, Alice. There's another body by the river in Wapping. Hancock's on his way there now.'

The next hour felt like being dragged along by a riptide. Local police had cordoned off the crime scene when I arrived, and the press were already massing. The set of Burns's shoulders revealed that his tension had hit a new high. The discovery of a third body would raise the media's interest from high to stratospheric. He nodded but didn't say a word when I joined him by the cordon. Pete Hancock ambled towards us; the SOCO's face was as impassive as ever, but his body language exuded gloom.

'Have we got a name?' Burns asked.

'Julian Speller. His driving licence was in his pocket.'

'What condition is he in?'

'The worst yet, boss.' Hancock disappeared behind the forensics van abruptly, as if events had suddenly overwhelmed him.

'Did you get my message?' I asked Burns, but he shook his head. 'Mark Edmunds, the student I told you about, was rejected by Jude, just before her attack. He's in the team that's been excavating here. The bloke's obsessed by the history of the Thames.'

'I'll get someone to run another check, but so far everyone at King's has come up clean.' Burns's expression showed that he was too concerned about the new attack to absorb the information. 'Guy Shelley went missing two nights ago. He slipped out of his flat when his security guard was on the phone; he hasn't been seen since.'

'Why didn't anyone tell me?'

Burns's scowl deepened. 'What could you do? Pound the streets searching every alley?'

He strode back to the CSI van and left me processing what had made Guy run from his own home. He was still on my suspect list, guilt or panic about the likelihood of being caught making him escape from his bodyguard. I watched the SOCOs completing their work, a line of white-suited drones crawling across the tarmac on their hands and knees. The crime scene was metres from Execution Dock, where Amala had been found – the killer seemed to be claiming the area for his own. I glanced back towards St Katharine Docks. The High Street was at its narrowest there, surfaced with old flagstones and cobbles. It was easy to see why the area would attract a history fanatic. Horse-drawn carts would have brought goods to the cargo ships docked below; and a sign pointed towards King

Henry's Stairs – a reminder that the crime scene was a stone's throw from the Tower of London, the Tudor royals' favourite home. Tania appeared while I was trying to make sense of the new killing. Her expression had darkened from tiredness to disgust.

'Don't ask how it's going,' she said. 'We've made fuck-all progress and now this happens. This one's even younger than Amala.'

'When's the last time you had a break, Tania?'

'Christ knows.' She smoothed her hand over her short hair. 'Sorry, you caught me at a bad time.'

'It's not surprising. You must be exhausted.'

'Knackered is too mild a word. You'd better wait here; they'll call you when they're ready.'

She handed me a Tyvek suit and plastic overshoes then hurried away. By now the crime scene was in full swing, uniforms manning the outer cordon and keeping the press at bay. A few dogged photographers were pointing foot-long lenses at the blue plastic curtain that screened Wapping Old Stairs. They seemed to be hoping a sudden breeze would reveal the murder scene in all its glory.

My discomfort grew when the team trailed back up the steps. Nothing neutralises people's smiles quicker than observing a corpse, and today even the seasoned veterans looked unsettled. Burns appeared just as my instincts were advising me to make a quick exit.

'You don't have to do this, Alice. You'd be better off looking at the photos.'

'I need to see the victims. You know that.'

Burns's protectiveness irritated me. Witnessing the bodies in situ always helped; the chance to see the killer's handiwork explained more about a perpetrator's mind-set than photos ever could.

I pushed past him towards the steps trailing down to the riverbank, stone worn smooth by a million tides. My plastic shoes slipped on the wet surface as I saw the man's corpse lying directly ahead. The river seemed to have tired of him suddenly, his body splayed across the stairway as if he'd been dropped from a height. One of his feet was bare, the other still wore a pointed shoe, neatly laced. As I knelt down I saw that his hands were grotesquely swollen, but it was the wounds on his wrists that disturbed me – they were so deep that the pain must have been excruciating. His clothes revealed how comfortable his life had once been, a Jermyn Street label inside his jacket proving that he'd had taste as well as money.

Burns's wide shadow appeared on the brick wall, reminding me that my time was almost up. The specialists were impatient to take over: crime-scene photographers, a police medic and Home Office pathologist. I stared at the victim's body again. There was no doubting that the killer was the same person who'd attacked Jude. A sharp-edged piece of flint, a couple of inches long, had been tied around his neck. The same neat incision circled his face, flesh ripped from bone until nothing was left, his broken jaw wrenched into a lopsided yawn. River water dripped from his ragged eye sockets in dark brown tears.

I fought my nausea and stumbled back up the steps. Burns was standing at the top, issuing orders into his phone. I wondered how he could carry on a conversation while the cacophony raged. Engines revved in the background, and a radio blared from a squad car's window, but he seemed oblivious.

'Julian Speller was a UK national, twenty-eight years old,' he said. 'Oxford law graduate, living near the Oval. Take a guess who he worked for.'

'The Shelleys?'

'At Westminster.' Burns gave a slow nod. 'He was a parliamentary adviser to the Minister for Employment, a key team member.'

'It looks like anyone inside Shelley's circle is vulnerable: his daughter, then his priest, the children's ex-nanny, and now a close colleague. You could call it a homicidal fixation: anyone who's touched his life is fair game. Failing to kill Jude the first time probably deepened his obsession.'

'You think he'd try and hurt her again?' he asked.

'It's unlikely. He'll still be haunted by his mistake, but he's moved on to new targets.'

'I'll put more security at the hospital just in case.'

I tried to gather my thoughts. 'The factor linking the victims could be intimacy. Jude knew every family secret. Father Owen had heard all the family's confessions, and Heather and Jude confided in Amala. Maybe Julian Speller knew the minister's professional secrets.'

'You think he's killing people the Shelleys confided in?'

'It's possible,' I rubbed my hand across my eyes. 'I still think the river's our best hope. It's worth patrolling stretches where he's picking up his calling cards: London Bridge, Southwark and Vauxhall. He's leaving the bodies at the most important sites for ritual sacrifice.'

His eyes narrowed. 'Where did you learn that?'

'From an academic at King's College.'

Burns's eyebrows shot up. 'I got a message from their top man this morning, Hugh Lister. He wants the crime-scene objects for his archive, as if we didn't have enough to worry about.'

'That doesn't surprise me. The guy's a world authority on the Thames, and a first-class obsessive. He's Mark Edmunds's supervisor. I need information on both their alibis.'

He nodded. 'Lister's coming to the station to talk about the calling cards. I'll speak to him then. Where are you going now?'

'To see Heather Shelley.'

'Can you stay for the press briefing?'

I'd have felt the same in his shoes. There's nothing lonelier than announcing bad news while the entire nation watches you squirm. Tania and I flanked him while he made his statement, his Scottish accent more pronounced than ever, a sure sign that his stress levels were spiralling.

When the cameras stopped rolling, a police photographer disappeared between the plastic shrouds covering the stairway, and I caught a last glimpse of Julian Speller's body, lying where the river had discarded it. He was starting to attract a more sinister type of interest than the police and the media. Crows were already massing overhead, hoping for a free meal.

34

My urgent tone must have done the trick because Heather Shelley agreed to see me immediately. Security was thick when I arrived at her house, two armed guards stationed outside her door, more officers in plain clothes milling in the square. It interested me that even though her son was missing, it looked like she had been on her way to an official function. Her blonde hair was swept into a French pleat, and she wore discreet pearl earrings, her tailored blue dress accentuating her slimness. She looked like a typical cabinet minister's wife: so perfectly in control that a controversial statement would never escape from her mouth. It was only up close that her distress showed itself, her lips trembling with suppressed fear.

'It's Guy, isn't it? Something's happened to him.'

I shook my head. 'That's not why I'm here.'

Her hands flew up to her face. 'Thank God. I've been going out of my mind.'

Heather led me into her cavernous living room. 'I'm due at a fundraiser in twenty minutes. Tell me what's happened, Alice.'

'You might want to cancel your appointment.'

'That's impossible, I'm their keynote speaker.'

'It's bad news, unfortunately. Have you met Julian Speller?'

'Of course. I've known him for years.'

'I'm afraid he's been killed. His body was found by the river at Wapping.'

Her eyelids fluttered. 'He came here last week. We had dinner together.'

'I'm so sorry.' I touched her hand but she snatched it away.

'Tim will be beside himself. I should call him.'

She paced around the room as she made the call, high heels clicking on acres of parquet. My eyes caught on a pair of Guy's drawings. One showed an old coat draped from a hanger, its hem unravelling. Beside it was an image of a broken lawnmower, lying on a patch of grass, the mechanism severed in two.

'I can't reach him.' Heather frowned as she dropped her mobile on the coffee table. 'The press are blocking the lines. They'll be all over us, like they were with Jude.'

'What kind of work did Julian do for your husband?'

'Tim sits on the Ethics Committee. Julian had the best legal background to advise him on human rights and ethical business practices.' Shock had slowed her speech dramatically; it sounded like a radio announcement, the battery running low.

'Can I get you anything? A glass of water?'

'I can't stand much more of this.' She stared down at her hands. 'I should get in the car.'

'You mustn't drive until you calm down.'

She stood up abruptly and walked to the bay windows to pull the curtains. 'The bloody snoopers'll be here soon.'

Heather switched on the huge TV that hung on the wall as the one o'clock news began, cameras panning the crime scene. Wapping High Street had been cordoned with so much yellow tape it looked like it had been gift-wrapped. Angie stood in the foreground, lips pursed for once, keeping her thoughts to herself. The next clip was a close-up of Burns with me and Tania flanking him. We all wore matching expressions, shock mixed with anger that another life had been stolen.

'A young man's body was found at nine this morning,' Burns announced. 'It's likely he was attacked by the same killer who has struck twice by the Thames in recent weeks. The victim has been identified as Julian Speller, and his family have been informed. If you saw anyone acting suspiciously in the Wapping area last night, or in the early hours of this morning, please call the helpline.'

The image changed to a melee of news photographers on the steps at Westminster, jostling like rugby players. Timothy Shelley was caught at the centre of the scrum. For once his professional calm had deserted him; his skin was taut and shiny, eyes reddened. He cleared his throat before attempting to speak.

'Julian Speller was an extraordinary young man. He was a gifted and thoughtful member of my team for five years. He will be irreplaceable. My thoughts and sympathies are with his family.'

Shelley held up his hand to end the interview but the cameras pursued him, eager to catch every ounce of distress. He turned away abruptly, but not before his tears were captured on prime-time TV, his face bunched in misery.

'Oh God,' Heather muttered. 'Poor Tim.'

Her own appearance had changed radically in the past half-hour. She had kicked off her high heels, her chic hairstyle unravelling like one of her son's artworks.

'Did Speller know Jude at all?' I asked.

She nodded absently. 'He helped her choose her law course; it's partly due to him that she studied at King's.'

My heart rate quickened. 'Do you know if he ever visited her in hospital?'

Her eyes were still blurred. 'A few times. I think he went with Tim two or three weeks ago.'

I rocked back in my seat. All of the victims had known Jude

198

and her father. The killer seemed intent on hurting people close to them both, which made me concerned for Heather's own safety. My thoughts were interrupted by the bleep of her mobile phone. She pressed it to her ear without saying a word, her face even paler when the call ended.

'Tim's on his way. He sounds in a dreadful state.'

I sat forwards, trying to get her full attention. 'Heather, you realise this changes everything, don't you? The attacks are linked directly to your family. There's a secret you need to tell me, isn't there? Someone hurt Jude when she was a child. Who was it?'

She gasped in a long breath. 'My son,' she whispered. Her eyes were glassy with distress. 'After he learned he was adopted, I couldn't leave them alone together, even for five minutes. It was the worst kind of physical bullying. One time Guy pushed her so hard she broke her wrist. He used to hit other kids at school too. The psychiatrist gave him medication, and things settled down, but Jude was terrified. They only grew close again in their teens. Normally he can control his outbursts these days.' Her gaze trailed back towards the window.

'Why didn't you tell me?'

'I didn't want Guy to be questioned. He's too vulnerable.'

'You've covered for him before, haven't you? Where was he the night Jude was attacked?'

Her mouth trembled. 'He was at his flat, but he had no way of proving it. It was my decision to tell the police he was with me. He wasn't strong enough to deal with them after Jude got hurt.'

'So you both lied about that evening?'

Her hands flew up to her face. 'He was cracking under the strain. I couldn't lose them both.'

'Where is Guy now?'

'I don't know, he's not answering my calls. Something terrible could have happened to him.' Her voice was raw with guilt.

'You were right to tell me the truth. I'll find out if there's any news.'

As I walked into the kitchen, I realised that Guy's claim that his family was held together by secrets had turned out to be true. His closest relatives had concealed his violence for over a decade.

It took several attempts to reach Burns, a hum of noise in the background as I explained what I'd learned about Guy's background.

His reply was a dull monotone. 'We've put out a nationwide search for him and his car, but had no sightings.'

He sounded so tense that there was no point in asking questions. I switched off my phone and returned to the living room. Heather had dissolved into floods of tears. I rested my hand on her shoulder, but my thoughts veered towards her missing son. If he'd been disturbed enough to lash out as a child, his aggression could have returned. Guy might be unbalanced enough to kill anyone within his reach.

I waited with Heather until her husband returned. We stood side by side, peering through a gap in the curtains. A crowd of photographers had occupied the steps, cameras flashing furiously. Giles Moorcroft pushed through them, with Timothy Shelley following. I got a taste of how punishing it must be to spend every waking moment in the public eye as I watched the minister stumble inside. When I reached the hallway, Moorcroft was laying his boss's briefcase on a table carefully, as though it held bone china. He shot me a look of concern but the MP glared in my direction, his eyes red and glistening.

'You should leave,' he hissed. 'My wife and I need time on our own.'

'Of course,' I replied.

Heather's tone was apologetic as she said goodbye, but it was her husband's reaction that fascinated me. The loss of Julian Speller had brought him to his knees, his public guard evaporating. Neither of the two earlier murders had bleached the colour from his face in the same way. This time he looked ready to collapse.

'Thanks for staying with me,' Heather said quietly.

Over her shoulder I saw Moorcroft, stiff backed and awkward, tending to his boss. The civil servant would obviously have preferred to be at his desk, but he was steadfastly doing his duty. He wore a look of pity on his face as he helped Shelley out of his coat, as though he was undressing a poorly child.

I looked at Heather again. 'Would you mind if I visited Guy's flat? I'm concerned about him.'

I felt sure members of Burns's team would be waiting there to intercept him, but she gave me a grateful look, then produced some keys from her handbag. 'Phone me if he's there, won't you?'

'I'll go this afternoon.'

'Promise me you'll call.' She gripped my arm tight enough to burn.

'Of course I will.'

The panic on her face made me feel guilty. I was torn between concern for her son's mental health, and a nagging suspicion that he might be the murderer.

35

I left the Shelley's house by the back exit, but some photographers had set up an ambush, cameras snapping as I hurried past. After two blocks I pulled out my phone and called Burns again. 'I've got permission to visit Guy Shelley's flat, but I need an escort.'

'You think he's been taken?'

'He could be the killer, Don. Violent kids can become violent adults.'

I heard him draw a sharp breath. 'Where are you? I'll pick you up.'

'No need. Meet me there in half an hour.' I read out the address and heard his footsteps quicken, as if he was racing for his car.

I tried to put my thoughts in order during the short train ride. Maybe my certainty that the killer was suffering from twin obsessions with the Shelley family and the river had blinded me to more obvious suspects. I tried to recall my first impressions of Guy Shelley. Concealed stress had been obvious in his jittery body language. He seemed to hate talking about his sister, even though a year had passed since her attack, and soon after our meeting he'd slipped back into his anxiety state, hiding himself in his room. I'd felt sure he had something to confess, but his revelation about family secrets had been too vague to pin down. Pins and needles pricked my spine as I remembered Father Owen. Guy had said that he sometimes went to confession – perhaps he'd admitted something that he'd later regretted. If he was seriously mentally ill, that might have triggered his attack on the priest.

When I reached Waterloo, I raced through the crowds. The South Bank was packed with strollers, enjoying a respite from the endless rain. Tourists stood in clusters on the Millennium Bridge, its frets so fine they looked ready to snap, like one of Guy Shelley's sculptures. My sense of unease was mounting steadily. The FPU had employed me to appease the Shelley family, but the truth kept getting in the way. If Guy turned out to be the killer, Whitehall would have an epic public relations battle on its hands. Timothy Shelley would go down in history as the first cabinet minister with a mass murderer for a son.

Guy's apartment was in the heart of Borough's trendiest neighbourhood. The cafés on Gabriel's Wharf were doing a roaring trade, couples topping up on caffeine and junk food. Burns was waiting outside an art gallery, looking like a displaced giant, head and shoulders taller than the Japanese tourists scurrying by. The circles under his eyes showed that he'd been catnapping at his desk instead of taking a full night's sleep. His expression was unreadable as he gazed down at me.

'Are you okay?' he asked.

'Fine, but I couldn't go in there alone. Hancock wouldn't like me messing up his crime scene.'

Burns blinked at me. 'You seriously think it's him?'

'Maybe Guy's just gone walkabout, but he could have reverted to infantile aggression.'

'You're talking like a shrink, Alice.'

'Infantile aggression is when adults experience the kind of rage they felt as a child, which can be dangerous. Children don't have clear moral boundaries.'

'At least we can search his place. I got an emergency warrant authorised.'

Guy's apartment block looked bland and inoffensive: three storeys of pale yellow brick. Despite the stylish wooden shutters and Juliet balconies, my stomach was tying itself in knots. Burns stopped to greet the two police officers standing by the entrance, then fell into step beside me as we climbed to the top floor. I rang the bell several times but there was no response, so I slipped the key into the lock.

'Christ almighty,' Burns hissed as the door swung open.

The air stank of chemicals and a bitterness I couldn't identify. The source was obvious when we reached the living room. Open bottles of white spirit and linseed oil stood on a large table, paint congealing on saucers and palettes. A window spanned the width of the room. Miles of grey sky had unfolded above the city, the river dark as charcoal, fractured by bridges.

'What are we looking for exactly?' Burns asked.

'Evidence that he's been searching the riverbank would be a good start. Like I said, Guy's very disturbed, with a history of violence. He wouldn't be the first person to attack the people closest to him.'

'Surely his parents would have noticed him changing?'

'Families are often last to guess. How many parents want to imagine that their son's a cold-blooded murderer?'

Burns's shoulders heaved in a reluctant shrug. 'You'd better use these.' He gave me a pair of sterile gloves. 'Where do you want me to start?'

'The bedroom, please.'

I glanced around Guy's disordered living room. His studio doubled as a kitchen, a tower of dirty dishes piled in the sink. But the most eye-catching thing was the artwork – delicate line drawings of houses and trees, united in decay. Buildings were falling apart, pavements littered with fallen masonry. Guy seemed to see destruction wherever he looked.

I stood back to survey the room. Proof of his chaotic mental state covered every surface, but I reminded myself that he might just be a sensitive young man whose equilibrium had been destroyed by his sister's tragedy. I was starting to feel foolish about my suspicions when Burns called from the room next door, his voice rising to a shout. He stood by Guy's unmade bed, gazing at a sketchbook which hung open in his hands. The word 'Jude' was scrawled on the front in large red letters.

'These are as sick as it gets,' he muttered.

The first drawings showed Jude before the attack, sitting on a chair, hands folded neatly in her lap. She wore a quizzical smile, as though posing for her brother amused her. But the next image was horrifying. It was a close-up of Jude's ravaged face, scarlet ink picking out exposed sinews and the gash where her lips should have been, her unblinking eye surrounded by raw flesh. One of the pages held dozens of thumbnail sketches showing her hooked to a life-support machine. Guy must have sat in his sister's hospital room while she slept, making endless drawings of the ruined landscape of her face.

'They're like anatomical paintings,' Burns commented.

'What do you mean?' I always forgot that he'd spent time at art school.

'It started in the Renaissance. Leonardo drew corpses in the operating theatre, long before anyone knew how our muscle groups worked.'

I gazed down at the images again, trying to understand Guy Shelley's mind-set. Either he'd taken pleasure in studying his sister's wounds in forensic detail, or it was a form of acceptance. I remembered Heather saying that he would lock himself in his room after visiting his sister. The pictures explained how he'd spent those hours of solitude.

'You'd better tell me what you know,' Burns said.

I passed on the information I'd gathered from Heather, and my terse conversation with Timothy Shelley. He scribbled in his notebook, then released a low whistle.

'Guy was so messed up after Jude's attack that he dropped out of college; he spends days sketching her wounds, and he's got no social life. Why would he give his bodyguard the slip? He left here in his black VW Passat and hasn't contacted anyone since.'

I tried to think straight. 'I can see why Guy would attack Jude. Adopted kids often feel like misfits, overwhelmed by rage about being excluded from the biological family. In a few cases it becomes obsessive. But why would he target his priest and the nanny he adored as a child, then one of his father's advisers? Maybe he hates himself enough to hurt anyone in striking distance.'

Burns held up his hands. 'You saw the drawings, Alice. He's seriously screwed up. Why look at all that pain, unless it gives you pleasure?'

Something about the argument struck me as wrong, but I couldn't pinpoint why. I stared out of the window while Burns made phone calls. He was checking progress on the search for Guy and barking out instructions about river searches, evidence files and press calls. When we finally got outside, dusk had fallen, that odd light which turns everything flimsy and insubstantial. A barge drifted in the middle of the water-way, lights flickering from Albert Embankment. A wave of anxiety crossed Burns's face when I told him I needed to phone Heather.

'I won't disclose anything,' I reassured him. 'All she needs to know is that you're searching for her son.'

There was a note of relief in Heather's voice when I told her that Guy's flat was empty. Maybe she'd been afraid, like me, that he was capable of suicide. I said nothing about discovering the sketchbook, or my fears that Guy could be the killer. Until there was hard evidence it was just conjecture, and the relentless media attention on her family was more than enough for her to handle.

Burns was unfurling his umbrella when I caught sight of a familiar figure and did a double take. Hugh Lister, the irascible history lecturer, was twenty yards away, sauntering towards the river, lips moving in a quiet monologue. He was dressed in shabby trousers and a black coat, a far cry from the glamorous young man who had presented his TV show twenty years before. I wondered whether he was heading to the foreshore to search for more treasures. He looked in my direction, nodded once, then scuttled away.

'That's the Thames expert from King's,' I said, pointing him out. 'Have you found anything on the history lecturers?'

'None of them have any convictions. Angie's getting a team to do in-depth checks and interviews.' Burns looked down at me. 'Where are you going now, Alice?'

'Back to mine, but we could grab a quick meal first.' It broke my promise to keep contact between us safely inside working hours, but there was no point in going home while my head was bursting with information.

We walked past the Globe Theatre to Simply Greek, where I ordered chicken souvlaki and mineral water in an effort to stay clearheaded. Burns was checking his phone for messages. I wondered again why he affected me so deeply. His image was in need of an overhaul, with a shapeless jacket and messy hair, black stubble emphasising the pallor of his skin. His wide shoulders looked tense with strain, yet it required all my willpower to stop myself touching him. I pushed my feelings to one side and gave the waiter a brisk smile as he delivered our orders.

'Go on then, give me an update,' I said.

'It's moving too slowly for my liking. The Battersea team's done street searches and house to house, and forensics spent days at Father Owen's vicarage. The vagrants who slept in the community centre are all accounted for, and we've gone through his congregation with a toothcomb. The bloke didn't have any enemies.'

'Apart from the one who cut him to shreds then threw him in the river.'

He gave a thin smile. 'It's no joke. His congregation want him beatified.'

'I'm just stating the facts. Is there any news on Amala?'

'A witness called after the last *Crimewatch*. She saw a blond man watching Amala at the bus stop, in a dark coat and hat. She says he boarded the same bus, but images from the on-board camera are too grainy.' Burns's face tensed with frustration. 'And you were right about Shane Weldon. He hasn't put a foot out of line. They're still testing the van he drives at work, but so far it's clean, and so's his girlfriend's car. Nothing in their living accommodation either.' He spoke slowly, as if the words pained him.

The childish part of me felt like crowing, but I bit my tongue. My thoughts flashed to Sue Rochford in her grim apartment, so unconcerned about her boyfriend's violent past that I'd alerted social services. 'Did you read the updates on my profile report?'

Burns nodded. 'You think the killer's obsessed by Timothy Shelley, not Jude.'

'That's why my alarm bells rang today. Guy could be carrying unresolved anger about his adoption and the close relationship between Timothy and Jude. Now that he's ruined his sister's life, he could be lashing out at anyone his father trusts.'

'Do people really set out to destroy their parents' lives?'

'It's not pretty when it happens. Remember the Craig Leonard case? He made it look like a stranger had bludgeoned his mum to death while she slept. He killed two of her closest friends the same night, in exactly the same way. I interviewed him for the prosecution.'

Burns sucked in his cheeks. 'Sounds like a fun job. Did he confess?'

'On my fifth trip to Belmarsh. His mother used to dress him in girls' clothes and humiliate him in front of his sisters.'

His eyebrows rose. 'And that's a reason to kill people?'

'He thought so. All I had to do was flatter him into a confession.' I pushed my plate away. 'When's Julian Speller's autopsy? I should be there.'

Burns lopsided smile reappeared. 'Your wish has come true. It's tomorrow afternoon. The coroner's office rushed it through.'

I groaned quietly. 'Something to look forward to.'

The rest of the evening passed in a blur of conversation. It felt like we'd slipped back into the old routine, when we'd debrief for hours, odd facts from our private lives rising to the surface. It was eleven by the time my espresso arrived. Burns was studying me so closely, I thought he was about to deliver a lecture on the dangers of late-night caffeine.

'Are you seeing anyone, Alice?'

I put down my cup. 'How is that any of your business?'

'Curiosity got the better of me.'

'You should learn to control it then.' My temper was coming to the boil as I grabbed my coat and headed for the exit, but Burns was beside me when I got outside. He caught hold of my arm before I could escape.

'I still think about you, Alice.'

'Why tell me that now? It's too late.'

He held my arm so tightly I could feel the pressure of each fingertip. Light from the streetlamps caught his

209

clenched jaw and the curve of his cheek, then he leant down and kissed me hard enough to make my head spin. I did my best not to respond, but it took me a while to regain enough presence of mind to pull away. As soon as I came to my senses I gave his face a resounding slap, then marched away without looking back.

36

At midnight the man stands alone on Westminster Bridge, and for once he feels content. The river hums in his ear, soft as a lullaby. He gazes at the black water a hundred feet below. In a split second he could scale the railings and let himself fall. He closes his eyes and imagines the water's cold embrace, currents drawing him to its heart, but he's not ready to join the other souls. The thought of it terrifies him. He raises his gaze and stares into the darkness. The Houses of Parliament are illuminated, every window ablaze with light. For the first time today, the police vans have disappeared. If the armed guards spot him, they will see nothing more than a speck in the distance: a tourist marvelling at the grand architecture. The man has crossed the bridge so many times he knows every brick and paving stone. He saw Timothy Shelley on the evening news tonight, stumbling down the steps, drunk with shock. The image shamed him, but the river whispered its approval in his ear.

There's hardly anyone around, just a few couples strolling home from a night out. With luck they're too drunk or distracted to remember him loitering on the bridge. He turns his attention back to his task and pulls his binoculars from his pocket. He knows the building like the back of his hand, but he checks the location of the security points once more, and where the CCTV cameras are positioned. Anyone could approach the building; no security cordon to keep pedestrians away. It still amazes him how easy it would be to blow the building sky-high.

He feels satisfied as he walks back towards Waterloo. In the station car park he drops into the driver's seat of his car. He might be giving in to paranoia, but he's too nervous to return to his flat. There's a possibility that the police might be waiting there, ready to question him. He will drive there at daybreak and check whether it's safe to enter. Tonight he will rest here. He takes a pillow from the back seat and tries to get comfortable, but soon a man's voice disturbs him.

'You can't sleep here. You'll have to move on.' A security guard peers at him through the glass, face gleaming with rain and anger.

The man opens the window and presses a bank note into his hand. 'Will this cover it?'

'All right, mate, but make sure you're away by eight tomorrow.'

'I'll be gone long before then.'

The guard leaves him in peace, and the man's eyes finally close. The river's song is the last sound he hears as he slips into unconsciousness.

37

Will answered the door when I reached my mother's flat on Saturday morning, his face tense with strain.

'I didn't know you were here,' I said, smiling.

'I came over last night.'

'You don't have to do everything, you know.' His body stiffened in my arms as I embraced him.

'I said I'd sort this out, remember?' His scowl was deep enough to silence me.

Despite his foul mood, it was clear that Will had attended to Mum's every need. She was reclining on her sofa against a mound of cushions, and gave her usual cool nod when I greeted her.

'There was no need to come, darling. Will's been the perfect nurse.'

'I wanted to see how you are.'

She looked disgruntled. 'I had a fall, Alice. It could happen to anyone.'

Under her bravado she seemed frailer than before. The tremor in her right hand made her fingers twitch uncontrollably, the bruise on her forehead turning every colour of the rainbow. But it was clear she was enjoying her newfound power. She picked up her coffee cup and waved it at Will.

'Could I have a refill, darling?'

I watched with amazement as my brother loped into the kitchen. A few weeks ago he could barely mention her name, and now he was at her beck and call. Mum waited until he was out of earshot before launching her attack.

'You're not in my good books,' she murmured.

'Why's that?'

Her grey eyes had frosted over. 'You know how worried I've been, but you never said a word. Why didn't you tell me he'd recovered?'

'Bipolar disorder's cyclical. It never goes away.'

She rolled her eyes. 'Anyone can see he's well again. You can be so thoughtless sometimes.'

I had to count to ten, but managed not to snap. If she chose to ignore Will's condition, that was her concern, but professional experience reminded me that one missed dose of chlorpromazine could send his mood on a manic roller-coaster ride. When Will returned, he was exuding so much suppressed rage that anyone in their right mind would have cleared the room.

'You forgot the biscuits, darling.'

He gritted his teeth. 'I'm not your slave, Mum.'

'Why don't I get them?' I suggested.

'Stay where you are,' Will said, glowering. 'I'm handling this.'

A look of amusement crossed Mum's face as he stalked out of the room. I'd forgotten how much she loved the drama of conflict. Before Dad's violence ran out of control she had stage-managed their rows, as if she was starring in a biopic about Elizabeth Taylor and Richard Burton. Will looked slightly calmer when he returned with a plate of digestives. Maybe he'd called Nina from the kitchen to discuss coping strategies. He passed me a crumpled piece of paper.

'This is what I've arranged,' he said quietly.

The list covered all of Mum's requirements. He'd booked a health visitor, and an agency was providing an assistant to shop, cook and clean. He'd even contracted a specialist company to install a stair-lift.

'I can't believe how much you've done, Will.'

My thanks didn't reach him. He sat on the edge of his chair, hands locked together as if he was trying not to punch something. When my mother spoke again, she sounded completely relaxed.

'I did most of it. All your brother had to do was make the calls.'

Her ingratitude must have been the final straw. The next thing I saw was the side table bouncing off the wall, a black pool of coffee soaking into her cream wool carpet. He'd vanished in the time it took to blink, followed by the front door crashing. I felt like congratulating my mother on goading him to breaking point, but her hands were fluttering in her lap like caged birds. One-upmanship against someone so frail would have been cruel, even though it was the perfect moment to remind her that Will's condition was permanent. I kept my mouth shut and spent the next half-hour swabbing the carpet with diluted bleach.

Mum's new assistant arrived at two p.m., a no-nonsense Croatian woman called Elise who wore a blue overall and a look of fierce determination. She set to work scouring the bathroom immediately, intent on exterminating every germ. By the time I put on my coat, my mother looked exhausted, and it was clear that the conflict had hit home.

'I won't see him for months, will I?' Her voice quaked.

'Why not send him a text, thanking him for his help?' My suggestion fell on deaf ears – when I leant down to kiss her goodbye, she turned her head away.

I arrived at the mortuary fifteen minutes early, feeling uncomfortable about seeing Burns. I had decided to ignore last night's debacle and put it down to the stress we were both under, but there was no sign of him as the assistant scribbled my name in his attendance book. The familiar odour of disinfectant and formaldehyde hung in the air as I entered Lindstrop's theatre, to find her already studying Julian Speller's corpse.

'You're early, Dr Quentin,' she murmured. 'A lesser crime than being late, in my estimation.' She looked the same as before, rotund with florid skin, grey curls scraped back from her face. 'Are you developing a fascination with pathology?'

'Not exactly, but the details help me understand the killer's approach.'

'Quite so.' Lindstrop's shrewd eyes met mine. 'Every wound enlightens us, if we're paying attention.' She turned away to check her instruments; lines of saws, probes and scalpels, arranged on a metal tray.

Burns arrived at the exact moment when the autopsy was due to begin. He gave me a sheepish look, as if he was still smarting from the slap I'd delivered.

Lindstrop pointed at the clock. 'By the skin of your teeth, Inspector.'

'The traffic's shite out there. Cut me some slack.'

'Slack isn't available when I've sacrificed eighteen holes to be here.'

'I know you, Fiona. You'd rather chop people up than walk round the fairway.'

She gave a snort of laughter then turned away. Their intimacy reminded me that Burns must have spent countless afternoons watching murder victims being sliced apart. He gave me a tense smile before I focused my attention on the procedure.

The pathologist began by taking an inventory of the marks on Speller's body, muttering into her microphone. I forced myself to study the man's injuries. Even in death his youth was evident from his slim build and taut skin. Pronounced biceps and chest muscles proved that he'd made regular trips to the gym; there was a peppering of black hair across his chest. Now that the ropes around his wrists had been removed I could see the raw depth of his wounds. Lindstrop was peering at his scalp, parting his dark hair with her gloved hands.

'A twenty-millimetre-wide occlusion and bone fragmentation to the central crown.'

Speller's facial injuries were worse than I remembered, a mass of exposed muscle and bone. His broken jaw hung at a grotesque angle, revealing a grin of perfect white teeth. The sandwich I'd eaten for lunch shifted in my stomach, and I had to lean against the wall to steady myself.

'Are you okay?' Burns was peering down at me.

'I'm fine.' His concern had triggered a childish impulse to slap him again.

By now Lindstrop was doing unspeakable things to Speller's body, but I was determined to keep my eyes open. I watched her remove his lungs, liver and heart without once looking away.

'Tragic,' she said quietly, as she placed the organs in a weighing dish. 'Transplant patients would give anything for a perfect heart like this.'

The procedure took an hour and a half. Only brute determination stopped me from keeling over. Lindstrop wore a thoughtful expression as she dumped her scalpels into a steriliser.

'What do you want to know?' she glanced from Burns's face to mine.

'A cause of death, if you've got one,' he said.

'Drowning. He was alive when he hit the river, like the others.' She held up a vial full of the brown liquid she'd emptied from his lungs. 'But there's something else you should

217

know.' She pressed a forefinger against the corpse's forearm, leaving a deep indentation. 'This level of skin saturation means he was underwater for at least twenty-four hours.'

'And the wrist wounds?'

'Rope fibres have chafed through the epidermis into soft tissue.' Lindstrop's frown deepened. 'I'd say he cut himself to the bone trying to get free.'

'What about his face?'

'Same as the priest. He made a circular incision round the hairline, from temple to jaw, then wrenched upwards. But this time he did it posthumously.' She gazed down at the victim. 'He cut out the eyeballs too. The optic nerves were severed cleanly; he'd have needed a sharp knife or a scalpel.'

Burns groaned. 'I shouldn't have asked.'

We were about to leave when Lindstrop pointed out some narrow cuts on the victim's shins. 'What do you think these are?'

'I dread to think,' he muttered.

'Care to hazard a guess, Dr Quentin?'

'Rat bites. If he was tied up in dirty, shallow water, he'd have been powerless to keep them away.'

'Excellent.' She shot me a look of admiration. 'You're welcome in my theatre, any time you like.'

On the way out I peered down at the sharp piece of flint that had been tied around Speller's neck, then took a photo with my phone. It looked antique, but I would need to ask Hugh Lister to identify it.

Burns gazed at the pavement in silence when we got outside. We seemed to have reached a tacit agreement not to mention what had happened the night before, but his shoulders were raised as if he expected another blow.

'That was pretty conclusive, wasn't it?' I said. 'Speller was tied up by the river, where the rats could get at him at low tide. He knew he was drowning, so he fought hard to free himself.'

'Jesus, what a way to go.'

The rain had stopped, but the clouds still looked ominous. Burns's hands were buried deep in his pockets, gloom emanating from every pore. I was furious with him, so I don't know what made me reach up and kiss his cheek as we said goodbye. Maybe the gesture was inspired by sympathy as well as desire. He looked stunned as I pulled away, as though I was a constant source of confusion.

The double whammy of visiting my mother then witnessing the autopsy had left me desperate for a boost, so I called at Morocco Street. Lola gave me a tight hug, then reclined on her chaise longue.

'Shouldn't you be in labour right now?' I asked.

'Tell me about it. They'll have to induce me soon.' She gave her stomach a gentle pat. 'He's too lazy to stir his bones.'

'Who can blame him? He's got peace, quiet and a private Jacuzzi.'

Lola giggled, then her cat-like eyes focused on me. 'How's the historian?'

'Too mysterious for my liking. He's got a picture of a woman just like me on his phone. I'm sick of all the intrigue.'

'What about the policeman?'

'Still stuck in my head like a bad tune.'

Her grin widened. 'That's not like you. If things get tricky, you're normally first out the door. What's so special about him?'

'There's a connection. It's more than just fancying him, I think about him all the time.'

'Husband material, you mean.'

I rolled my eyes. 'He's married, Lo, and you've been reading too much Nora Roberts.'

'Why not declare your interests, then let him make up his mind?'

'Good plan. When hell freezes over, I'll tell him just how I feel.'

She spent the next half-hour explaining all her attempts to kick-start the birthing process. 'I've tried vigorous dancing, chicken vindaloo, and shagging morning, noon and night.'

'Being pregnant sounds like heaven.'

At nine o'clock the Greek God returned from giving a music lesson, and I stayed for another cup of tea before hugging them both goodbye. The rain had set in again as I followed the river home. I sheltered under my umbrella and stared at the lights of Wapping. Guy Shelley was hiding somewhere, so gripped by mental illness that he couldn't even phone home. It was possible that stress had tipped him into a state of infantile rage and he was killing anyone close to his father, even attacking his sister because she'd received more affection. But it was hard to imagine the sensitive young man I'd met using such sadistic methods. Julian Speller's last hours had been horrific: tied up somewhere alone, waiting to drown. Someone had revelled in watching him gulp down his last breaths. When I opened my eyes again, an odd light had gathered over the river. Mist or a sheen of smoke hovered above the water's surface, like a company of ghosts.

38

It's late on Saturday evening when the man reaches Putney. He parks his car on a quiet street, then walks towards the bridge. He has no idea why the river has brought him here, its voice urging him to follow the embankment. Now it's telling him to stop and rest. When he goes into a pub, the bar is almost empty, a TV flickering in the corner. The bartender seems preoccupied and points at the screen as the ten o'clock headlines appear. Julian Speller's face fills the screen.

'Nasty business that, isn't it?' the bartender says.

'Terrible.' He nods in reply.

'Such a young guy, his whole life ahead of him.'

When the man glances at the screen again, he feels a pulse of shame. The reporter looks grave as she describes the gloom that has settled over Westminster. Pictures of the priest and Amala flash in front of him, but the man feels no pride. The actions don't belong to him and neither does the river's victory.

The man takes a sip of beer; when he looks up again, a new film is playing. A detective with a hulking build is talking directly to the camera, his gaze fixed. He claims that he will stop at nothing to find the killer. The detective's spirit is buried so deep in his core that it's hidden from view. He is so much broader than the blonde and brunette on either side of him that he looks like a giant. It's the dark-haired woman that catches the man's eye. Her soul is so powerful that he can see its dark outline, shrouding her features like a widow's veil.

A bubble of anger bursts in his throat as he looks at the detective and his two lackeys. He can read their determination to stop him in his tracks, and suddenly the voices are screaming so loudly that he can hear nothing else. The man scans all three faces again. The river must have brought him here to reveal his new path. Now that his mission is complete, his only duty is to save himself.

39

I'd arranged to meet Heather in a French café on Battersea Park Road after she'd attended church on Sunday morning. The place was almost empty when a black sedan car with smoked-glass windows dropped her outside. I watched her cross the street, swaddled in a dark raincoat. She collapsed in the seat opposite, outsized sunglasses eclipsing her cheekbones, and I couldn't decide whether they were for anonymity or to hide the fact that she'd been crying. It was obvious from the way she picked at her brioche that she had no appetite.

'Have you heard from Guy?' I asked.

'Not a whisper. I'm sure something's happened. He'd have called by now if he was all right; he hates making me worry.'

'Maybe the pressure got too much. He needs time alone.'

Her glasses slipped down, revealing her reddened eyes. 'The police have asked for his credit card details and passport number. They think he's been taken, don't they?'

'They're just concerned for his welfare.' I didn't have the heart to say that he was the main suspect in their manhunt. 'How's your husband coping with all this?'

'Not well. Number Ten have told him to stay at home and for once he's not arguing.'

'Heather, I want you to think carefully about Guy's behaviour. How's he coped since Father Owen died?'

When she removed her glasses, her frailty showed itself, deep shadows circling her eyes. 'He dealt with going back to college well. He called most days and came over at the week-ends, but things got worse after Amala died. He went to see Jude, then he was in bits afterwards. He had one of his outbursts.'

'What kind of outburst?'

Her hand skittered across the table. 'It's an anger management thing. He struggles to control his feelings.'

'He lashes out, you mean?'

'Sometimes.' Her voice fell to a whisper, and I knew she would clam up if I carried on pushing.

'And Guy visited Jude the day Amala's death was announced?'

She nodded. 'He thought she'd take the news best from him.'

'I still don't really understand Guy and Jude's relationship.'

Her coffee cup hovered in front of her mouth. 'Guy was eighteen months old when we adopted him. He couldn't walk properly, and his speech was slow to develop. The hospital told us he might have been shaken as a baby but I thought it was an emotional thing after so much neglect. He hated school until he discovered his talent for drawing, then things got easier. His jealousy about Jude being our biologi-cal child passed after a while. They've been incredibly close since their teens.'

'But you think he's still angry?'

She took a deep breath. 'Guy's temper comes from frustra-tion, not anger. He hates being unable to help her. He struggled for years to feel accepted, then she got hurt. Maybe it was more than he could stand.'

'Did you know he's been sketching Jude since her attack?'

She nodded. 'It's how he makes sense of things.'

'How's Jude? When I phoned the nurse said she can't have visitors.'

'She's so weak, all she can do is look out of the window. I haven't told her about Julian, but I'll have to sooner or later.' When she leant forwards a tear splashed onto the table. 'It's like I'm losing them both.'

I touched her hand but her barriers quickly rose again. She dabbed at her mascara with a tissue then shielded her eyes again with her sunglasses. Our meeting had only lasted half an hour but her driver was already impatient, the sidelights of his sedan flashing as he waited to deliver her back to Chelsea.

'It's Ben I feel sorry for,' she murmured as she buttoned her coat.

'Who's Ben?'

'Julian's partner. They were very close.'

'I don't suppose you've got his number?'

She looked uncertain. 'The poor man should be left in peace.'

'That won't happen, unfortunately. The police will be with him right now.'

She gave me Ben Altman's number reluctantly. 'Where are you going next? Do you need a lift?'

I accepted her offer because I was due to meet Burns in Pimlico, to interview Mark Edmunds. Travelling in the ministerial car showed me how it must feel to be escorted between appointments, diplomats waiting to welcome you. The back seat was more like a leather sofa than a car's interior, the air tinged with expensive perfume, peppermint and smoke. Heather must have sneaked a cigarette on the way over to combat her stress. The effort of discussing her situation seemed to have exhausted her, but she kissed my cheek as we said goodbye. The gesture increased my sympathy, and made me wonder how many genuine friends she could rely on while her life fell apart.

There was no sign of Burns as I stood on the pavement at Millbank, but his lateness gave me the chance to call Ben Altman. His refined voice was cold with outrage that a complete stranger was contacting him so soon after his partner's death. But when I explained that Heather Shelley had given me his number, he agreed to let me visit the next morning. Burns appeared as I was slipping my phone back into my pocket, unfolding himself from a taxi then swaggering across the road towards me.

'I've just arranged to see Julian Speller's partner,' I said.

Burns gave a dismissive nod. 'Good luck with that. I spent an hour with Altman, but all I got was monosyllables.'

'He must still be in shock.'

'His apartment's like the inside of a fridge. If you can defrost him, try and find out why Speller's colleagues say he'd been tetchy for the last few months.'

'I'll do my best.'

Burns scanned the street. 'Pretty posh for a student, isn't it?'

'Edmunds's family's wealthy.'

'They must be. He wasn't best pleased about our visit; apparently we're interrupting his research.'

'Have you found anything about his background?' I asked.

'There's a connection with Guy Shelley; he was the year above him at school. His university records say he saw a counsellor the whole time he was at Cambridge. They nearly chucked him out for stalking an ex-girlfriend.'

'That's interesting. He comes over as lonely, rather than violent. Did he threaten the Cambridge girl?'

'Not physically, but he sent her letters and texts, and followed her around for weeks.'

'That's bad enough.' I gazed up at Edmunds's Victorian mansion block and remembered the mildness of his smile.

Maybe his appearance was deceptive, and he'd been disturbed enough to attack someone who had refused his advances, then go after her friends and family. We walked through the swing doors of his block into a stylish lobby. The parquet floor and Art Deco wall tiles were evidence of taste as well as money. Burns insisted we take the lift to the seventh floor. I would rather have used the stairs, to avoid the inevitable surge of claustrophobia. A band of panic tightened round my ribcage when the metal doors closed, or maybe it was the effect of proximity. Burns stood so near I could smell him – a mixture of fresh rain, espresso and the musk of his aftershave.

Mark Edmunds looked shocked when he opened his front door. 'I didn't know you worked for the police, Alice. Is that why you spoke to me?' His baritone mumble filled the hallway.

'We just need some information, Mark. Can we come in?'

His apartment seemed more suitable for a pensioner than a PhD student. Book-laden shelves covered the walls, antique furniture and knick-knacks crowding every room.

Edmunds looked uncomfortable. 'I inherited the flat from my grandfather. I haven't got round to decorating yet.'

'You've got a great view,' Burns commented.

Fifty metres away, the river was unwinding like a spool of dark brown wool. Edmunds remained silent; his pleasant smile was absent and dark rings shadowed his eyes. His frown made him look even plainer, blond hair sticking up in awkward curls.

'You knew Guy Shelley at school, didn't you?'

'Not very well. Our paths didn't cross that often.'

'When's the last time you met?'

He hesitated. 'At a party in January. We know some of the same people.'

'What about Jude? She remembers you from her time at King's.'

His gaze was unblinking. 'To be perfectly honest, I found her a bit stuck up.'

'Yet you asked her out six weeks before she was attacked.'

His dark eyes locked onto mine. 'I hope you're not accusing me of hurting her, because I can account for myself that evening. I was in the library until it closed, then I came home. The concierge saw me unlock my door. It was a horrible shock to see the reports the next morning.' Edmunds's vulnerability had been replaced by a simmering tension that I could hear in his voice. 'I was friendly towards her, but that's not a crime, is it?'

Burns shifted in his seat. 'Polly Sampson says you scared her at Cambridge. You sent hundreds of texts and followed her home from lectures, didn't you?'

'That was three years ago. I've had other girlfriends since then.'

'Have you?' Burns studied his face then handed him a piece of paper. 'Write down their names and contact details, please. And make a note of where you were on each date on this list.'

Edmunds's scowl deepened. 'You can't threaten me in my own home.'

'It's a request, not a threat. You can do it here or at the station. Take your choice.' Burns gave a loud sigh.

Recording personal information seemed to make Mark Edmunds nervous. His foot tapped incessantly on the floor as he copied information from his phone. We were about to leave when I noticed a row of stones lined up on the mantelpiece.

'What are those?' I asked.

'Sharpened flints, a thousand years old. They were used as primitive cutting tools.' Despite his anger, he seemed prepared to launch into a history lecture.

'Shouldn't they be in your exhibition at King's?'

'I found them years ago. I used to visit my grandparents here as a kid; searching the riverbank's something I've always done.' He made a show of checking his watch. 'If we're finished, I should get back to my thesis.'

Edmunds said nothing as we left, but when I looked back his brown eyes were still glowing with anger.

I heard Burns issuing orders into his phone as soon as we hit the pavement, requesting immediate surveillance and a search warrant. He flagged down a cab without breaking his stride.

'Thank God you didn't go in there alone,' he said as the taxi pulled away. 'What do you make of him?'

'I'd say he's got a perception disorder. He lacks self-awareness and doesn't understand relationship boundaries; it often goes hand in hand with paranoia and obsessive behaviour.'

'And violence?'

I shook my head. 'No worse than the rest of the population. Sufferers often have a high IQ; they realise they're different but struggle to integrate. The fact that he knows two of the four victims worries me. Maybe Jude's rejection sent him over the edge, and now he's attacking anyone in her circle. He could have disguised himself and followed Guy, for all we know.'

'Christ almighty, I see what you mean about historians being a weird bunch.' Burns closed his eyes. 'His supervisor'll be at the station by now.'

'You're interviewing Hugh Lister?'

He shook his head. 'We've found nothing on him. He's talking about the calling cards at today's briefing.'

A throng of photographers was still blocking the front steps of the police station, so Burns asked the driver to drop us in the car park. Angie was the first person I saw as I headed for the incident room.

'Is the crime scene clear at Wapping?' I asked. 'I want to go back to the riverbank this afternoon.'

'It's fine to visit this afternoon. Tania'll be there, looking after the *Crimewatch* guys.' Her impish smile returned. 'The girls in the office have all fallen for Dr Lister.'

'Really?'

It took a stretch of the imagination to see the dishevelled academic as a sex symbol, but everything fell into place when I stepped through the door. Jake stood beside Hugh Lister at the front of the room and I felt a twinge of discomfort – Angie must have got their identities confused. Maybe he'd come along to keep Lister's odd behaviour in check. I observed them from the back of the room. Jake wore jeans and a plaid shirt, while Lister sported an ill-fitting suit, his hatchet features carved in a scowl. When he began to speak, his voice was a cold, west London snarl.

'The objects you've found belong in a museum, not a police station. It's a travesty that these pieces have become trinkets for a murderer.' Lister's hands trembled as he gestured towards the photos projected on the wall. 'I'll start by telling you their history.'

He explained that the Bronze Age arrowhead would have been cast into the river to appease the water gods, or as a dedication for victory in war. The flint found with Speller's body was a prehistoric cutting tool, just like the ones at Edmunds's flat. It would have taken a long time to hone, in the days before metal existed, and its high practical value would have made it an important sacrifice. Lister fixed the crowd with an irate stare.

'The Thames has been a sacred site for millennia, the most powerful and unpredictable river in England. Settlers near its banks were terrified it would wipe out their communities. That's why they performed sacrifices and attached precious possessions to the bodies of the dead. Maybe the man you're looking for worships the river in exactly the same way.'

A collective hush fell over the room as I made my escape, as though everyone in the room was visualising the killer performing his rituals. Jake caught up with me in the empty corridor while the rest of the team were still in the incident room, firing questions at Hugh Lister.

'Why did you disappear again, Alice? It's driving me crazy.'

'I saw my lookalike on your phone. It was a little unnerving.'

He looked startled. 'I can explain. Let's meet tomorrow and talk about it.'

'I'm busy tomorrow.'

'The next night then.'

I gestured towards the incident room. 'I should get back.'

He moved closer but my expression stopped him in his tracks. 'I'll call you later. Please don't let this stop you seeing me.'

I watched him heading towards the exit, wishing I'd given a categorical refusal. When I turned round, Burns was blocking the corridor. His expression revealed that he'd witnessed the whole exchange. I strode back into the incident room to hear the forensics team's report, reminding myself that he deserved no loyalty whatsoever.

40

Ben Altman's flat was on the tenth floor of an apartment block in Battersea. Even on an overcast Monday morning the building shone like a glass citadel, mirroring the pale grey sky. The stress of the investigation must have been getting to me because the lift felt impossible. I jogged up the stairs instead, pausing to admire the view from the landing. Rows of transparent buildings filled the skyline, the red-brick streets of Wandsworth sprawling south into the distance.

The grief on Altman's face made me feel guilty for disturbing him. He was a thin-faced thirty year old with short black hair, hazel eyes still glazed with shock. His handshake felt icy and I got the sense that he was following the rules of social etiquette on autopilot.

'You'd better come in,' he said quietly.

His flat was the opposite of Mark Edmunds's. It was the epitome of minimalism: pristine white furniture vanishing into the walls. On a bright day, his lounge would have been ablaze with light.

'Thanks for letting me visit. This must be a difficult time for you.'

Altman's eyes stared straight ahead. 'The night he was taken we'd been planning a weekend away.'

His hands gestured his disbelief and I noticed how beautifully manicured they were, with long, tapering fingers. Despite his suffering, his appearance was immaculate: cotton sweater perfectly ironed, not a hair out of place. He seemed to be using neatness as his strategy for keeping pain at bay.

'You had to identify Julian, didn't you?'

His head bowed. 'That's why I let you come. I'll speak to anyone if it helps find the bastard who did that to his face.'

'How long had you been together?'

'Eighteen months. I met him through work.' He rubbed his hand across his forehead, as if he was trying to clear his thoughts.

'You're at Westminster too?'

'God, no. I'm not smart enough.' He gave a strained laugh. 'I'm an account manager for a PR agency. We were polar opposites.'

'But you connected anyway?'

He gave a fierce nod. 'I wanted him to live here with me.'

'I can see why. This is a beautiful place.'

He looked uncomfortable. 'The mortgage company owns most of it.'

'Julian had a place at the Oval, didn't he?'

'It's pretty squalid.' He stared down at the polished floor tiles. 'He wasn't bothered about comfort. There was a naive side to him, I suppose. He was an idealist.'

'Had you set a date to move in together?'

He hesitated. 'A few weeks ago, Julian said he needed time to think.'

'The commitment scared him?'

'I don't know.' He blinked rapidly. 'He was working so hard, we hadn't spent much time together recently. We had a drink the night he was taken, but he went back to his place to finish a report.'

'His specialism was ethical advice, wasn't it?'

Altman's mouth twisted. 'Most politicians only want human-rights experts to help them take the moral high ground.'

Given what he'd been through, Altman's cynicism wasn't surprising. 'Did Julian get on well with his colleagues?'

'Westminster isn't the best place to be out and proud, but no one was gunning for him if that's what you mean.'

'What about previous boyfriends?'

'We didn't talk about the past.'

'You never traded secrets?'

Altman's expression hardened. 'I gave the names he told me to the police.'

'I'm sorry this is so intrusive, but it could explain why he was targeted.' I studied his elegant hands again, his fingers twisting in his lap. 'Did you know that Julian sometimes visited Jude Shelley in hospital?'

His face tensed with anger. 'It upset him terribly. I told him to leave well alone.'

'You thought he shouldn't go?'

'He didn't owe that family anything.' His voice was rising in outrage.

'But Mr Shelley gave him his first job, didn't he?'

'Julian was desperate to leave Shelley's team and find something else.'

'Really? Heather thought they were friends. You had dinner with them last week, didn't you?'

'That was on sufferance. Shelley held all the power; he could have got Julian sacked.' Altman surveyed the glass-walled room. 'He wouldn't say why, but I know Shelley often made his life hell.'

I stayed for another half-hour, hoping he would give more insights. But it was clear that he didn't know why his boyfriend had been at loggerheads with his boss. Altman remained dry-eyed throughout the rest of the interview, even when he spoke about his grief. The last thing I did was to show him photos of the objects from the crime scenes.

'Do any of these things have a meaning for you?'

He gave me a blank-eyed stare. 'I've never seen them before.'

I tucked the pictures back into my bag. 'Have you got anyone to keep you company?'

'I sent them away. Last night I drove around for hours. Christ knows where I went, but it calmed me down.'

He looked so brittle that I wondered how he'd coped with identifying Speller's body. Normally the mortuary attendants can make corpses look presentable, but injuries that severe would have been impossible to disguise.

I checked my emails on my phone after leaving Altman's flat. No progress had been made in tracking down Guy Shelley's car, which reminded me that – whether or not he was the killer – he was a high suicide risk. The accident and emergency departments of the city's hospitals had been placed on alert. I climbed back into my car, hoping the drive would clear my head.

By the time I reached Wapping, the *Crimewatch* team were huddled at the foot of King Henry's Stairs, positioning their cameras, but there was no sign of Tania. It was low tide, the water moving slowly eastwards as though it was reluctant to rejoin the sea; pungent smells of chemicals and effluent tainted the air. As I picked my way across the muddy ground, Tania walked towards me, huddled inside her long coat, face drawn from lack of sleep. Her sharp gaze met mine as we drew level.

'Back for another look, Alice?'

'It's my best chance to stand in the killer's shoes. I want to walk from the site where Julian Speller's body was found to where Amala drowned at Execution Dock. It's more than a double crime scene – he's passionate about it. He must have waded out, waist deep, in the middle of the night, carrying

Amala's body in his arms. We could be looking for a man who loves the river more than anything else.'

'He must be bloody lonely then.' There was no sympathy in her voice, only cold rage.

'Are you okay, Tania?'

'Fine, except we're getting nowhere and my daughter's winding me up. Burns is in a foul mood too.'

'Is he here?'

She nodded. 'They're filming him on the stairs where Speller was found.' Her face set in a grimace. 'He's been a nightmare for days. Fuck knows why, but it's hammering team morale.'

Tania looked as glamorous as ever, eye make-up immaculate, despite the weather. It annoyed me that we always struggled to communicate when there was so much to admire. She had serious grit, combining a tough career with being a single mum. I still believed that her attitude towards me alternated between friendliness and dislike because she held a candle for Burns.

'How's Sinead these days?'

She gave a rapid grin. 'A handful most of the time. It doesn't help that she hardly sees me.'

'But she must be proud.'

Tania gave a short laugh. 'That'll hit her when she's twenty-five. Right now she's just pissed off I'm working again tonight.'

'What are you doing?'

'Coming here for the reconstruction. It kicks off at ten.'

She set off to check on the actors and camera crew, who were starting their dress rehearsal. It surprised me that she'd revealed her frustrations instead of hiding them behind her glossy shell. I tried to focus again on the task in hand. By now I'd reached the spot where Amala's corpse had been tethered to a mooring ring. The embankment towered above me, twenty feet of exposed brick, metal and wooden bulwarks designed to contain the highest tides. Even if she'd freed herself, no one could have climbed such a sheer wall of bricks, slick with algae, mortar worn flat by endless tides. I was still studying the river sidings when Burns tapped me on the shoulder.

'How did it go with Altman?' he asked.

'He let slip that Julian Speller was planning to move in, then a month ago he cooled off for no apparent reason.'

'You got more out of him than me. Maybe Speller had someone else.'

'I'd like to know more about his movements for the past few months.'

Burns nodded. 'We're checking his phone and email. He only used his work diary for official meetings.'

'Altman said Speller had been hunting for a new job. He didn't have a good word to say about our friend the minister.'

He gave a frustrated groan. 'I need a one-to-one chat with Shelley, but the press office are still blocking it. Their official line is that the minister's privacy mustn't be disturbed. They're stonewalling every step of the way.'

'Maybe his wife could fix a meeting.'

'It's worth a try.' He gazed down at the murky water lapping at our shoes. 'The river keeps pulling our man back, doesn't it? I've got uniforms checking for his hiding places.'

On the opposite bank I could see a troop of uniforms scouring the foreshore. 'He can't keep operating under this kind of stress. He'll slip up before long.'

Burns gave a half-smile, as if he appreciated the encouragement but didn't believe it. 'Christ knows whether the TV bulletin's worth the effort.'

'It only has to jog one person's memory.'

'Let's hope it does. The heat from the top's unbelievable. They want the case solved immediately but won't let me interview the key players.'

I stared at the water's dark surface, wishing I could teleport myself to the safety of my flat. The case had escalated from examining a single brutal attack to a nationwide hunt for a serial killer. The tension in Burns's face indicated that he was finding the pressure brutal too. I was about to say goodbye when he turned to me.

'You could have told me you were seeing someone.'

I did my best to keep my voice neutral. 'Was I meant to put my life on hold while you got on with yours?'

He looked so crestfallen that I wanted to touch him, but reminded myself that he had a wife and kids waiting at home.

'Where are you going now?' he asked.

'Back to mine to switch off for a few hours.'

Burns gave an abrupt nod. 'Don't go out alone tonight. Most of the attacks have happened inside a mile of your flat.' He walked away at a brisk pace, leaving me to study the river churning at low ebb, cutting through an expanse of dark brown mud.

41

The man waits outside the police station at six p.m. He's disguised as a tourist with a camera around his neck, a London guidebook clutched in his hand, wearing sunglasses even though it's overcast. He leans against the railings, pretending to be waiting for someone. In reality he's expecting his next victim. He knows nothing about her apart from the set of her features, memorised from the TV news. With luck she'll appear soon and he can follow her home.

The river's voice hisses out warnings, but it's quieter than before, almost silenced by the rush-hour traffic. The delay frustrates him. He's forced to watch and wait, pretending to be absorbed in his guidebook, glancing up frequently to see if she's arrived. But the police station is quiet today. He can hear the journalists' complaints. Most of the officers are on the riverbank, and he wishes he was there too. If he had the choice he would sit on a bench facing the water, lulled by its quiet conversation. The pain in his head has returned, pulsing behind his eyes like a drum beating, impossible to ignore.

The man allows himself to imagine the future. Once he's killed the people who are chasing him, he can live just as before. He will have no regrets because he's not a coward like the victims he's taken. There will be time to concentrate on his own comfort for once.

He looks up again but still no one emerges from the police station. Two of the journalists walk by, one of them mentioning an address in Wapping. Relief floods his system as the river's voice grows louder. It has a way of saving him. Whenever he's lost, it comes to his rescue. He fiddles with his camera, scans the street to check that no one is watching, then saunters away.

42

My phone rang when I got home at half past six. The voice at the end of the line was a genteel London drawl.

'Are we still meeting tonight?'

'I can't, Jake. I'm too busy.'

'The department's throwing a party to celebrate getting our funding. If you drop by, we could go for a drink after? I want to clear the air.'

Part of me wanted to see the history team again because I knew the killer was obsessed by the river's past, but the photo on Jake's phone still bothered me. 'I can only stay an hour.'

'That's better than nothing.' He sounded relieved, as if he'd been expecting a flat refusal.

I hung up swiftly, promising myself to find out his secret then make a quick exit.

The celebration was in full swing when I arrived at King's College, salsa music spilling from the exhibition hall. There was no sign of Jake, so I grabbed a glass of wine and surveyed the crowded room. It was filled with students and academics, bunting trailing between display cases, an atmosphere of refined euphoria. Some discreet flirting had begun, and I could tell that gentility would soon fly out of the window. The event would morph into a riotous student hoedown when the lecturers went home.

Plenty of familiar faces were in evidence. Paul Ramirez, Jude's old flame from the law department, was basking in his colleagues' reflected success. I took care not to catch his eye. It still seemed odd that Jude had been attracted to him; the only reason I could fathom was that she'd been too naive to spot that he was a sleaze-ball. Ramirez was so absorbed by a stunning brunette that he didn't notice my scrutiny. Many others in the room must have known Jude when she was a law student; most of the lecturers and postgraduates would have rubbed shoulders with her in the corridors. I found myself studying their faces, trying to guess who might have spoken to her.

The history department had turned out en masse, clearly relieved that jobs had been saved. The only person missing was Mark Edmunds, probably nursing his bruises from his interview the day before. Hugh Lister stood alone, brooding over his beer, as if social contact was torturous, even though he'd been so committed to the Thames excavation. Jake appeared before I'd touched my wine. For once he looked less than immaculate, with creases in his shirt, his hair uncombed.

'It's good to see you.' He leant down to kiss my cheek. 'The party started hours ago, I'm already hungover.'

'How come your friend Hugh looks so unhappy?'

'End of term isn't his favourite moment; he prefers keeping busy. The guy's been through a rough time.'

'Meaning what?'

'A bad divorce, he doesn't see much of his kids.'

'He's alone, you mean.'

'Even during the holidays, he comes in most days.'

My eyes travelled back to Lister. It fascinated me that some people could isolate themselves in the middle of a crowd. His colleagues were keeping a respectful distance, as if his loneliness repelled them, like an invisible force field.

'You're doing it again, Alice,' Jake whispered. 'Let's get out of here before you psychoanalyse my whole department.'

The Globe on Bow Street had undergone a transformation since my last visit. It had changed from a spit and sawdust inn to a gourmet eatery. The waiter looked unimpressed to hear that we only wanted drinks. Jake pulled his phone from his pocket and a petulant, child-like part of me felt like hurling it through the window. The rum he'd bought me left a burning sensation at the back of my throat, but it took effect fast, the knot in my stomach quickly unravelling. Jake was classically handsome, even at his most dishevelled. His wide blue eyes looked so dreamy, half his attention seemed to be focused elsewhere.

'The girl in your photo left her stuff in your bathroom, didn't she?'

'It doesn't mean anything. It ended last year.'

'What's her name?'

He stared down at his drink. 'Emily. I met her at college; we got married the year we graduated. She's an archaeologist like me.'

'Why did you split up?'

'She got a job on an excavation in Peru. The dig was meant to last three months, but she never came back.'

I gaped at him. 'She died out there?'

'Nothing so romantic. Emily met an American guy and wanted a quick divorce. After six weeks she emailed to say she wasn't coming home.'

For once I had his undivided attention. His eyes latched onto my face as if he expected me to evaporate into thin air. The story explained why he was locked in the past. Maybe he thought that a doppelgänger could answer all his questions about why his wife had left. The sudden loss must be the reason why he slept with the light on, to keep nightmares at bay.

'Why did you keep her stuff?'

'I hoped she'd come back at first. Then I didn't know what to do with it.'

'Sleeping with her double doesn't seem like a great recovery plan.'

He shook his head firmly. 'That could be why I spotted you, but it's not how I feel now. I want to spend time with you.'

'If I'd chosen you because you were the spitting image of my ex, how would you feel?'

His smile narrowed. 'We're in the same boat, Alice. You've still got feelings for someone else – maybe we can cure each other.'

'Relationships aren't my immediate concern.'

'The case is still causing headaches?'

'Migraines, more like. I shouldn't have let myself be flattered into taking it on.' I pulled out my crumpled map of the Thames and brandished it at him. 'I've even been dreaming about where he leaves the bodies. None of it makes sense.'

Jake studied my scrawled notes. 'It looks like he understands tides as well as estuarine history.' His finger tapped the Battersea shoreline. 'Dropping the priest's body here guaranteed it would be carried straight to the House of Commons.'

'Delivered like a birthday present.'

'Exactly. Whoever he is, he's probably spent hours researching tidal flow.'

I stared at the river's sinuous profile. But the only face that came to mind was Guy Shelley's, pinched and obsessive, struggling to conquer his demons.

'Want another?' Jake held up my empty glass.

I checked my watch. 'I've still got work to do.'

His hand closed around my wrist. 'Forget about the photo. It doesn't mean anything to me now.'

'You look at her every day, Jake. Her face is your screensaver.'

I leant down to kiss him goodbye, and his grip tightened as I pulled away. I felt a pang of sympathy, but knew there was no point in meeting again. I'd always be wondering if it was me he was looking at or his ex-wife's shadow. When I got outside I considered walking the half-mile home, but Burns's warning about staying safe rang in my ears. I gazed across the river and waited until a cab's hire sign flashed gold in the dark. Maybe the killer was alone on the foreshore, looking for relics. Locating him by the riverside would be miraculous even if the search team was a thousand strong – the waterway meandered through the city's twisted heart for dozens of miles.

43

The man's heart beats too fast as he steps onto the escalator at Wapping Station, the night-time faces surrounding him pale and distorted. All he can hear is the muffled sound of his own breathing. If he lingers here too long, someone might see through his disguise. When he reaches the turnstile, he pulls down the brim of his hat, shielding himself from the cameras overhead.

The river's whisper begins when he steps outside and a surge of relief overwhelms him. Recently its voice has grown weaker; he only hears it when he shuts his eyes. But for now the river is guiding him, its murmur louder with each footstep. He presses his back against the wall of an old warehouse, hiding in its shadow. The wide expanse of the river lies directly ahead, reflected streetlights breaking across its surface like glass shattering. His nostrils fill with the odours of brine and pollution.

From here he can see the film crew at work. He wants to laugh out loud at their mistakes. An actor stands in the dark water, holding a young black girl in his arms, but she's nowhere near beautiful enough. Their attempts to mimic him are pathetic. When the filming ends he watches the camera crew carry their equipment back to their van. One man walks past so close that the vapour of his soul trails across his face, leaving behind a peppery taste. Maybe his journey has been wasted. None of the detectives are here, only three men in uniform climbing back into their squad car as the film crew departs. He watches them drive away with a sense of disappointment until a woman emerges at the top of King Henry's Stair: tall and slender, black hair eclipsing her eyes. Her soul is breathtaking, dark and glittering like a skein of silk.

He follows her in silence, pulling on his gloves as she turns down a narrow side street. When he seizes her shoulder he can tell she's different from the rest. Her blue eyes fill with panic but she doesn't scream.

'Give me your phone and your car keys,' he says. When she tries to pull away he slaps her hard across the face. 'Don't waste my time.'

'My daughter's waiting. You can't do this.' She fumbles in her pocket and pulls out her phone.

The man hurls it down the stairway into the river. 'Now the keys.'

Her hands stay in her pockets. 'Too late. I pressed the panic button. If you fuck off now you've still got a chance.'

His punch sends her sprawling across the car's bonnet, then he hunts through her pockets. She's still unconscious as he folds her body into the boot, knees pressed tight against her chest. Now he lets himself relax. The city breathes itself into his lungs, sulphurous and filthy, with an aftertaste of sweetness. For the first time in days, the river is singing his name.

44

My mother was waiting for me in the Neurology Department at Bart's Hospital on Tuesday morning. From a distance she looked stronger, sitting upright in her chair. The bruise on her forehead was a rainbow of different shades, and her left hand fluttered violently in her lap, but she greeted me with a calm smile.

'You look better, Mum.'

'I am, darling. You shouldn't have come; I'll probably have to wait ages.'

'It's fine, honestly. How's Elise doing?'

'Efficient but dull,' she said, grimacing. 'The woman's got no conversation whatsoever.'

'You employ her to shop and clean, she probably thinks you'll be angry if she wastes time chatting.'

She gave a snort of disapproval. 'Monosyllables are all she can offer. She only managed a grunt for the stair-lift people.'

'Did they finish installing it?'

'They'll be done tomorrow. It's a dreadful waste of money.'

I gritted my teeth. 'Not if it stops you falling.'

Fortunately the receptionist called her name before the discussion turned sour. It took my mother a long time to cover the short distance to the consulting room. She insisted on walking unaided, refusing to take my arm. The consultant Dr Kumar looked close to retirement age, his wizened face wearing a gentle smile. My mother relaxed visibly when she realised

248

he was a senior consultant. He listened intently while she described her symptoms, then flicked on a light-box to study her brain scan. He asked her to perform gait and coordination tasks, observing her shuffling walk and poor balance. Afterwards Dr Kumar leant forwards to observe my mother's face.

'You'll have to stop fighting, Mrs Quentin. That's the hardest part. I can tell you're a strong person, and that will help, but you mustn't tire yourself. Parkinson's progresses faster when you're exhausted. If your tremor worsens, we can talk about surgical options. In the meantime, I'll prescribe stronger medication and keep a close eye on you.'

My mother simpered with gratitude, and even her walk seemed lighter as we left. 'What a relief to see someone who knows what they're talking about.'

Dr Kumar had given us remarkably little information, but I'd learned a lesson in bedside manner. Maybe I could copy his brand of serene professional certainty when I returned to my consultancy.

'Ready for a coffee?' I asked when we got back downstairs.

'Please, darling, if you've got time.'

We ended up in an Italian café by Smithfield Market, waiters racing past in crisp white aprons. I could see that she was tiring, her gaze blurring out of focus.

'Have you spoken to your brother?' she asked.

'Not since last week. Did you ring him?'

She shook her head. 'I don't know why he made such a fuss.'

'It's his illness, Mum. You know he has mood swings.' There was no point in reminding her that their relationship had always been volatile, two huge personalities battling for supremacy.

'Would you like a lift?'

'There's no need. I'm going to the Tate Modern to see the Paula Rego show before it finishes.'

My mother's only concession to her illness was to lean on a railing as she waited for a taxi. I felt a surge of admiration as her cab pulled away. No matter how irritating she might be, she deserved credit for recovering from so many knockout punches.

I was heading back to my car when I spotted a maternity shop and remembered Lola stranded on her chaise longue. A tiny red jumper caught my eye, not much bigger than the width of my hand, perfect for a boy or a girl. I couldn't resist ducking inside. My phone rang just as I was tucking the parcel into my handbag. The voice at the end of the line was a low Scottish grumble, words racing much too fast.

'Slow down, Don, I missed half of that.'

'Tania's missing. She never went home last night.'

'And you've checked all the logical places?'

'Of course we bloody have,' he snapped. 'There's no sign of her.'

'Where are you now?'

'I'm going to see her family.'

The facts still hadn't sunk in when I met him at Limehouse Basin. Tania couldn't be in danger. She was glossy and invincible, the kind of person who sensed danger from miles away. But reassurance would have been pointless. We both knew that she would never vanish without telling anyone, her daughter was always top of her concerns. He sat on the edge of a bench, his huge shoulders hunched.

'Tell me what happened, Don.'

'I left her with the *Crimewatch* boys. They finished around eleven thirty and the uniforms buggered off home. The wankers didn't even walk her back to her car.' His face contorted with rage. I wanted to tell him to save his energy for the chase, but he and Tania had been friends for twenty years. This time the search would be one hundred per cent personal. 'Her sister Louise called at one a.m. She'd been looking after Sinead. We traced Tania's phone signal to Wapping, but it hasn't been found.'

'What about her car?'

'Missing.' His eyes were so dark, no light reflected there.

'What makes you think she's been taken? All the other victims had a direct relationship with the Shelleys.'

'So does she. We're protecting them, aren't we? Our team's hunting him down.'

Louise Goddard was waiting on the grass outside Tania's apartment building. She was performing an odd dance-like movement, shifting her weight from foot to foot to keep warm or displace her anxiety. She stared up at Burns's face through eyes glittering with shock.

'Have you found her?'

'Not yet. I need a few more details, Louise.'

Her hands shook as she fumbled with her keys. She was a smaller, rounder version of her sister, with the same sea-blue eyes. I put the kettle on while Burns took her into the lounge, noticing a row of photos stuck to the fridge with bright red magnets. Tania looked different from the hard-as-nails task-master she pretended to be at work, so slick and professional that no criticism ever scratched her surface. She was clowning for the camera, relaxed enough to pull faces. There were snaps of her daughter too. In a few years' time, Sinead would be as gorgeous as her mum, with the same willowy figure and sleek black hair. Reality suddenly hit me so hard that I almost dropped the kettle. Tania was missing, and we had hours, not days, to find her. So far every victim had died within forty-eight hours of being taken.

When I opened the door, Louise was sobbing into one of Burns's large white hankies, his hand on her shoulder. The furniture in Tania's lounge looked like second-hand IKEA, a battered sound system standing beside an ancient TV. Burns had told me that Tania was going through a bitter divorce, her ex wrangling over custody of Sinead. Her legal bills must have eaten up her salary, leaving nothing for home comforts.

'Talk me through it one more time,' Burns said quietly.

Louise's hands balled in her lap as if she was planning to punch someone. 'She was too tired to cook, so we ordered pizzas. I stayed over because she had to go out again. When I called her around midnight, there was no reply. That's when I rang you.'

'What have you told Sinead?'

'Nothing. The kid's got enough to worry about. I said Tan had left for work early then packed her off to school.'

'It'll be on the next news bulletin; you don't want her hearing it from a stranger,' Burns said.

The expression on her face soured. 'Don't tell me what I want. This is your fault for leaving her alone. Go and tell Sinead that a fucking madman's got her mum. How do you think she'll take it?'

Louise flew at him suddenly, hands flailing, but I didn't intervene. She was half Burns's size, so she was never going to leave a mark. He restrained her gently, holding her arms until she collapsed, sobbing, on his shoulder. I waited in silence for her tears to subside. Burns was still comforting her when the family liaison officer arrived. That raised my anxiety even higher. If Burns genuinely believed Tania would come home safe and sound, he would never have summoned Millie Evans. She was a pretty, middle-aged woman, brown curls swept into an untidy bun. Her mild expression hid the fact that her job exposed her to every variety of human suffering. Normally she exuded calm, but today she looked tense. The team at St Pancras Way must have heard already that their second-in-command was missing. Burns instructed her to stay put until he'd collected Sinead from school.

His face was two shades paler when we got outside, his walk shambling, as if he'd downed half a litre of Scotch.

'Are you okay to drive?' I asked.

'Don't be ridiculous.'

'I'll come with you.'

He shook his head firmly. 'She needs to hear it from me, and no one else. I've known her all her life.'

Burns's machismo seemed to be the only thing holding him together as his car sped away. I didn't envy him having to tell a twelve-year-old girl that her mother was missing without putting the fear of God into her. The challenge facing us was growing bigger every minute. If we didn't act fast, Tania's body would be cast into the river, just like the rest.

45

I tried to visualise where Tania was being held as I exited Westminster Tube station. It was two p.m., and she had been missing over twelve hours. She could be in the water already, screaming for help. Until now I'd been certain that the abductions were linked directly to Timothy Shelley, someone so near his inner circle that Jude had recognised his voice. But now he was attacking anyone who stood in his way. It still seemed possible that Guy was disturbed enough to target his adoptive father. He had been missing three days, without a single sighting. But there might yet be an unhinged history fanatic out there who believed that Shelley had wronged him in some way and was attacking anyone in his sphere. The minister had already shown that he had no intention of opening up about professional or personal matters. My only option now was to prise secrets from his allies.

I came to a halt beside Big Ben, the huge clock tower casting its shadow across the road. A gang of Italian tourists had blocked the pavement, oblivious to the weather, cameras clicking in time with the downpour.

The receptionist eyed me with suspicion when I reached the House of Commons. 'Do you have an appointment?'

'I think Mr Moorcroft will see me without one.'

'Normally you have to book weeks in advance.' She inspected my ID card then disappeared behind her counter, returning a few minutes later. 'You're lucky. He's got twenty minutes free.'

Giles Moorcroft looked exactly as I remembered. His features were pale and forgettable, and he wore the same discreetly expensive suit, dark hair greying at the temples. His expression was as calm and unreadable as ever.

'I'm afraid Mr Shelley's not here. Didn't the receptionist explain?'

'It's you I came to see, Mr Moorcroft. Can we talk privately?'

He gave me a curious look then led me away. Disraeli's portrait gazed down with a baleful stare when we reached his office, and I wondered how Moorcroft had been occupying his time while his boss was away.

'You realise I'm not at liberty to share private information.' His refined, old-fashioned speech made him sound Victorian.

'I'm not asking for state secrets, but you're in the best position to know if anyone's been harassing the minister.'

Moorcroft's eyebrows shot up. 'I've worked for Mr Shelley for many years, first at his constituency office, then as his diary secretary. Nothing untoward has happened in that time.' His stare was icy, as if he was prepared to safeguard his employer's reputation at any cost.

I glanced at the leather-bound volumes on the shelf behind him. 'Are those Mr Shelley's diaries?'

He nodded. 'I've kept them all since he's been in post.'

'Every one?'

'Of course, they're an important archive. It's a requirement of my job.'

It fascinated me that Moorcroft seemed to believe he was working for a political genius. I wondered how many letters and emails he had salted away for posterity in case Shelley ever graduated to Number Ten.

'Could I take a look?'

'Not without the minister's permission.'

I took a sharp breath. 'People close to your boss are being killed, Mr Moorcroft. He may be vulnerable too. I'd like you to think hard about anyone who disliked him. Did you ever hear raised voices coming from his office?'

His gaze shifted to the window. He studied the river intently, as though it might jog his memory. 'I'm not sure how much to disclose.'

'Another policewoman went missing last night; you could help us find her.'

Moorcroft's eyes blinked rapidly with concern. 'Mr Shelley's son is sometimes very agitated. Guy made quite a scene here last month. I don't know what the argument was about, but he was shouting at his father. He had to be driven home.'

'Did Mr Shelley argue with anyone else?'

'I don't think so.' His gaze slid to the floor.

'Please, Mr Moorcroft.'

He gave an evasive shrug. 'There was friction between him and Julian Speller.'

'Do you know why?'

'Professional differences, I think. They worked closely on the ethical employment bill, but weren't always in accord. Speller was an exceptionally brilliant adviser. He saw himself as indispensable, which irritated the minister at times.'

'And you heard them arguing?'

'Frequently.' His lips shut tight, as if he had no intention of yielding another word.

I held his gaze. 'If you show me Mr Shelley's appointment diaries, I promise not to tell him.'

'That could get me sacked,' Moorcroft bridled, but in the end he handed over the diaries from the last eighteen months.

His phone rang constantly as I flicked through the pages, and I heard Moorcroft advising journalists that Mr Shelley

256

wasn't available for interviews in a firm tone of voice. I concentrated on pages relating to the months before Jude was attacked. The entries proved that Shelley's career had reached a new high. His days often included lunches at Downing Street, press briefings and trips abroad. There had been a flurry of meetings with Julian Speller, often after late sittings in the house. It seemed odd that such a close working relationship had been so conflict-ridden.

Things changed dramatically after Jude got hurt. Shelley's appointments were cancelled for a fortnight, days gradually refilling when he returned to work. Shelley seemed to work incredibly long hours, starting before seven and continuing late into the evening, relying on a small group of advisers. I spent over an hour studying the pages detailing the time and purpose of every appointment, hoping that a name would spring out at me. When I glanced up again, Moorcroft seemed oblivious to my presence. His fingers were balanced on his keyboard, but he was staring blankly out of the window, lost in his thoughts. Maybe he was concerned about the future. Despite his efficiency, his fortunes rose or fell with the minister's.

'Do you work the same hours as Mr Shelley?' I asked.

'Fortunately not. I wouldn't have the stamina for a political career.'

'Mr Moorcroft, are you certain there's nothing else? Your information could help keep the minister safe.'

He looked regretful. 'I've already been indiscreet. There's really nothing more I can say.'

Moorcroft gave a tense smile when I said goodbye. The diaries had given me new insight into the feverish pace of Shelley's lifestyle, with his assistant ensuring that he reached each destination properly briefed. I'd also learned that his relationship with his son was even more strained than I'd realised, and his most frequent adviser had been Julian Speller, despite Ben Altman's claim that his boyfriend hated his job. Part of Shelley's grief could have stemmed from knowing that Speller had been pivotal to his career. He seemed to have depended on the younger, more brilliant man to help him make decisions.

It was early afternoon when I reached the FPU, and the first person I saw was Christine Jenkins. She was standing in the reception area, her arms tightly folded.

'I've been waiting for you, Alice. Join me in the meeting room, please.' For once the CO's sang-froid appeared to be slipping. Her expression was agitated when we reached the empty room, closing the door firmly behind us. 'I'm afraid things have escalated.'

'In what way?'

'The seniors want a change of personnel.'

I gaped at her. 'You're sacking me?'

She drew in a long breath. 'You were appointed to look at Jude Shelley's case. We both know that Whitehall wanted to silence her mother's complaints, but the fall-out's been worse than they expected. Three murders and now this latest abduction.' Her voice tailed away.

'That's precisely why you should keep me on the case.'

She shook her head slowly. 'No one could have worked harder than you; I know you haven't taken a day off since this started, and your profile report's very comprehensive. I'm in a difficult position. They want a profiler with an international reputation like David Alderman.'

'David retired two years ago. He'd take weeks to get up to speed.' I tried to rationalise why I was fighting. This was my chance to withdraw from the case gracefully and forget about the horrific attacks, but logic had fallen by the wayside. 'I've got in-depth knowledge of the killer's approach, and I gave

Jude Shelley my word that I'd track him down. It took a long time to win her trust.'

'I'm sorry, it's out of my hands. I can get you one more week, then they'll insist on replacing you if there's been no progress. For what it's worth, I think they're making a mistake.'

She gave me a tense smile then left me alone. The conversation had made me so angry that I kicked the wall hard, leaving scuffmarks on the magnolia paint. I'd ruined my peace of mind for the sake of the case, yet my only thanks was the threat of being sacked, which would hurt my professional reputation. It took several deep breaths before I was calm enough to call Burns. There was a dull roar of traffic in the background when he answered. It sounded like he was beside Niagara Falls, torrents of water thundering past.

'Where are you, Don?'

'Hammersmith Bridge. We've found Guy Shelley's car, but he won't be driving it any time soon.'

'How come?'

'The tyres have been nicked, windows smashed too. It's making Hancock's job a nightmare.'

'It's been there a while?'

Burns's voice sounded grim. 'Long enough for someone to strip it to the chassis.'

'Have his parents been told?'

'Not yet. That's my next job.'

'Let me do it; I'll go there now. Is there any more news?'

'Mark Edmunds has hardly left his flat since we saw him. We've checked all Guy's art-school contacts, but so far there's no sign of him. Tania's car was picked up by street cameras heading west around midnight on the night she was taken, then it slipped off the radar. He used her own car to abduct her.'

When I put the phone down, images rushed through my head: Tania struggling to fight off her attacker, then anxiety spreading across Heather Shelley's face. She was bound to fear the worst. Her son's car had been found in pieces beside the river. No doubt her fighting spirit would hold her together, but Guy had been missing for three days and she'd seen the depth of his suffering. We both knew that stress could have overtaken him. It was possible that he'd waited until nightfall, then dived from the embankment into the racing tide.

46

Security was still high outside the Shelley residence when I arrived at seven p.m. Two burly guards stood either side of the door and a squad car was parked outside, but most of the journalists had dispersed. Tania's disappearance must have sent them scurrying back to St Pancras Way in search of a hotter story, the last remaining photographers snapping at me, despite my lack of celebrity. Eventually the door opened by a foot and I squeezed through, expecting to see Heather's anxious face. But the cabinet minister stood there, swaying gently from left to right. The smell on his breath was easy to identify – the peaty odour of undiluted whisky.

'You again, Alice.'

Drunkenness had finally placed us on first-name terms. He no longer looked like a slick MP as he led me into his living room. He could have been any middle-aged dad after an exhausting day, hair falling in lank waves, dressed in ill-fitting jeans and an old grey sweatshirt.

'Is Mrs Shelley at home?'

'She's at Guy's flat. One of us should be there when he comes back.' His words were slurred and a bottle of Laphroaig sat on the drinks table beside an empty glass. The sight triggered my sympathy for the first time. If he was upset enough about his son to drown his sorrows, he must be capable of human emotions after all.

'Guy's car has been found vandalised by the river in Hammersmith, Mr Shelley, but we've had no sightings of him. I think it's time to explain the difficulties in your family before anyone else gets hurt.'

He let his body slump into an armchair. 'If this gets out, it'll hurt Heather and the kids.'

'I'm afraid I can't promise to keep it confidential.'

The stink of booze hit me again. 'We've been in trouble since we adopted Guy. I even considered calling the Adoption Agency to tell them we couldn't cope. The tantrums were unbelievable; he used to hurl himself round the room, literally bouncing off the walls. I know my wife told you about him hitting his sister, but that's the least of it. Last month I found Heather on the kitchen floor. He'd punched her to the ground.'

'Did you call an ambulance?'

'God, no. My wife's always protected him, and she was afraid of negative publicity. Heather cares far more about my career than I do. There have been times when I've wanted to stand down, but she wouldn't let me. She thinks we've sacrificed so much, we shouldn't waste our chance.'

I blinked in disbelief as his words spilled in a drunken gush. The truth must have existed midway between his version of events and Heather's. 'I appreciate your honesty; it's helping me to understand.'

'I found Guy at Jude's bedside a few weeks ago, drawing one of his vile pictures.' His face twisted into a sneer. 'I can't tell you how much they disgust me. It's the worst violation yet, staring at her when she's too weak to refuse. We had a dreadful shouting match in my office afterwards. Poor Giles couldn't look me in the eye for days.'

'What are you saying, Mr Shelley?'

His head swayed drunkenly. 'Guy's attacked Jude and

Heather many times, and he picks verbal fights with me. You can see the shame in his face after he calms down. It makes him hate himself.'

I remembered Jude's words the first time I visited her. Her attacker had been ashamed, just like Guy, begging forgiveness before abandoning her to the river. And the killer spoke in her own accent; Guy may have been adopted, but he'd acquired the family's verbal mannerisms perfectly.

'Where do you think your son's hiding?'

'God knows. We've phoned all of his friends.'

'Can you tell me one more thing? You were close to Julian Speller once. Why did he want to quit his job?'

Another blast of Laphroaig hit me as Shelley's mouth gaped open. I couldn't guess whether he'd bawl at me or laugh hysterically, but when he finally spoke his voice was soft as a lullaby. 'I had no idea he was unhappy.'

'There must have been professional trust between you once. It would help to know what happened.'

'Everything went wrong for us.' His voice cracked suddenly, eyes blurring with tears.

The emotion on his face was unmistakable, and the facts slowly clicked into place. His dead adviser was the cause of his pain, not his missing son. 'You were having an affair with Julian?' Shelley gave a minute nod of confirmation. 'How long had it been going on?'

'It started a few months before Jude was attacked. Then I broke it off, but it was impossible. We were always together at work. We'd started meeting again recently.' Now that he'd admitted to the affair, words gushed from his mouth like a floodgate opening.

'You need to give me the name of everyone who knew.'

His bland professional mask melted away, lips twisting in a rictus of distress. 'Jude found us here once, and she told

263

Guy. I begged them not to tell Heather. It would have broken her.'

'What about Father Owen?'

He hesitated. 'I confessed to the affair, but didn't name Julian.'

'And Amala?'

'She was so close to my children; it's possible one of them let it slip. But I'm certain no one else knew.'

When I looked at Shelley again, tears were seeping from his eyes, and my cynicism evaporated. No one cried such bitter tears over the end of a political career. That kind of pain only surfaced when someone lost the love of their life. I almost felt guilty that soon I would have to report his revelation to Burns. The story was making my head spin. It added weight to the theory that Guy was the killer. Knowing about his father's affair might have destabilised him to the point where he vented his rage on everyone who knew his father's secret. When I stood up to leave, Shelley was too grief-stricken to notice, head bowed, weeping into his cupped hands.

47

It's eight p.m. when the man returns to the garage. Even before the light flicks on, he knows the woman's alive; her spirit hovers above the car in a dense cloud, particles glittering like mica. He wishes he could stand there admiring it, but there's so little time. When he pulls open the boot, the gaffer tape is still covering her mouth. There's anger in her eyes, but no panic. Maybe this one will be wise enough to accept her fate. He pulls back the tape and forces a bottle of water to her lips. She accepts the liquid without fighting, her shoulder relaxed against his hand. Her voice is quiet as he screws the lid back onto the bottle.

'I'm glad you came back,' she whispers. 'I've been waiting.'

'Flattery won't work. The decision's already made.'

'Is it?' The woman's dark eyes pinpoint him.

'The river wants me to save myself. It told me to bring you here.'

She looks surprised. 'That's weird. I hear the river talking sometimes too.'

'You're lying.'

'It's loudest at night when I can't sleep.'

He binds the rope tight around her wrists. When he looks at her face again, her gaze is steady. 'What does it say?'

'The words aren't clear. They just run through my head when I'm tired.'

'That's not true.' But the man doesn't know what to believe. It started that way with him too, the river's quiet babble mingling with his thoughts.

'I need to go home now, but you should come with me. We were meant to meet. No one else hears what we hear.'

'I'm not letting you go.' Something in her expression lets him know she's lying, even though her spirit remains constant, not even flickering as she speaks.

'You'd be safe in my flat.'

He stares at her. 'It's too late. You'll never see your family again.'

'My daughter needs me.'

'Shut up. I can't keep the river waiting.'

He silences her with a fresh strip of tape. Her lips twitch behind the sheen of black rubber, fear shining in her eyes, revealing that her bravery was just an act. He slams the lid shut then turns out the light. Her feet drum against the metal, a rhythmic thud of protest, muffled and pointless. He stands in the dark, planning the next stage. It's too early to drive east – he must wait until the city sleeps before sacrificing her to the river. He locks the garage door behind him, with the water's voice humming in his ears.

48

I gave up biting my nails when I was eight years old. It was an easy decision: the habit made my hands look ugly and did nothing to soothe my nerves, so I steeled myself and quit overnight. But by nine p.m. the impulse to gnaw at them was back with a vengeance. I stood in my kitchen dialling Burns's number, but there was no reply. The investigation team needed to know about Timothy Shelley's secret, but Angie's phone went straight to voicemail too. My coping strategies were wearing thin; images from the autopsies I'd witnessed kept drifting into my head.

I slipped on my running shoes and left the flat, in spite of Burns's warning to stay indoors. I was desperate to burn some adrenalin, but promised myself to stick to well-lit roads. Deep puddles still covered the pavement, but I quickened my pace and soon my muscles were working so hard that the dank air made no difference. The steady rhythm of my footfalls calmed me, even though my anxiety about Tania refused to shift. My thoughts flicked through the evidence as I ran at full pelt down Tooley Street. Why had the killer waited a year to strike again, and this time with even greater ferocity? Had each attack been linked to Shelley's affair? He seemed to believe that the river had a mythic importance, sending the faceless bodies of his victims into the Thames as if he was baptising them. He must have spent days scouring its banks for talismans to carry them into the next world.

When I got back to Tower Bridge Road, I ran on to St Katharine Docks. The houseboats were packed tight as sardines. Through the window of the *Bonne Chance* I could see Nina alone in the galley, reading. I'd had no contact with my brother for days, despite sending regular texts. She looked as though she'd just woken up, white-faced, with tousled hair.

'Come in, Alice. You must be cold.' She fussed over me, pressing a mug of tea into my hands, but her distraction was obvious. 'If you're looking for Will, you're out of luck.'

'Do you know where he's gone?'

She sat down opposite, black lines of script circling her wrists like bangles. 'No idea. He stuck a note on the fridge saying he'd be back soon. I'm trying not to worry.'

'Me too. He slammed out of Mum's flat in one hell of a state.'

Her frown deepened. 'It's not the first time he's done this. Will's an escape artist. When the pressure gets too much, he ups and leaves.'

'That's how it was when he lived at mine. He'd be steady for months, then he'd go back on the road without any warning.'

'So long as he doesn't start using again, I don't care. It's his past that's pushing him away, not the present.'

'He'll be back soon. He's crazy about you.'

'The feeling's mutual.'

'He's lucky you feel that way. Some people would find him too challenging.'

She attempted a smile. 'We're in it together, aren't we? Fully paid-up members of the fucked-up childhood club.'

'That's for sure. What was yours like?'

'French aristocrat mother, with a chilly heart. When my dad left she sent me and my sister to a public school two hundred miles away. I spent a year in a psychiatric hospital in my twenties but she never visited. Her last piece of advice before she died was to get my tattoos removed.'

I glanced at her wrists. 'That would be a pity. I'd love to know what they say.'

'Quotes from Byron and Yeats, Emily Dickinson between my shoulder blades.' Her smile reappeared. 'My body's a library.'

'What made you get them?'

'Comfort, I suppose. There's solace in beautiful words, isn't there?'

Nina's face was sombre again, and it was clear she wanted to be left alone to wait for Will. She allowed me to embrace her before I left, and promised to phone when my brother returned. Rain was falling again as I ran home, light as teardrops on the back of my neck.

Burns finally rang back just before midnight. His voice was quieter than before, as if he was too tired to catch his breath. 'We got a trace on Tania's phone. It's at the bottom of the river, near where her car was parked. I'm sending a dive team down in the morning.'

The facts were too bleak to register. 'Can I do anything?'

'Help me find the maniac who's doing this.' He spat the words out like expletives. 'I've got teams sweeping the riverside twenty-four seven. Apart from that, there's fuck-all anyone can do.'

'I'm sorry, Don.'

'Me too.' There was an odd choking sound. 'Stay safe, Alice. Don't take any risks.'

He rang off abruptly, and a surge of guilt flooded my system. I'd looked at the evidence from every angle yet still drawn a blank. I was beginning to wonder if the Met's executive board had been correct after all. Maybe they were right to want me removed from the case.

49

The man returns at one a.m. He fixes the false number-plates in place, then backs the car through the narrow opening. The woman makes no sound. Either she understands that fighting is pointless, or she's conserving her energy. He drives east at a steady pace, careful not to trigger any speed cameras. The river hums softly as he makes his journey. His pulse rate doubles when he drives through Shadwell, past a row of stationary police cars. Luckily none of them notice him.

When he reaches the wharf, he parks by the side of the road to peer through the entrance gates. The site looks the same as before, builders' rubble and abandoned steel girders strewn across fractured concrete, but another police car is parked by the trap door. A sick wave of panic crashes over him. They will find his basement, and see the metal brackets screwed into the wall, rats scurrying from their torch beams.

Only the river's voice prevents him from losing faith. East, east, it whispers as he drives on, looking for safety. Eventually he finds a narrow turning between two factories, a stairway leading to the river, no one in sight. He opens the boot of the car and the woman's bound fists strike at him. Her body is rigid as he drags her to the riverside, a siren screaming in the distance. The sound is coming from the opposite bank, an ambulance racing through Rotherhithe.

The woman writhes under his grip as he ties her ankles to a mooring ring. The tide is coming in fast, reassuring him that she will drown before first light. Her breathing is harsh, screams muffled by the thick layer of tape, blue eyes glinting in the dark. The woman's soul touches his face like steam from a boiling kettle, making it hard to breathe. He rips the tape from her mouth to hear her last words.

'You haven't even got the guts to do it yourself. Cut these ropes off me, you freak.'

The man punches her so hard that her head bounces from the siding. 'It's not my decision.'

She gives a loud moan. 'Why not chuck yourself in and let me go?'

He pulls the tape from his pocket and seals her mouth once more. Then he pins an ancient brooch to the lapel of her coat, a piece of the past connecting her to the river's memory. He tightens the bonds around her wrists and ankles then walks away. Much as he would love to see the tide claim her soul, he knows it would be too dangerous.

The drive back disturbs him. Flashing lights appear in the rear-view mirror, and he's afraid he'll get pulled over. He's exhausted by the time he drives through Poplar, Canary Wharf lit up like bonfire night. He parks the woman's car on waste ground near Virginia Quay. The water is smooth as glass. Blackwall Tunnel hides below its depths, but the spirits are oblivious, drifting east to join the sea. The man takes a long breath before performing his final task of the day. Paraffin splashes over the car's upholstery then he drops a lighted match on the driver's seat. The flames grow steadily until they reach the fuel tank. He's a hundred yards away when it explodes, metal and debris scattering across the tarmac. The river sings his praises, but he's already vanishing into the shadows, running too fast to look back.

50

'Thank God you came.' Millie grabbed my wrist and pulled me into the hallway of Tania's flat. 'The doctor gave her tranquillisers, but she's no better.'

A voice keened in the background, its pitch rising and falling like someone singing out of key. I'd heard the sound before. That thin wail of despair must be the same in every country, the universal soundtrack of grieving. Louise was slumped on the sofa in a pool of thin morning light. A wad of tissues was clutched in her hand, cheeks glistening as she released her wail. On a professional level, it was a straightforward case of situational hysteria. The normal treatment would be to wait for the diazepam to take effect, but there was a child to consider. Sinead huddled in an armchair, wide-eyed with terror. The girl seemed determined to hold herself together. An iPod rested in her lap, wires trailing from her ears, muffling her aunt's cries. She eyed me cautiously as I knelt down.

'My name's Alice, I work with your mum. Are you okay here, or do you want to wait in your room while I help your auntie?'

'I'm not leaving.' Her voice was no more than a whisper.

'Of course, that's fine.' Her aunt's eyes had opened by a few millimetres. 'I hear you've been up all night, Louise. Why don't you rest now? We can wake you when there's news. You'll feel stronger after you've slept.'

272

Soon she let me lead her to Tania's bedroom, the sedative finally taking effect. She lay down on the bed fully clothed, exhaustion felling her before her head hit the pillow. I took off her shoes and laid them at the foot of the bed before joining Millie in the kitchen.

'Did you get any sleep?' I asked.

Her face was drawn. 'Not much. She's been like that since dawn. It's the kid I feel sorry for. And it would help if the boss didn't snap all the time.'

'Burns?'

'He's in a hell of a mood. He bit my head off again last night.'

'The stress is getting to him.'

She gave a nod of agreement. 'The poor sod's split from his wife.'

I blinked at her. 'I thought they were back together.'

'It didn't work out. He let slip to Pete that he'd moved out yesterday. Talk about bad timing.'

An odd feeling passed through my stomach, like a knot unravelling. When I looked back into Tania's living room, her daughter was frozen in her chair, silencing the world with music. The idea that Burns had left his children failed to make sense.

Millie looked anxious as I put on my coat. 'What if Louise gets upset again?'

'Comfort her and let her cry it out; tears are a natural reaction. Try and keep Sinead busy though. Board games are better than TV. Are there any grandparents who can help?'

'Her grandma's been in Florida on holiday. She'll be here tonight.'

'That should give them some support.' I still had no idea how Millie coped with helping victims through tragedy after tragedy. The work would have brought me to my knees. The upside of being a shrink is seeing people recover: if a treatment works, patients gradually shed their burdens over a course of months, but she stepped from one crisis to the next, witnessing endless suffering.

I chose the wrong day to arrive late for my meeting with Burns. He was sitting in a café on Wapping High Street, scowling at a computer printout. The pulse of attraction was stronger than ever. It annoyed me that my body was following its own instincts, while Tania's family fell apart at the seams. His face was deadpan when he shunted a coffee cup across the table.

'That'll be stone cold by now.'

'Millie asked me to check on Tania's sister. I had to call there first.'

His eyes narrowed. 'Is she okay?'

'She's reacting to the shock. Has there been any news?'

'We found Tania's car at Virginia Quay.'

I stared back at him. 'Her phone's in Wapping, but her car's three miles east?'

'It's been torched. The forensic evidence is blown, and the rain's washed away any footprints.' Only the subdued rage in his voice signalled that he had no intention of giving up. 'You had quite a day yesterday, listening to Shelley's confession, by the sound of it. Odd to think he'd been seeing Speller for over a year. Politicians are meant to be pillars of the community, aren't they?'

'It could have been the final straw for Guy. When Shelley told me about his violence, it sounded like he'd accepted he could be the killer.'

Burns shook his head in disbelief. 'Do you agree?'

'If you'd asked me a week ago, I'd have said Guy was too frail. But it's pointing that way, isn't it? Shelley thinks that the only people who knew about his affair are Guy, Jude, Father Owen and possibly Amala. I still think Jude can give us the answer. She's ninety per cent of the way there.'

'How do you mean?'

'Recovering buried memories is partly a conscious choice. If you're brave enough, you can fight your way back. All it takes is courage.'

'And you think she's got enough?'

'She's braver than anyone I know. I'll see her again straight after this.'

We talked for another twenty minutes, but I got the sense that he'd stopped listening to my theories, and he seemed immune to comfort. When I got up to leave he was staring at his stack of papers, as if the killer's identity was concealed between the words like a crossword clue. My thoughts strayed to the reason why he'd left his wife. Some crisis must have triggered it after he'd shown so much determination to stay.

I bumped into Angie when I left the café. Her tone was upbeat when I asked how she was doing.

'My lot are keeping busy. We found where he kept Julian Speller, in an abandoned basement that floods every day. Search teams are scouring all the buildings on the wharfs.' She pointed towards the river. 'The divers are dragging the riverbed.'

'They won't find her. Tania'll have him wrapped round her little finger.'

Angie's smile had vanished. 'I'd have said that about Amala, but she ended up at Execution Dock.'

A fine mist of drizzle clouded my vision as I walked back to my car. But something caught my attention by Alderman Stairs. A police boat was anchored ten metres from the shore, a cordon of red plastic buoys drifting from the bank. One of the divers appeared at the surface with powerful lights strapped to his wrists. I caught a glimpse of his oxygen tank and the tips of his black flippers before he disappeared. The diving conditions must have been atrocious. They were searching for a tiny object, constantly resurfacing to check the GPS signal. And they weren't just looking for Tania's phone. They were hunting for her body, in water so dense with silt that even the strongest lights could barely penetrate it.

I felt a renewed sense of urgency as I drove away. If Jude failed to remember her attacker this time, Tania wouldn't survive. The look on Burns's face had concerned me too: rage mixed with the kind of anxiety that saps your strength.

Security was tighter than ever when I reached the Royal London, uniforms and plain-clothes police mingling with visitors and hospital staff. A young woman checked my ID card before allowing me upstairs. At least the procedures meant that Jude was safe. If the killer targeted her again, he would need the nerve of the devil to con his way inside.

The sister on duty looked less upbeat this time. When I asked after Jude, she just shook her head and pushed the door open carefully, as if she was trying to minimise noise. Heather was hunched beside her daughter's bed. It was clear that Jude's condition had worsened. She lay prone on the pillows, her exposed eye fixed on the ceiling, flawless hair rippling across her pillow. The only sound was the pump of the respirator keeping her alive. Heather was clutching her daughter's hand. Her pale face was free of makeup as she threw me an unsteady smile. I felt a stab of sympathy as I thought of her husband's drunken revelations, knowing I was about to cause her even more pain, but I had to witness her reaction.

'They can't lower her temperature.' Her focus stayed on her daughter's ruined face, and it finally hit home that she was slipping away. If Jude didn't open up soon, her secrets would vanish forever.

'I need to speak to you, Heather,' I said quietly. 'Could we step outside?'

'We can talk here. I don't keep anything from Jude.'

'The police will question you later, but I thought you'd prefer to hear it from me.'

'Hear what?' She chose not to meet my eye.

'I'm afraid your husband's been having an affair.'

The last trace of her calmness went up in smoke. 'Do you think I care?' she snarled. 'I stopped asking about his weekends away years ago.'

'Did you know who he'd been seeing?'

'Some tart from his office, probably, an intern sleeping her way into a job. Why are you bothering me with this?'

Jude's hands twitched helplessly, but she made no sound. 'I'm afraid he's admitted to an affair with Julian Speller. It had been going on some time.'

The shock on Heather's face would have been hard to fake. Her skin blanched, lips trembling with distress. Her chair clattered against the wall, and before I could say another word she'd rushed from the room. I approached Jude's bed as soon as she'd gone. Her ribcage rose and fell, the plastic tube funnelling oxygen into her throat. I had no idea whether she could hear me.

'I'm sorry, Jude, but it's too late to protect anyone. It's time all the secrets came out. The police will interview your mum about Speller, and they're talking to your dad too. Have you remembered anything else?'

Her glazed eye held mine. 'I hear his voice, that's all.'

'Is it Guy? Is that why you won't let yourself remember?'

The respirator wheezed out a long breath. 'Deeper,' she whispered.

'Sorry?'

'His voice. It's a man, not a boy.'

'You're sure it wasn't your brother?'

'He lashes out sometimes, but it's never planned.'

I didn't have the heart to suggest that Guy might have changed his style, shame making him disguise his voice. Part of me felt guilty for pressing her, but I knew it could be my last chance.

'You know who did it, Jude. Tell me before someone else gets hurt.'

Her words were a raw sob. 'I wish I knew.'

'But there's something else?' I squeezed her hand.

'Jamal. I want to see him.' As the words left her mouth, her shoulders convulsed and I watched in panic as the numbers on her monitor plummeted, her body giving up the fight. Her grip on my hand tightened as a bell peeled in the corridor. A doctor arrived immediately, with Heather pacing behind, her eyes red from tears.

'What's happened?' Her voice was shrill with anxiety.

The doctor studied the bank of machines above Jude's bed, then twisted a dial. 'It's an oxygen imbalance, this should bring her round.'

The machine hissed even louder and I felt myself shaking. It was impossible to tell whether it was the prospect of Jude dying or the memory of the divers dragging the river for Tania's body that made it hard to breathe. I saw Jude's body shudder as she regained consciousness, then stepped out onto the landing. My hands shook as I fumbled for Jamal Khan's card in my bag. I tapped out a quick message, asking him to visit Jude while he still had the chance.

51

It's midday when the man returns to the spot where he left the woman. The risk terrifies him, a buzz of panic spreading through his system, but there's no other way. He takes a cab east from the city, then walks the last half-mile through narrow back streets. Every passer-by fills him with alarm. He's angry with himself for losing confidence. The river's voice used to offer comfort and reassurance, but today all he hears is criticism.

It's a relief when he reaches his destination. There's no sign of the police, and nothing has changed. He glances around cautiously before approaching the steps, the river's smell rising from the silt, acidic as sour wine. He expects to see the woman's spirit hovering above the water, but there's no sign of it as he paces down the stairs.

The truth dawns on him when he sees the rope hanging from the mooring ring. The woman has gone. He slumps on the cold ground and stares at the opposite bank, unable to accept that she has escaped. Only one thought reassures him. She may already have drowned, the river's currents loosening her ties then dragging her into its depths. Something moves at his feet, making his whole body shudder, a rat scurrying across his shoe. The river hisses, and the weight of his failure overwhelms him. He stands at the water's edge, head bowed in shame.

52

I stood outside Jude's room trying to catch my breath. I was still recovering from watching the medic bringing her round. Her life had hung in the balance, vital signs dipping towards zero, but at least she was alive. The experience had brought home how much I wanted to find her attacker, to give her the pleasure of seeing him captured. I regretted having to tell Heather about her husband's affair while her daughter fought for her life, but there was no way to protect her from the questions Burns's team would throw at her.

I pulled my phone from my pocket and listened to my messages. The first was from Christine Jenkins asking me to touch base. I deleted it immediately, aware that she couldn't help, despite her sympathetic tone. I would end up venting my anger about the threat of being removed from the case, even though it wasn't her fault. The next message was from Lola, bored senseless by the long wait for Greek God Junior to arrive and begging me to visit. Her voice lifted my spirits – normality still existed, and with luck I could return to it soon.

Burns sounded more relaxed than before when I dialled his number. 'Guess who we just brought in?'

My brain was too frazzled for games. 'Who?'

'Guy Shelley. He was wandering round Borough Market, talking to himself. Can you come and assess him?'

'I'm on my way.' There was no point in asking about Tania. He would have told me straight away if she'd been found.

The press must have got wind of a new development because the crowd outside the station had thickened. I considered using the back entrance, but knew there was no point. Photographers would be blocking the car park, hoping to catch new suspects arriving. Flashguns blinded me as I trotted up the steps, but the atmosphere inside was subdued enough to hear a pin drop. Most of the seniors were on the riverbank coordinating search teams, but those left behind were working at full pelt, not a smile in sight.

Burns was closeted in his office with Pete Hancock. I scanned the room while they finished their conversation. A battered suitcase and two holdalls were piled by the wall beside a heap of cardboard boxes. It reminded me of the eccentric historian, Hugh Lister, his office crammed with possessions. Burns turned to face me as soon as Hancock had left.

'Guy Shelley's doing a good job of acting like a nutter. The search team found a blond wig hidden behind a cupboard in his flat.'

'That doesn't automatically make him guilty. And people aren't nutters, they're mentally ill.'

He snarled something under his breath. 'I stand corrected. He's not answering questions, and he won't cooperate.'

'What won't he do?'

'Fingerprints, compliance form, registration, the whole nine yards. The bloke's talking gibberish.'

'Have you interviewed his father today?'

'For an hour, before Guy was picked up. He tried to hold back about the affair with Speller, but he cracked eventually.'

'Heather said it's not the first time, but she's turned a blind eye. When she heard he'd been seeing a man, she went into shock.' I stared down at the scratched surface of his desk. 'I felt terrible saying it all in front of Jude.'

He took a step closer. 'She had to be told. It'll be a miracle if the press don't get wind of it.'

'Does Heather know Guy's here?'

He nodded. 'She can't see him till he's been interviewed. The lad punched my desk sergeant – it took three uniforms to put him in a holding cell.'

I felt a surge of pity for Heather as we left Burns's office. If Guy was responsible for the murders, she would need an iron will just to survive. I noticed how edgy Burns was when we reached the interview room, twitching with caffeine and frustration. If I was distressed by Tania's disappearance, his anxiety must have been raging out of control, his shield of professionalism cracking apart.

'Let's see what he's got to say for himself,' he growled.

'We can't interview him. I can do a risk assessment, then we need to wait for the solicitor.'

Burns stared at me like I was missing the point. 'The lab are running tests on the wig hidden at his flat to see if it matches the fibres on Amala's carpet. If it's him, I've got to know where he's hiding Tania.'

'But it may not be. Plenty of students own fancy-dress costumes, and Jude thinks her attacker was older.'

He looked unconvinced, but there was no time to argue. Guy Shelley's protests were audible as he was marched down the corridor. His two escorts looked unnerved, as if they expected him to lash out at any minute. When he finally arrived, my concern intensified. His lips were moving rapidly, releasing a stutter of words. There was a long smear of dirt on his cheek; his hair was matted, clothes covered in mud. The raw state of his hands suggested that he'd either been fighting or punching walls. His appearance reminded me that Will was still missing. Guy looked like my brother when his bipolar disorder was at its worst; the strain of watching a close relative fall apart must have added to Jude's suffering.

'We've been looking for you,' I said. He didn't reply, but his muttering quietened. 'These officers need to fingerprint you. Will you allow that?'

'None of it's my fault.' He still wouldn't meet my eye.

'Everyone's fingerprinted – you're not being singled out. Your parents have been so worried. Can you tell us where you've been?'

His face contorted. 'Walking, sleeping, standing in the rain.'

'Why didn't you go home?'

'I can't look any more. It's my fault she's like that.' His head bowed over his knees.

Burns lurched forwards. 'Are you talking about your sister?'

'I hurt her more than anyone.'

'You're telling us you harmed Jude?' His eyes blazed. 'Did you attack the others too?'

'Guy, if you've hurt anyone else, we need to know,' I said.

I put a restraining hand on Burns's arm. The whispered conversation Guy was holding with himself was too garbled to make out. I knew he could slip beyond our reach permanently, and without a solicitor present, his statements wouldn't stand up in a court of law.

'Do you want to say anything else before your fingerprints are taken, Guy?'

He didn't reply, making no protest when the uniforms led him away, but it was obvious that Burns was struggling to control his rage.

'I think he was talking about when they were kids, Don. He's very agitated. I hope you've got him on suicide watch.'

Burns scowled. 'He could have tied Tania to a barge some-where and left her to drown. When the solicitor comes, he'll be straight back in here.'

He shut the door more forcefully than was necessary. Everywhere I looked, people were falling apart: Tania's sister hysterical with shock, Heather fighting to keep her daughter alive, and Burns buckling under an overload of guilt. If the pressure continued, he'd be a gibbering wreck.

I found an EF1 form in my briefcase and recorded my assessment of Guy's mental state, marking high scores for agitation, aggression and volatility. His panic condition had worsened to the point of breakdown. I guessed that he'd been skipping medication, which could explain his violent outburst. Sleep deprivation would be increasing his confusion. If he was a cold and calculating murderer, he was doing an impres-sive job of pretending to be disturbed. But I remembered the complex psychology behind his sketches of Jude's wounds. Either he had been revelling in his handiwork, just as some serial killers keep photos of their victims, or he'd been striving to accept his sister's injuries.

Guy's behaviour was calmer when he returned half an hour later. He was accompanied by his solicitor, a tall blonde with a haughty expression who must have insisted that he be allowed to tidy himself up. His clothes still looked filthy, but the streak of dirt had vanished from his face and someone had bandaged his damaged knuckles. He rocked silently in his chair while Burns fired out questions.

'Nowhere to hide,' Guy chanted softly. 'Nothing to say.'

'My client's exhausted,' the solicitor said. 'Can't you see he's distressed? He should be allowed to see his parents and have access to a doctor.'

'All in good time,' Burns snapped. 'Your client could be facing a multiple murder charge.'

The solicitor muttered something about human rights, but a dismissive gesture from Burns silenced her.

I tried to make eye contact. 'Guy, you need to tell us if you abducted a woman in Wapping. The police think you took her somewhere, then set light to her car.'

'Ripped apart,' he murmured. 'Everything in pieces.'

'Try and focus on my questions. Do you know where Tania Goddard is?'

He was humming softly to himself. Burns carried on throwing questions at him until it grew obvious that Guy was unable or unwilling to answer. The uniforms were about to lead him away when he swung round to face me, his eyes burning with anger.

'Did Dad tell you his secret?'

'I know he was seeing Julian Speller.'

His stare smouldered and it was a relief that he was hand-cuffed. 'I was seven the first time I saw him kissing a man. He made me promise not to tell.' Guy's face relaxed the instant he'd vented his father's secret.

Burns stood by the door rubbing the back of his neck after he was led away. 'But is he sick enough to kill?'

'It's possible. He carried that burden for years. Maybe it exploded out of him in the form of violence. He could have been attacking people his dad relied on: his priest and his lover. But the others make less sense. He loved Jude and Amala, and Tania's a complete stranger.'

'He's given us nothing. We'll have to wait till forensics send in their results.' Burns's skin was growing paler by the minute.

'When's the last time you ate?'

'Can't remember.' He was too busy gathering his papers to look up.

'The pub on the corner does food.'

'I can't leave here.'

'Then order something, before you keel over.'

He almost cracked a smile. 'Thanks for the health warning, Dr Quentin.'

Guy's statements buzzed around my head like bluebottles until the noise was deafening. I stared through the window as I tried to describe his body language and demeanour, knowing that my psychological evaluation had to hold up in a court of law. More journalists were massing outside. Now that Guy Shelley was being held, the pressure on his family would be even heavier. My old nemesis Dean Simons stood at the heart of the pack, dirty grey hair spilling over the collar of his leather jacket. Hopefully he remembered the eye-watering fine he'd paid for invading my privacy. I understood the need for a free press, but hacks like Simons wrote without conscience, touting their fabrications to the highest bidder. I pulled down the blind and concentrated on my summary.

It was nine p.m. when I returned to Burns's office. The evening had been spent scouring my notes, looking for connections between each attack, head fogged by over-think- ing and lack of food. Burns was gazing at his computer screen as if he was peering into a black hole.

'There's no news,' he said. 'He's left her somewhere to drown.'

'It still might not be Guy Shelley.'

Burns rubbed his hand across his face. 'Whoever it is, Tania hasn't got a prayer unless we find her. He won't just turn himself in.'

'It can happen. The last woman the Baltimore strangler abducted persuaded him to drive her home, safe and sound. Somehow she talked him out of it.'

His eyes blinked shut. 'Let's get that meal. There's bugger all I can do here.'

We ended up in a Chinese on St Pancras Way with paper

lanterns suspended from the ceiling. The garish synthetic flowers on every table were a poor match for Burns's gloom. He talked nonstop about the investigation, swallowing mouthfuls of food too fast, as if it had no flavour.

'Why don't you think it's Guy?' he asked.

'He's neurotic, not psychotic. I'm not sure he's deranged enough to destroy his sister's face. There's a big leap between bullying your sibling, and butchering her then leaving her to drown. You've got no evidence he did it, unless the lab results prove he was at Amala's flat.'

Burns gave an exhausted shrug. 'I hope to God they do.'

'I still think we're missing something. The killer's left clues all along that he's obsessed by the river's history. I can't believe the trail led us in the wrong direction.'

'Maybe Guy took us down a blind alley on purpose.'

I studied him again. 'You've been working flat out, Don. Why not rest your brain for half an hour?'

'Easier said than done,' he said, pushing his plate aside. 'How's your boyfriend these days?'

I shook my head. 'I haven't seen him recently.'

'You were an item last time we spoke.'

'People haven't been items since the Seventies. Your vocabulary needs updating.'

His gazed locked onto mine. 'Are you seeing him or not?'

'Not, as it happens. I called it quits.'

'Me too.' The anger in his eyes dwindled. 'All the old rows started again. The boys are in a bad way – trying to keep it together did more harm than good.'

'I'm sorry. You'll still see plenty of them, won't you?'

'Every weekend.' Burns's gaze intensified. 'There's another reason why I had to leave.'

'What?'

'You, obviously. It's been that way for years.'

Something shifted inside my ribcage. It felt like a heavy piece of furniture was being dragged across my chest. I remembered Lola's speech about honesty. I'd spent my whole life concealing my emotions, determined to protect myself. I opened my mouth to tell him how I felt, but no sound emerged. The impulse was there but not the words.

'Where are you staying?' I asked, when I caught my breath.

'A shite hotel on Gray's Inn Road. The guy next door's into heavy metal.'

'Stay at mine.'

Burns's slow grin unfurled. 'Are you serious?'

'In the spare room. At least you'll get a good night's sleep.'

'I need to go back to the station. I can't just walk away.'

'Come to mine when you're ready.'

Burns's phone rang as we were splitting the bill. The full range of emotions crossed his face as he listened: first he looked stricken, then his smile slipped back into place. 'Tania's alive,' he said. 'The ambulance is taking her to Guy's Hospital.'

'Thank God.' I reached across and touched his hand.

'They think she'll be okay. I'll go there now.'

When we stood up to leave, my stomach was twisting into knots. My emotions were pulling in different directions – relief that Tania had been found, combined with fear about letting Burns get close. The tables had turned so quickly it hardly made sense. I could have stood there watching him for hours, but we behaved like sensible adults, putting on our coats and heading for the door.

The deluge had started again when we got outside. Rain was cascading from the sky so fast that the pavement had become a river, but Burns didn't seem to notice. When I looked up his face was bleached by the streetlight as his thumb skimmed my cheek.

'I just need to see she's all right, then I'll come round.'

I watched him stride away before hailing a taxi. When I settled on the back seat, a senseless grin unfolded across my face as the cab raced into the night.

53

I waited an hour before calling him. The news about Tania had lifted my spirits, but I was still impatient to see Burns shambling down the hallway in his outsized raincoat. There was no answer from his mobile, and I knew that something must have delayed him. When I finally got through to the incident room, there was a barrage of noise. Phones jangled frantically in the background, the clamour of voices so loud I could hardly hear Angie's voice.

'It's mayhem here. Did you know Tania's been found?' she said. 'A few of us are going to see her now.'

'Is Burns with you?'

'I'll check his office.' There was a pause before she spoke again. 'He's set off for the hospital already.'

The muffled cheer in the background made me wish I'd stayed put. I wondered whether Tania's sister and daughter had been given the news, suddenly so keen to know how she was that I couldn't stay indoors. I threw on my coat and left the flat.

Tiredness must have been catching up with me when I reached the hospital, because I was worrying about Tania's injuries, even though Burns had said she would recover. I was afraid that her face might have been slashed to ribbons, just like Jude's. By the time I arrived at accident and emergency my tongue was glued to the roof of my mouth. A nurse told me that she had been taken to a surgical ward, which raised my anxiety another notch.

A small crowd of police was hanging around outside her room, and Hancock was the first familiar face I spotted. His expression gave no clue as to the severity of Tania's injuries. His black monobrow was in its usual place, a centimetre above his eyes. Only his demeanour let me know that he was relieved, and for once he didn't bark at me.

'How is she?' I asked.

'Pretty beaten up. Her back took the worst of it, apparently.'

'Do you know what happened?'

'A patrol boat found her wedged in a concrete overflow. Two of the blokes pulled her out, unconscious. She's swallowed so much water they'll have to pump her stomach.'

'Poor her.' It would be a cruel twist of fate if Tania had survived an encounter with a serial killer, only to succumb to the river's toxins. 'Where's the rest of the team?'

'At Rotherhithe shore, where she was found.'

After a few minutes, someone tapped my shoulder. I expected to see Burns but when I spun round it was Millie, her face blank with tiredness.

'God, what a relief,' she said quietly. 'Louise and her mum are in no state to leave the flat. I told them to rest till morning, then bring Sinead over.'

'Have you seen Tania?'

'No one has. The doctors are stabilising her.' The tense expression on her face made me realise that she shared my fears about Tania's injuries.

A medic appeared as we were talking. He explained that two of us could see her, and Millie and I were first through the door. The room was such a hive of activity that I couldn't see the bed, nurses crawling over each other, but when I finally got close enough, Tania was lying face down on the gurney. A ragged wound ran from the middle of her spine up to her hairline. One of the doctors was taping surgical dressing to her torn skin. When I turned to Millie, she was two shades paler than before.

'God, I could kill that bastard with my bare hands,' she murmured.

One of the medics spoke to us. He was a middle-aged man with the face of an eternal optimist. 'It looks worse than it is. The wound's superficial, so it should heal nicely. But she may need a skin graft on her arm. It looks as if she scraped her wrists over raw brick to loosen her ties.'

'What about the head wound?'

'There's no skull fracture, just subdural swelling. A concussion, in other words.'

'When do you think she'll come round?' Millie asked.

His smile widened. 'She's already regained consciousness. She was so exhausted and traumatised we gave her sedatives to help her sleep. You can talk to her tomorrow.' The man's hopeful expression faltered for a second, as if he was contemplating a worst-case scenario. 'She's been lucky. Most people don't survive a fall into the Thames. It's a blessing she was found.'

Millie's colour improved when we returned to the corridor. 'Thank God she's out of the woods.'

'Have you seen Burns anywhere?'

'Not since we left the station.' She gave me an absent smile as she punched numbers into her phone. 'Wherever he's hiding, he must be over the moon.'

54

Silence rings in his ears. The river is no longer murmuring a word, but at least the man's patience has been rewarded. An hour ago he stood outside the police station, unnoticed in the scrum of journalists, while the detective announced that his colleague had been found, a sickening look of triumph on his face.

The man lingered at the back of the crowd until Burns emerged again. He watched him walk between the press vans in the car park, then slip down a narrow alley. The detective stood by his car, face tipped to the sky, accepting the rain like a benediction. All it took was a powerful blow to his skull to make his body crumple. The keys were hanging from the lock of his car, but the man couldn't lift the detective's dead weight into the boot, so he dragged him onto the back seat instead.

Now he's sitting in the driver's seat, hands fused to the wheel. He's too afraid to twist the key in the ignition. Police cars are racing down St Pancras Way, their lights flashing. He needs to return to the river, but without its voice to instruct him, he doesn't know how. When he peers into the rear-view mirror, the detective's soul is drifting like smoke. The light it casts is so fierce, he's afraid that someone will see it glowing through the car's locked windows.

55

I ran down the corridor at the police station searching for Burns. The incident room's atmosphere had changed from gloom to celebration, empty bottles of Cava littering the table, a dozen people letting off steam in a roar of chatter. I was hoping to find him asleep at his desk, felled by exhaustion, but his office was empty. I inhaled his familiar smell of coffee, musk and fresh air. I tried telling myself there was no reason to panic, but the reassurance brought no comfort.

I found Angie putting on her coat, her elfin face shadowed by tiredness.

'Shouldn't you be home by now?'

'Burns is missing, Angie.'

She stared at me. 'He's still at the hospital with Tania.'

'He never made it. And he's not answering his phone.'

She sighed loudly then punched a number into her mobile. Her expression was only slightly less sceptical when there was no reply. 'He's probably gone home.'

'He never switches his phone off, and anyway, he split up from his wife. He's staying at a hotel on Gray's Inn Road.'

Her gaze grew more focused. 'Tell me what you know, Alice, slowly and clearly.'

'I was with him when Tania was found. He said he was going to the hospital, but he never arrived.'

'He's been under so much pressure. Maybe he went for a drink.'

'No way. He was desperate to see her.' I felt like saying that he was equally keen to get to my flat, but Burns would hate his secrets being spilled.

She suppressed a yawn. 'I'll get my lot to find him, then someone'll ring you at home.'

'You know he had bypass surgery three years ago, don't you? He could be lying somewhere by the side of the road. Or maybe he's been taken, just like Tania. You have to take charge, Angie.'

The mention of her newfound responsibility had the desired effect. Once she realised that she was now first in command, Angie raced away like a small tornado. I stayed silent while she handed out duties. One team began phoning hotels on Gray's Inn Road, another worked on tracing his car, someone else called his wife. I was left with nothing to do except observe the shock on people's faces. Things like this didn't happen to men like Burns, with the heavyweight build of a boxer, six foot five, tipping the scales at over two hundred pounds. Attacking him would be an act of bravery, or madness.

'You're shaking like a leaf.' Angie appeared again at my side.

'Give me something to do. Anything.'

She shook her head. 'He was staying at the Kingsway Hotel, but there's no sign of his car.'

'And he's not with his wife?'

'She hasn't seen him.' She stood there, eyeballing me. 'Go home. There's nothing you can do. We'll call when there's news.'

'I'm getting in the way, you mean?'

'You look like you need a rest.'

Arguing would have been pointless. Angie was like a pit-bull terrier, prepared to fight to the death to win her point – but leaving felt negligent. My body fizzed with anxiety, as though I'd downed half a dozen espressos on an empty stomach. I stood on the pavement, waiting for my head to clear. I could have called someone, but sympathy didn't interest me. The overriding need was to find Burns, worry building inside my skull like a new migraine.

I decided to visit Jude again, even though it was clutching at straws. Guy had fallen from the suspect list because he'd been in a holding cell when Burns was taken, but I still felt sure she could identify her attacker. She knew his voice, a man older than her brother with a familiar accent. A single, well-aimed question could send her hurtling back into the memory. The idea of forcing her to relive her terror filled me with guilt, but it might be the only thing that could save Burns.

The night sister grumbled loudly about my late arrival when I reached the Royal London, and I had to work hard to convince her to let me see Jude. The air in her suite had the cloying odour of medicine and fever, yet I found myself smiling. Jamal Khan was clutching Jude's hand; he gave me a brief nod, then his gaze returned to her as if I'd ceased to exist.

'How is she?' I asked.

'Drifting. We've been talking whenever she comes round.'

'Is Heather here?'

'Asleep in the next room. She was exhausted.'

Khan's appearance had changed since we met in Tottenham. The tension had left his face, as if seeing Jude again had wiped the past clean.

'Could I have a moment with her? I've got a question to ask.'

He rose to his feet reluctantly and a thought arrived before I could silence it. How would I cope if Burns was dragged from the river with the same horrifying injuries? Did I have the guts to sit there, willing him to recover? Jude looked weaker than ever, but her bloodshot eye still stared intently – even this close to death she didn't miss a trick. The monitors above her bed revealed that she was hanging on by a thread.

'You again.' Her voice was a low rasp, but her face twitched as if she was attempting a smile.

'Jamal beat me to it. Is it good to see him?'

'Scary at first, not any more.' The statement was little more than a rush of air.

'Jude, I still need your help. We know it's not Guy, but have you remembered anything else? Anything at all.'

'Has another one been taken?'

'Tell me the words he used. It doesn't matter if they're jumbled.'

Air gasped from the oxygen machine. 'Souls, lonely, forgiveness, history.'

'History? You never said that before.'

'The river's hungered for souls since the start of history.' Her speech was a slow west London drawl, deeper than her normal voice, as though she was imitating someone. The tone sounded familiar, but I couldn't place it.

'Is that what he sounded like?'

'Pompous. Like he knew everything.'

A yellow light flashed on the panel above her bed as Jamal returned, her blood pressure dropping below eighty, vital signs on the verge of crashing. 'Thanks, Jude, you've helped so much. I'll come back tomorrow.'

When I left her room my own pulse quickened at the thought of Burns. The man who had destroyed Jude's face had taken him somewhere, and he would die if I made a mistake. I forced myself to stay calm as I called Angie, but she had nothing new to report. Burns's car hadn't been found. I could see nothing beyond the hospital's windows except silhouettes of empty buildings and the city's grubby darkness. Jude had used the word history for the first time, mimicking her attacker's opinionated delivery. And that's when I made my decision. Even though their alibis had been checked, I had to follow my hunch and look again at the historians from King's. I set off down the stairs with renewed energy, vaulting two steps at a time.

56

The man knows he must act fast because the detective is coming round, his voice a groggy string of expletives. He parks by his favourite bridge and wrenches open the car's back door. Burns carries on grumbling curses, his soul bright as a halogen flare.

'Get this fucking blindfold off me. My lot'll be here soon, they'll track my phone.'

'I threw it away. Now stand up,' the man barks. 'Do as I tell you.'

Burns refuses to move and he has to haul him by his shoulders until his huge form spills onto the tarmac. It takes all his energy to drag him inch by inch across the walkway. A hard shove sends him falling, fifteen feet to the shore below. There's a splashing sound as his body hits the mud, followed by a groan. The man stands still for a moment. There's a grind of night buses in the distance, and a woman's laughter, false and high-pitched. But the river is silent. Whatever he does now, he must cope without its guidance. All he can hope is that the conversation will resume when the new victim is delivered.

The man runs down the steps. One of Burns's arms twists at an odd angle, as he drags his inert form into the water. His eyelids flutter as he slips in and out of consciousness. The man binds his wrists, then ties them to the scaffold cladding the bridge. The pain of Burns's injury is waking him again.

'Who the fuck are you? I recognise your voice.' His feet kick out with wild strength, but the man drags the rope back and secures his legs to the iron bar. 'Why are you doing this?'

'It can't be explained.' The man kneels to secure his ties.

'My bloody arm's broken, in case you hadn't noticed.'

'You should have followed my instructions.'

Burns gives a gasp of pain. 'You can't do this, someone'll see you.'

'Keep your voice down or I'll gag you.'

'What have I got? Two hours till the tide's over my head?'

'No more than an hour. You need to hear why you've been chosen first.'

'Untie me and I might listen.'

The man beats his clenched fist against the detective's broken arm, making him release a sharp moan. The water is already up to his knees and he's desperate for someone to hear his story. He's never felt more completely alone.

'The sacrifices have a reason. The river understands because of its history, it's always craved souls.'

Burns gives another loud cry of anger or pain. The man ties a sharp piece of metal round his neck, then gazes across the river. The water's rising fast tonight, blacker than memory, threatening to knock him from his feet.

57

'It's the middle of the night.' Jake sounded half asleep. I pictured him under his bare light bulb, mobile pressed to his ear, rubbing his eyes.

'Someone else has been taken. I need your help.'

There was a slight pause. 'Give me ten minutes, then come to mine.'

He was fully awake by the time I arrived, listening to me babble as he led me into his lounge.

'It's the detective running the case,' I explained. 'I know it's a long shot, but you have to predict the next kill site. There's hardly any time left to find him alive.'

Jake looked startled, then pulled his river map down from the wall. Outside his window the Thames snaked past, streetlights casting a glow over its oily surface. 'So far he's gone for Battersea, London Bridge and Execution Dock. They're all places where human blood's been spilt for centuries. If he's taken the top man, this is his big finale. That would have to be at Vauxhall Cross.'

'Why?'

'More victims died there than anywhere else. He'd see it as the best site for a sacrifice.'

'The search team already looked there. Now they're working east, towards Wapping.' I rubbed my hand across my face. 'I've thought all along that the killer's obsessed by the river's history. The calling cards have to mean something, and your team have been looking for exactly the same objects. Can you think of anyone who could be doing this?'

Jake blinked at me. 'You're asking me to identify someone on my team as a serial killer?'

'Have any of them been behaving strangely?'

His mouth twitched. 'Mark Edmunds is the only one with mental health issues, but he told me he was leaving for a dig in York on the last day of term.'

'Anyone else?'

There was a moment's pause. 'Hugh had a row with the dean last week; I heard him yelling that she had no reverence for history. It sounded slightly crazed.'

'Where does he live?' I remembered Jude saying that her attacker sounded pompous, as if he knew every answer, just like Lister.

'His flat's by Gabriel's Wharf. But surely you don't think it's him?'

'It's worth a visit. The killer knows the Thames like the back of his hand, and Lister's a world expert.' I was already tapping out a message to Angie on my phone.

'That doesn't make him a murderer, for God's sake.'

'He kept calling the crime line, asking for the objects. I thought he was just an eccentric but I have to check.'

'If you seriously think he's dangerous, you're not going there alone.'

I was too grateful to argue. Even though Angie would send officers to Lister's flat, I wanted to see him myself. By now my shock about Burns's disappearance was turning physical. Rain smeared my face as we paced towards the building; it felt colder than before, my legs weakening as we ran upstairs.

There was no answer when I rang Hugh Lister's doorbell, but the commotion had roused his neighbour. An elderly man peered from the doorway opposite, his bathrobe wrapped tight across his chest.

'He's not in,' the old man said briskly. 'I heard him leave about seven o'clock.'

'Do you know where he went?' I asked.

He looked surprised. 'Dr Lister never speaks to anyone. He comes and goes as he pleases. Has something happened?'

'I work for the police. We need to get into his flat.'

'He won't like that one bit. He hates people invading his privacy.'

'Then we'll break down the door.'

Lister's neighbour looked horrified. 'Wait there. He gave me a key years back.'

I took a sharp intake of breath when we finally entered the living room. The scene was a textbook definition of hoarding. Boxes were piled to the ceiling, newspapers in vast bundles, parcelled with string. His kitchen was even worse. A crate overflowed with empty cartons and egg boxes, and the air stank of sour milk, burnt food and decay. The shrink in me wondered how much loss the historian must have endured to hide behind such an impenetrable wall of rubbish.

I turned to Jake. 'I'm clutching at straws. Lister knows all about the crime scene objects, and his path could have crossed with Jude's at King's, but the police believed his alibis. There's nothing solid connecting him with the other victims.'

He nodded. 'I can't see why he'd hurt anyone. Hugh's got a temper, but he's never seemed violent.'

My panic was leading to bad judgements. I had wasted precious time chasing someone the police had already checked. But my certainty that there was a link to the river's history hadn't faded. Knowing that the killer might already be completing his business made it hard to stand still. Burns could be tied to the riverbank, his murderer planning to return later to butcher his face. I took a step backwards as a police siren wailed outside.

'Wait here,' I said. 'Tell the police everything you know about your team, and get them to search Mark Edmunds's flat.'

I heard Jake protest as I rushed outside, but there was no point in taking him with me. If Burns had been left to drown, he could be stranded anywhere beside a river that stretched for miles.

58

The river is higher now, its wide sweep pulsing with energy as it races inland. The water has reached the man's waist, but he doesn't feel the cold. Its contact is reassuring as an embrace. The detective's teeth are gritted as he listens, the pain from his broken arm clearly overwhelming him.

'Your soul's reflected in the water,' the man says.

'Yeah? Take off this fucking blindfold so I can take a look.'

'It's like a force field.'

The detective gives a dull laugh. 'Lapsed Catholic, mate. Eternal souls stopped working for me. What does mine look like?'

'A cloud of light. White, yellow and gold.'

'Sounds like Guy Fawkes Night. Why don't you finish your story?'

The man hesitates. 'I learned a secret. I knew it was my duty to safeguard it.'

'And that's when you heard the river talking?'

'Whispering first, then begging for souls.'

'Is that why you took Jude?'

'There was no choice. The river wanted her, like it wants you.'

'Why do you hate the Shelley family so much?'

'I don't hate them. The secret concerns them, but I feel no ill-will.'

Burns twisted towards him. 'It must be getting light by now. Let me go before someone sees us.'

'There's no need. If the police come, I'll slit your throat.'

'Christ, you really are a freak. It's ironic really – I've just met the girl of my dreams. That's another reason to free me.'

'Perfect women are an illusion.'

'Not her. She's as real as they come.'

The man falls silent as the water reaches his chest. The current is so strong he must return to the shore or risk being swept away. Soon the river will claim its new victim and his crimes will be erased. The waters will sing his name again, lulling him to sleep. He leaves the detective tied to the scaffold, dragging himself along the metal pole to dry land, as dawn bleaches the sky. He plans to return to watch his final victim die.

59

Rain pounded my windscreen, the wipers struggling to clear it. I knew it was a wild goose chase, but anything was better than sitting still. Angie had sent out teams to search the killer's regular stamping ground, the riverside from Wapping to Canary Wharf, while I drove west down Lambeth Palace Road, trying to suppress my panic.

Jake had seemed so certain about the next kill site that I'd picked Vauxhall Cross to search for Burns. I parked at Peninsula Heights and grabbed my torch from the glove compartment, knowing that Burns might be locked in a flooded basement somewhere or chained to a buoy in the middle of the river. But as soon as I reached the path, the torch was unnecessary. Tower blocks filled the skyline either side of the bridge, light gleaming from landings and stairwells, as if the residents never slept. At three a.m. I was completely alone, apart from a few tramps sound asleep under an archway.

If he'd dragged Burns down to the riverside, surely he would have been spotted by the flat dwellers above? Frustration was suffocating me as I gazed at the muddy shore and the fast-encroaching river. Burns could be anywhere except this shiny postmodern landscape. The killer preferred dank cellars crawling with rats. I yanked my phone from my pocket to call Angie but there was no reply. She was probably combing another stretch of riverbank with the same sense of hopelessness.

There was no point in going home to agonise. So I carried on walking, not caring that I was near the spot where Shane Weldon had thrown his unsuspecting victim into the river. I was so full of adrenalin that any attacker who dared approach me would get hurled in himself. I carried on pacing through the driving rain until Ben Altman's futurist apartment block appeared. The buildings west of Vauxhall Bridge were even uglier than the ones to the east. The towers looked like ziggurats, built to exactly the same design. Thousands of occupants must be saddled with colossal mortgages just like Altman, pinned to their day jobs forever like butterflies behind sheets of glass.

My eyes scanned the riverbank as I turned back, but there was nothing to see except abandoned bicycle wheels, carrier bags and crushed beer cans. The river had spat out all of the rubbish it had been force-fed during the day. I trotted back towards Vauxhall Bridge, determined to keep looking all night, even though Jake's prediction had turned out to be wrong. The best option was to drive to Wapping to join the police search teams. I studied the river again, my eyes lingering on the bridge itself. It was being repaired, ironwork covered in scaffold, life-sized statues adorning the arches. It was only when I drew closer that I saw something at the base of one of the pillars, ten yards out from shore, between the barges at anchor, and raindrops jittering like shotgun pellets.

My heart gave a quick somersault as I grabbed my phone and left a garbled message for Angie. I didn't hesitate before running down the steps to the muddy expanse below. My eyes had grown used to the artificial light on the walkway, but when my vision cleared I saw him. Up to his neck in water, blindfolded, his face whitened by moonlight. He had stopped moving now, and there was no way to tell whether he was alive. The killer had followed his pattern, abandoning him to the river.

The water was still rising as I called emergency services, knowing that Burns could go under at any minute. I dropped the torch on the shore and fumbled in my pocket. All I found was my car keys and the Swiss army knife Will had given me years ago, but I had to try. Currents snatched at me, eager to pull me under. I hauled myself along the iron bars of the scaffold, but the moment my feet lost contact with the ground I was in trouble. The water felt icy and had a mind of its own, tugging hard at my clothes. It took all my strength just to cover a few metres. It grew easier when I realised that Burns was still alive, fighting to keep his face above water. The sight of him battling gave me a new rush of strength. I thrashed on as fast as I could, pausing to cling to the scaffold and catch my breath. From a few metres away I saw that he was injured, blood oozing from a head wound, his skin unnaturally pale.

'I'm here, Don. Are you okay?' I pulled off his blindfold.

'Best day of my life,' he muttered, teeth chattering. 'You took your fucking time.'

'Keep your head up, that's it. Are you injured?'

'Broken arm, blurred vision. He wanted to give the river my soul.' He gave a dull laugh. 'He tied something round my neck.'

When I tugged at the string, a sharp piece of metal glinted in my hand. It was a long arrowhead, sharp enough to wound. I stuffed it into the pocket of my jeans.

'You can keep it for a souvenir.' I clung to the pillar and scanned the water's surface, but there was no sign of anyone. 'Hold still, I'm going to free your wrists.'

Burns's pain seemed to be defeating him, his head bowing. I clutched the scaffold as I dived into the blackness to stop the water wrenching me away. I slashed at the ropes round

309

his wrists with my small knife, surfacing for air. The emergency services had to arrive soon, but there was still no sign of them. Eventually the rope gave way, his hands fighting free of the water. At least now he could use his good arm to haul himself a few inches above the surface, but I could see his energy fading.

'Your feet are tied too?'

'Don't try it. The currents are too strong, you'll be swept away.'

'Shut up, you idiot.'

I kissed him hard on the mouth then dived again, fighting through six feet of oily blackness. When I came up, my first reaction was relief. As I rubbed the water from my eyes, I saw two squad cars pulling up on the north shore, but they were no use, distanced by fifty metres of racing tide. I dived once more, but the next time I surfaced, a different face was staring at me. A sharp pain shot through my arm. The man gazing at me was Giles Moorcroft, his grip on my shoulder agonising as he dragged me towards him.

'No,' I spluttered. 'The police are here, you can't.'

'Your soul's perfect,' he whispered. 'Spotless.'

I could see Burns lunging at him from the corner of my eye. If he lost his grip on the iron bar, he'd drown, ankles lashed to the fretwork, his broken arm useless to fight the currents. My mouth filled with liquid that I fought not to swallow, the water bitter with poisons. Moorcroft was yanking me under. I took a lungful of air then lashed out with the knife in my bunched fist. The blackness was so complete that I was afraid of striking Burns, but there was no choice. I was close to passing out and it took everything I had to kick my way back to the surface. The river spat me out by the scaffold and I grabbed hold to stop myself being swept away. That's when I realised that I'd dropped the knife. Moorcroft was thrashing towards Burns and there was no time to think before I pulled the arrowhead from my pocket. I coiled my arm back and slashed at his neck. He gave a dull whimper as he spun round, blood pulsing from the wound. His gaze cast down, as if he could read the river's secrets.

'I did what you asked,' he whispered. 'Please don't take me.'

Moorcroft's arms flailed wildly as the river bore him away. The tide moved so fast he was dragged ten metres upstream before I could blink. Then I was too busy fighting to keep Burns's head above water. His eyes kept closing, shock or the river's chill defeating him.

Relief came in the form of a police rescue boat. Two patrolmen dived down to cut the ropes from Burns's ankles, then I was lying on the hard deck of the boat, taking ragged breaths like a fish newly landed. By the time they hauled Burns over the side, I was sitting up with a blanket round my shoulders. They propped him beside me, and I clutched his hand. His arm was a mess, wrist bowing in the wrong direction, but the pain didn't seem to bother him. There was a dazed grin on his face.

'I saw them, Alice.'

'What?'

'The souls. Lights and faces under the water, beautiful.'

'You're delirious. Take some deep breaths.'

'Was it them kissing me, or you?'

'Me, you fool.'

'Even better.' Burns's head lolled back as he passed out, and one of the men pressed an oxygen mask over his face, but he needn't have bothered. His eyes burned fiercely as he came round. 'Get that fucking thing off me. I can breathe fine, it's my arm that's broken.'

Shock or the river's poisons were making me nauseous. The boat was travelling east at top speed as I hung my head over the side. And that's when my phone vibrated in my pocket. I was shocked that it still worked after a prolonged soaking. A woman's quiet voice was dulled by the roar of the boat's engine, and then I heard it. She was crying her heart out at the end of the line.

'Who is this?'

'It's me.'

'Lola, are you okay?'

'It's started, Al. I'm so scared. Can you come?'

I took a deep breath. 'Of course, sweetheart. I'm on my way.'

The boat's prow cut swathes of water from the river's surface like strips of tickertape as I gripped the rail. I'd never been more desperate to reach dry land.

60

When I arrived at Morocco Street, Neal was crouched beside the bed, with Lola clutching his arm, preventing him from bolting. She was in the middle of a contraction, clearly trying not to scream.

'You're soaked. Where've you been?'

'Stuck in a downpour, sweetheart. How're you doing?'

'It's fucking agony,' she said through gritted teeth. 'If men did this, the human race would be extinct.'

Lola gave Neal a withering look, but she was heroic during her labour, getting by on gas, air, and the midwife's constant encouragement. Her daughter Neve made her entrance at nine a.m. precisely, as though she intended to be punctual for the rest of her life. I'd witnessed plenty of births during my time at med school, but it's different when the mother is someone you love. Lola and Neal were weepy and elated, but Neve took it all in her stride. She lay on her mother's chest, taking minute breaths, observing the world through unfocused blue eyes. Her fingers were fine as tendrils, no longer than my thumbnail, wisps of coppery hair curling at the nape of her neck.

'She's a redhead,' I said.

'Damn right,' Lola purred.

It was the wrong moment to sit there admiring my goddaughter. Lola and Neal needed time alone to celebrate her arrival, so I kissed all three of them goodbye. My clothes had dried against my skin, but my jacket was still damp, so I left it behind.

A roar of traffic greeted me outside, the rush hour in mid-swing. By now I was swaying with exhaustion. It felt like days since I'd slept or eaten a meal, so I ducked into a café on Tower Bridge Road. My phone was still on silent, but I felt it buzzing in my pocket, Nina's name lighting the screen.

'Will's home, Alice. He came back this morning.'

Relief surged through me. 'How is he?'

'Calmer. He's been with friends in Brighton.'

'Tell him he's a godfather. Lola and her daughter are doing fine.'

There were eighteen messages on my phone, including one from my mother. I considered calling her, then thought better of it. Her frosty disapproval could wait for another day. With luck her assistant was learning to utter more than the odd monosyllable.

After two lattes, orange juice and a mountain of toast, my brain was functional again. The facts about Moorcroft were falling into place. He'd come across as a man so rigidly in control that no flicker of emotion ever reached the surface, and his repression must have contributed to the violence. His job had provided the perfect setting for a history obsessive. It allowed him to watch the Thames rolling past Westminster, his office filled with records of the past: volumes of Hansard detailing every bill since Parliament began. And the diaries he kept provided an archive of Timothy Shelley's career. I gazed out at the pedestrians walking north towards the City, umbrellas shielding their faces. But what had made Moorcroft kill? He had targeted two different types of victim: people Shelley loved, and those who knew about his secret affair. What had triggered such monstrous violence? My curiosity had returned with full force, even though exhaustion was threatening to topple me. More than anything, I was eager to know whether he was dead or alive.

Angie sounded tired but upbeat when I called. Tania had regained consciousness and her family was with her. Burns was in hospital too, having his broken arm set. The most surprising news was that Giles Moorcroft had been fished from the river alive, the wound on his neck so shallow that he'd only required a handful of stitches. Knowing he was at the station filled me with mixed emotions. Part of me felt relieved that I hadn't caused his death, but there would have been poetic justice if the river had claimed him. Although I'd never believed in capital punishment, the prison system would be saddled with a dangerous psychotic for the rest of his life.

I bundled myself into a taxi back to my flat. Cool air greeted me, scented by the roses I'd bought days before to cheer myself up. I couldn't face taking a bath before dropping into bed. The prospect of more water touching my skin seemed unbearable. My last thought was a pulse of relief that Burns was safe, then sleep closed over my head immediately, with no dreams to interrupt it.

My head still felt muzzy when I came round late that afternoon, but I knew exactly what I needed to do, so I forced myself under the shower, then dressed in a hurry and raced out of the flat.

Angie looked like an irate pixie when I tapped on her office door, her voice a shrill squawk. 'Why are you here? You should be resting.'

'I want to speak to Moorcroft.'

'No way on God's earth. A bloke from the FPU's assessing him tomorrow, the appointment's booked.'

'Cancel it. I'll see him now.'

'Burns would never authorise it.'

'He's not here, is he?'

She rolled her eyes. 'He might as well be. The super's told him to take a week off, but he keeps phoning for updates.'

'This is my one chance to talk to Moorcroft before the system swallows him. I need to understand why he did it.'

'You never switch off, do you? You're worse than the boss.'

'Please, Angie, just twenty minutes.'

She put up a strong protest, reminding me that it couldn't be a formal interview because I'd serve as a witness for the prosecution. It took serious persuasion to convince her that the meeting could be classified as a risk assessment, not a psychological interview.

Moorcroft came willingly to meet me. He was handcuffed, and kitted out in clothes from lost property, a shapeless navy blue jumper and outsized jeans. He looked like a different person from the slick civil servant I'd met at the House of Commons. Only his expression was the same, haughty and distracted, as if he was privy to national secrets. It was impossible to be objective; my head kept filling with images of the madness in his face when he'd tried to drown me. He looked relaxed as he sat opposite me and Angie, his gaze hovering inches above our heads.

'What can you see, Mr Moorcroft?'

'Your spirits,' he said calmly. 'Yours was clean yesterday, Dr Quentin, but now it's filthy.'

'What do you mean?'

'Our souls reflect our deeds. You should know that. You're a psychologist, aren't you?'

'People with neurological problems sometimes see a haze around objects and faces, called an aura. It affects migraine patients too. You'll need a brain scan.'

'An X-ray won't change anything.' He threw me a look of disgust. 'It's a spiritual gift no one else shares.'

'Can you explain why you carried out your attacks?'

He looked unconcerned. 'The river made the decisions, leaving me free to carry out my work to the best of my ability.'

'Which you did very successfully, by all accounts. Mr Shelley was stunned to hear about your arrest. Even now he can't believe it.'

His boss's name made him flinch. 'What did he say?'

'You've got strong feelings for him, haven't you? I can see why. You've known him a long time.'

'He's the finest politician of his age. No one should criticise him.' His face stiffened with conviction.

'You wanted to protect him?'

'I could see Mr Shelley was in danger. We're all vulnerable in matters of the heart, but the people closest to him weren't trustworthy. Those who knew his secret could have ruined his career.'

'What was it that concerned you?'

A look of disgust crossed Moorcroft's face. 'Julian Speller seduced him. I heard every word through the door: the promises and assignations. I even had to book their hotels. When it ended the first time, Speller used to phone up and beg to see him. It started again in May.'

'Is that why you killed him?'

'Speller would have sold his story. The minister is the best statesman the House has seen, but that man could have broken him. The river begged for his soul. When I heard the minister arguing with his wife about the police reopening Jude's case, it was my duty to protect his reputation.'

'That doesn't explain why you attacked Jude right at the start.'

A flicker of regret crossed his face. 'She knew about her father's affair. Once it ended I thought he was safe, but Amala visited her so often, Jude was bound to confide in her. The minister was vulnerable when the affair restarted. It was only a matter of time before Amala blabbed to her friends. The river confirmed my decision to silence her.'

'But the attacks upset you. They made you feel ashamed. Is that why you waited a year after hurting Jude?'

'Like I said, the river makes its own choices. The spirits are cleansed then returned to the sea. The minister told me once that he kept no secrets from his priest. That's why I had to kill Father Owen.'

'How did you find out about the history of the Thames?'

'From books, of course, and night-time walks. It's been my hobby for years. Stretches of the foreshore contain treasures no one else sees. The objects I found belong to the river and had to be returned.' A beam settled on Moorcroft's lips.

'Do you take responsibility for your crimes?'

His gaze latched onto mine. 'I had no choice. It was my duty to protect Mr Shelley.'

'And it's my duty to recommend a full psychiatric review before your trial. The guards will take you back to your cell, Mr Moorcroft.'

Angie pushed back her seat after the door closed, her expression dazed. 'Mad as a bag of snakes,' she muttered, as though his verdict was already sealed.

61

An unexpected phone call came the next morning. The calm voice belonged to Christine Jenkins. I pictured her standing by her window on Dacre Street, wearing a look of relief.

'I hear your work led to the arrest of the riverside killer. Your methods were unconventional, but you deserve congratulations.'

'Thanks, Christine. I'm still processing it all.'

'I knew you were the right person for the job. That's why I'm calling. I'd like to discuss a proposal with you.'

'What kind of proposal?'

'You'd be an ideal team leader. I'll be advertising for a deputy soon; I'd like you to apply.'

'But I'm going back to my consultancy.'

'The FPU needs someone dynamic. Think about it, then call me. You'd be a strong candidate.'

She hung up before I could reply, leaving me speechless. The rational part of my brain knew it would be madness to work in a building filled with a strange collection of obsessives, but it would provide access to the most fascinating cases on offer. Thank God she hadn't demanded an immediate decision. I was so stunned by all that had happened, I'd have agreed on impulse, then regretted it immediately.

Burns was waiting for me when I reached Butler's Wharf that evening, newly released from hospital. He was sitting at a table in the galleria, broken arm propped beside him, staring into space.

'A penny for them,' I said.

'Don't waste your money. I'm an empty vessel.'

'That's fine. I'm not expecting scintillating conversation; you can just gaze at me in silent admiration.'

His lopsided smile unfolded. 'I could try, but I've still got double vision.'

'Didn't the hospital want you for another day's observation?'

He shrugged. 'I can walk, talk and think. That's enough, isn't it?'

We ended up in a steak restaurant, sharing a bottle of prosecco, and even though we were both exhausted we talked until midnight. By tacit agreement we avoided the case completely and kept the conversation on terra firma. I found out secrets he'd never told me before. We talked about the countries we'd visited. He was twenty-five before he ever went abroad: a trip to Rome that almost blew his mind.

'It was unbelievable. Beauty and decadence on every street corner.'

'I've never been.'

'You're joking.' Burns gaped at me. 'Let's go to City Airport now and get one-way tickets.'

I laughed at him. 'The Crown Prosecution Service wouldn't be thrilled. We haven't given our statements yet.'

'Speak for yourself. Angie grilled me all morning.'

'You haven't told me what happened to you last night.'

'Why should I?' He rolled his eyes. 'I haven't got post-traumatic stress, Dr Quentin. I'm happy as Larry. This fizzy wine is mixing nicely with the codeine in my bloodstream.'

'Did you hear I interviewed Moorcroft?'

He gave a slow nod. 'What's your verdict?'

'He'll need the full battery of neurology and psychopathy tests. But if he's telling the truth, part of the problem could be physical, a slow-growing brain tumour perhaps. He's got a disturbed visual field. It might explain why he's hearing things too.'

He gaped at me. 'A tumour can turn someone into a serial killer?'

'Not on its own, but it could be a contributing factor. His problem's more likely to be episodic psychosis.'

'Which is what?'

'The sufferer has lucid intervals, then periods of hallucination and hearing voices. It can be stress induced.'

He shook his head. 'The bloke almost killed Jude, but carried on working as Shelley's loyal foot soldier. It doesn't make sense.'

'I think it does. Moorcroft was fixated on his boss. He killed people who knew about Shelley's affair with Julian Speller, believing he was protecting a gifted politician from losing his career. It gave him a mission when the rest of his life was empty. Angie says there's nothing much in his flat apart from history books. The guy started studying the Thames and its tide patterns when he began hearing voices.'

'At least Jude lived to hear that he'd been caught.'

I put down my glass. 'What do you mean?'

'Sorry, I thought you knew.' He hesitated before speaking again. 'She died this morning. Jamal Khan was with her. After he told her the killer had been caught, she stopped breathing.'

My eyes swam, even though I'd always known she was unlikely to survive. Maybe it was the fact that Moorcroft had finally stolen the life he'd ruined years before. Burns's hand settled on my arm, and when I looked up again, the familiar jolt of attraction slammed into me even harder than before.

His unblinking, no bullshit stare almost had me begging him to take me back to his hotel.

'You're pale, Alice. Do you need fresh air?'

'Definitely.'

As we walked away from Hay's Galleria, the river appeared in front of us without announcement. It looked sleepy and benign, half a mile of black water rolling by too slowly to hurt anyone. But when I looked closer, currents were twisting under its surface like ropes pulled taut.

'Jesus. Can you believe we were up to our necks in that last night?' he muttered.

'Thank God we're on dry land.'

'Speak for yourself. I'm completely out of my depth.' His shoulders blocked the streetlight as he leant down to kiss me, leaving me giddy when he pulled away.

'I wish I was taller.'

'God, I don't. I've got a thing for perfect, doll-like blondes.'

'Buy yourself a Barbie then.'

His smile widened. 'Is that how you see yourself? A knife-wielding Barbie with a terrifying IQ?' We carried on walking towards my flat, his arm slung across my shoulder. 'You're better than that. If I remember rightly, you saved my life.'

'I should have let someone else fish you out. I ripped my favourite top, and you're the reason my bike got nicked.'

'I'll make it up to you.'

I stopped to kiss him again, which delayed our progress, but the walk home didn't take long, the river tracking us every step of the way. We paused to stare at it one last time by Cherry Garden Pier. The headlights of passing cars on the opposite bank scattered splinters of colour across the water. Maybe it was a trick of the light, but with my eyes half closed, they could almost have been spectres trapped beneath its depths.

ACKNOWLEDGEMENTS

Many thanks are due to my agent Teresa Chris who remains my great advocate and an excellent companion on shopping expeditions. Ruth Tross is not only a brilliant editor, she is also unfailingly kind and charming. Nick Sayers remains the loveliest man in publishing. Rebecca Mundy is due great thanks for her constant work as my publicist, her encouragement and the regular miracles she performs. Many thanks are also due to my husband Dave Pescod for his unstinting support, Miranda Landgraf, Penny Hancock, Sophie Hannah, and the inspiring members of the 134 club. The Thames Police provided me with a tremendously helpful tour, which unlocked some of the river's murky secrets. Thanks also to the staff of the London Museum and the British Museum for educating me about the artefacts which have been dredged from the river in recent years. Thanks to Professor Sylvia Helman for advice about the symptoms of schizophrenia and episodic psychosis; your insights into the nature of mental illness helped a very great deal. Thanks to DS Dan Miller (I promise to include you in the next book, and to make you tall, dark and handsome). DC Laura Shaw, thanks also for excellent guidance on matters of police procedure. Finally, huge thanks are due to the hundreds of reviewers and bloggers who have taken the trouble to rate my work in recent years. Your thoughtful comments have boosted my confidence and helped shape me as a writer. That includes you, Julie Boon, Peggy Breckin and Claire Brown.

Note: Some of the locations in this book are real, but some are imaginary. Apologies for changing some of London's geography, history, and street names; my motive is always to tell the best possible story.

Alice Quentin returns in

BLOOD SYMMETRY

Coming June 2016

Clare Riordan and her son Mikey are abducted from Clapham Common early one morning. Hours later, the boy is found wandering disorientated. Soon after, a pack of Clare's blood is left on a doorstep in the heart of the City of London.

Alice Quentin is brought in to help the traumatised child uncover his memories – which might lead them to his mother's captors. But she swiftly realises Clare is not the first victim . . . nor will she be the last.

The killers are driven by a desire for revenge . . . and in the end, it will all come down to blood.

MULHOLLAND
BOOKS
HODDER